NEW YORK TIMES BESTSELLING AUTHOR

HANNAH HOWELL

HIGHLAND DEVIL

All New! First Time in Print!

**HAVE YOU
MET ALL
THE MURRAYS?**

EAN

ISBN-13: 978-1-4201-4307-2
ISBN-10: 1-4201-4307-7

WHEN YOU KISS A HIGHLANDER

Gybbon gently stroked her face and tucked the few stray locks of her hair that had come loose from her braid behind her ears. "Time to go inside."

They slipped in with only one lone kitchen maid noticing them and then went up the stairs. By the time they reached the top of the stairs, Gybbon had his arm around her waist. They had reached her door when he suddenly pulled her into his arms and kissed her.

Mora let herself sink into the kiss and enjoyed the heat it stirred within her. She knew what he wanted and she was uneasy. A large part of her wanted it, too, but she was neither a widow nor a tavern maid and she knew she should not. There had been no words of love or even need. No promises she could cling to for a future.

Then she thought of all that had happened. What good were promises to her when she had a man determined to kill her? She was filled with a grief and anger that had little place to go and his kisses eased all that, gave her a moment to forget them. He was evidently a man who liked to wander and she was one who ached to settle. So what harm was there in allowing herself to just forget all of it in his arms?

He looked at her and she was certain there was a question in his eyes. A strong reckless and rebellious part of her rose up to answer that question and she opened her door. His eyes widened when she tugged him into her room. Delighted by his surprise, she curled her arms around his neck and kissed him with all the fierce desire she had fought to keep under control. . . .

Books by Hannah Howell

Published by Kensington Publishing Corporation

HIGHLAND DEVIL

HANNAH HOWELL

ZEBRA BOOKS
KENSINGTON PUBLISHING CORP.
http://www.kensingtonbooks.com

ZEBRA BOOKS are published by

Kensington Publishing Corp.
119 West 40th Street
New York, NY 10018

All Kensington titles, imprints, and distributed lines are available at special quantity discounts for bulk purchases for sales promotion, premiums, fund-raising, educational, or institutional use.

Special book excerpts or customized printings can also be created to fit specific needs. For details, write or phone the office of the Kensington Sales Manager: Attn.: Sales Department. Kensington Publishing Corp., 119 West 40th Street, New York, NY 10018. Phone: 1-800-221-2647.

Zebra and the Z logo Reg. U.S. Pat. & TM Off.

First Printing: August 2018
ISBN-13: 978-1-4201-4307-2
ISBN-10: 1-4201-4307-7

eISBN-13: 978-1-4201-4308-9
eISBN-10: 1-4201-4308-5

10 9 8 7 6 5 4 3 2 1

Printed in the United States of America

Chapter One

The way her cousins burst into the house startled and frightened Mora. She paused in doing up her cloak. "What do ye want?" she demanded as she pushed Andrew behind her.

"We want ye gone," answered Robert, the eldest.

"Why? I have a right to stay here and hold the house for my brothers' return." She felt a chill at the look that crossed Robert's face.

"We can hold it for them. Now that your parents are dead, 'tis nay right for ye to stay here alone. How will ye fare with no one bringing in some coin?"

"The goats give me milk and I will have cheese to make and sell. 'Tis nay a bountiful living, but it will serve."

Robert looked at his brothers and nodded toward the back door. All three went in that direction. Mora tried to stop them, but Robert paused long enough to backhand her in the face, and she fell. She was just scrambling to her feet when she heard the first goat scream. Keeping an eye on Murdoch, who rushed out the door and tried to stop what his brothers were doing, she grabbed the bag she had packed for young

Andrew, handed it to him, and hurried over to a window to lift him out.

"Run with the goats if any get away. Go to Aunt Maggie."

"But ye should come, too," Andrew said. "We were supposed to stay together."

"Go. I will come when I can. Go!"

She watched him run to the woods and a moment later saw several of her goats bolting into the woods as well. Pleased her cousins had not killed all the animals, she turned around and saw a badly battered Murdoch leaning against the side of the door frame, watching her.

The elder three brothers came stomping back into the house, and she tensed. "Ye shouldnae have killed my animals. Glad some of them kenned the danger and fled."

"Ye willnae be able to gather them all back anyway," sneered Robert as he walked toward her. "Now we have taken care of your parents and your cursed goats."

Shock turned her blood cold and she said in a voice softened by horror, "It wasnae thieves. It was *ye* who killed my parents. Ye probably took what they had earned for their goods as well."

Robert laughed. "Of course we did. And it showed they had a good day at the market. They had no need of it and ye willnae either. And, curse it, where is that wee brat Andrew?"

"Ye expect me to tell ye where he is when ye have just admitted to killing our parents?"

"Aye, and if ye dinnae, we can easily make ye want to tell us anything."

"I think people would frown on ye torturing your own cousin, especially if that person is a newly orphaned girl."

"Nay when they are told ye are a thief and a killer."

"What nonsense is that? I have stolen nothing and killed no one."

"Ye stole money from our da and ye killed the mon who was caring for him."

"William has died? How did that happen?" She forced herself to speak calmly although she was deeply shocked. "He was verra hale and hardy when I last saw him."

"Aye, right before ye stabbed him with a sword ye stole from me, along with some coin our da had in a wee wooden box that has a carved dragon on the lid."

The description of the wooden box with money in it told her they had robbed her of her father's small savings. She also knew they did not have it, for it was stuffed deep in the bag she had packed. Mora suspected they had killed poor William, too, or Robert had, and she had the chilling feeling the man had died because he had suspected that the laird's illness was being caused by something being given to him. Worse, it was something his own son was doing.

"Ye have gone mad, havenae ye?"

Robert grabbed her by the arm, and it was so shocking, and painful, she could not silence a cry. She heard a recognizable hiss even as she saw her small cat leap upon Robert's face, her little paws scratching furiously at him. Robert screamed and his brothers Duncan and Lachlan started to rush to his side even as Robert grabbed little Freya and hurled her toward the fireplace. Since he had released her in his vain attempt to protect his face, Mora ran and grabbed the animal.

When she saw Murdoch signal with a motion of his head that she should run, she did not hesitate, but Robert still tried to stop her, grabbing her by the wrist and lashing out with a knife. He did not manage to stab her as he had clearly intended, but she knew he had scraped the flesh on her side for it stung and she could feel that there was some wetness, telling her that it bled. Breaking free of Robert, she then raced to the door while his brothers reached his side and clumsily tried to help him. He was screeching as if he had just been gutted.

She grabbed the bag she had packed, and while still in motion, shoved Freya inside and kept on running. The moment she espied a good place to hide, she ducked into the bushes and burrowed deep into the brush. Pulling the hood of her cloak up, she nestled down in the undergrowth all the while praying they would not search too hard for her. The light was fading as the sun began to set, so she also prayed that would produce enough shadow to keep her hidden. Once she was sure they had left, she would begin the long trip to Dubheidland and the distant relatives her mother had always insisted would help her. Mora was not sure what the Camerons could do to help her, or even if they would accept her word that the crimes Robert tried to hang her with were lies, but she had no other choices.

Night descended on Mora Ogilvy like a heavy fog, stealing the light and some of the warmth, and she shivered. She reached into the bag she carried and lightly scratched her cat's ears. The animal licked her hand and Mora sighed. It had been silly to bring her cat with her. She knew few people would understand, especially if they knew what she had risked to accomplish it. She shifted back, deeper into the bushes she was crouching in. Fear still gnawed at her, but she almost welcomed its sharp teeth because it kept her alert, something Mora felt sure would help her stay alive.

She could not be certain how long her cousins would chase after her, or how hard. Considering how often she had to dart off the road and hide, it would be months before she reached Dubheidland. The way Robert had carried on about his face, she suspected he would insist on someone tending to the wounds soon, and that should delay the hunt for her. There were also a lot of dangers for a woman walking the roads and pathways alone, especially at night. Mora wished she had been able to grab a horse to flee on, but she had barely gotten herself and her little brother away.

Thinking of her little brother, Andrew, made her start to cry, but she hastily wiped the tears away. He was only seven—a surprise child, their mother had called him—and he was so smart. He had not argued much when she had told him to run to the woman they fondly called Aunt Maggie and tell her what was happening. Mora just prayed she had not put the woman in danger, too.

It was time to move on, she decided as she stood up and closed her bag. The moon was now out, so she had some faint light to see by. It was not as much light as she would like, but she suspected too many rests by the side of the road would be risky. She had already had to duck into the undergrowth of the forest or into the hedgerows several times because she heard someone approaching.

Unable to resist, she opened her bag and her pet immediately stuck her head out, eager to look around. "I am verra glad that ye are so small, Miss Freya, as I suspicion I will be carrying ye the whole way."

Freya made a small chirping sound as Mora thought hard on where she was going. The clan she sought was a relation of her mother's, but Mora had only met them twice. All she could recall about them was a lot of boys and every shade of red hair. She prayed they recalled her mother or she could find herself facing a lot of confused and angry men.

Shaking her head, she fought to recall how hard her father and mother had worked to make certain she knew how to get to Dubheidland. The moment they had suspected trouble from her uncle's sons, they had begun to speak on where to run to. They had been very adamant about it being the best place for her to run to be safe, so for their sake she pushed aside her doubts and fears and started walking.

When Freya snapped her head around to look behind them, Mora turned and headed into the trees. The cat had proven to be very good at warning her of trouble. Mora listened carefully but it was several minutes before she heard the sound of a horse approaching. Freya crouched down into the bag, flattened her ears against her head, but made no sound.

A single rider came into view astride a magnificent horse. The animal had a white tail, a white mane, and a blaze of white down his face, but the rest of him appeared to be black. In a soft, deep voice the man spoke idly to the animal, and the way the animal's ears moved made Mora ready to believe that it was actually listening to the man.

Once the rider was out of sight, Mora looked back down the road and listened carefully but neither heard nor saw any sign of someone else coming. She glanced down at Freya only to find the cat idly washing herself, so Mora relaxed. She was as certain as she could be that there would be no more surprises, so she slowly returned to the road and started walking again.

"Mayhap I should have spoken up when that man rode by, Freya. He was but one man and I didnae recognize him as an acquaintance of my thrice-cursed cousins. Even if I had not met him before, I would surely have recognized that horse. He may have even offered us a ride. It would be much nicer if we could ride to Dubheidland."

Glancing at her pet, who was giving her what Mora could only see as an expression of disgust, she grimaced. "And, mayhaps not. Still, it would have been faster to be able to ride at least some of the way to our destination. And I would have someone to talk to aside from a cat. And, he could have provided some warmth, too," she grumbled as the air grew even colder and she tugged her cloak more tightly around herself. "Ye are all tucked up in the bag and have fur so ye dinnae notice, but there is a sharp bite to the air tonight."

Watching the road so that she did not stumble, Mora forced herself to keep a sharp listen out for the sound of someone approaching from any direction, although she wondered why she bothered as Freya could hear the sound of hooves long before she did. She carefully thought through all that had just happened and made herself believe it, forcing away all thought of how they were family. Her cousins wanted her and Andrew dead. She had not truly caught her parents' growing fear until they were dead, killed on the road back from the market. Even then it had been too easy to believe it had just been thieves. Then her cousins had come for her and Andrew and actually boasted of their killing of her parents.

Thinking back to that moment, she realized at least one of her cousins might not have been in complete accord with his brothers. Murdoch was just eighteen and, even through her own shock, she had seen how stunned he had looked at Robert's boasting. He had then protested when his brothers had gone out to kill her goats. Unfortunately, he was also the smallest of the group and Robert had just slapped him around until he could only sag against the side of the house. She doubted she could count on him to give her much more help than that.

Another stroke of luck was that her goats were not the completely brainless beasts the cousins had anticipated. They killed a few but the fear and blood of the murdered goats sent the others racing for the fence, which they easily cleared, and then they disappeared into the forest. She had had the time to send her little brother off, for which she was grateful. Murdoch had watched her and said nothing, then motioned with his head for her to move away.

As she had grabbed some things to take with her and picked up her cat, the others had returned. They had tried to slaughter her goats and Robert had then tossed her cat toward the fireplace. Mora could taste the fear she had suffered thinking she was about to watch her pet get burned alive, but Freya had twisted as she had flown through the air to land hard just to the side of the fireplace. Mora had grabbed her cat and, dodging Robert's attempt to stab her but still feeling the bite of his knife, shoved her cat in her bag, then bolted for the door, while Robert cursed and shrieked, his brothers trying to tend to him. She had raced down the road and hidden away, something she was getting very tired of doing, for she had begun weeks ago, when her parents had warned her there was a threat from her cousins.

She had briefly considered running to their father, her Uncle Tomas, but shook aside the thought. The man was still sick but she had no idea how bad he was. He could no longer be sensible enough to understand what she said or strong enough to stop his sons if they came after her. He had also proven impossible to convince that Robert could do anything wrong. Even her mother had complained about it. It was better to make her way to her mother's cousins in Dubheidland and pray that they believed her and were ready to help her.

After walking for what felt like miles, the small wound Robert had inflicted stinging badly, she stopped and sniffed the air, realizing she smelled the hint of smoke. Unsure what caused it, she scurried into the trees. As soon as she felt certain she was hidden in the trees well enough not to be seen by anyone on the road, she stopped and sniffed the air again. The smell of wood smoke was still there and had become just a little stronger.

Mora looked carefully through the trees trying to see where the smoke could be coming from. She finally spotted a faint flicker of light to her left. Moving forward as quietly as she could, she drew near enough to recognize a small campfire. Then she saw the horse. The animal she saw was enough to tell her who was crouched by that fire. A moment later the scent of what he was cooking drifted her way and her stomach growled. It smelled as if he had caught himself a rabbit. Mora was sorely tempted to walk right over to him and ask for a share.

Knowing that would be foolish, she turned her attention to his horse. With a mount like that she could keep well out of her cousins' reach and probably get to Dubheidland quickly, even with her poor riding skills. It would certainly be better and faster than walking every step of the way. There would be less need for camping out in the night all by herself as well. She looked back at the man and prayed he would wander away just for a little while.

She crept as close as she dared to his campsite, then settled down to watch for him to walk away. Mora decided she would not need much time to take the horse. As soon as she mounted the animal it would be easy enough to avoid the man if he came back and tried to catch her. Once she was on the road she would definitely have a strong advantage. Studying the horse carefully, she planned out the quickest way to saddle the animal, attach her bag, and then mount. While waiting for the man to leave for a short while, she kept going over the plan in the hope that she would be able to move fast.

Her mind kept reminding her that stealing a man's horse could get one hanged. Mora decided to ignore it. If she let it linger it would make her afraid and that could cause her to fail. Despite having many good reasons to be afraid, she refused to allow that fear to settle inside her.

The man abruptly stood up and stretched, then scratched his bottom. She rolled her eyes. Her brothers always did the same, stretch and scratch. Then she pressed her lips together to hide the sigh begging to be let out.

She missed her brothers, Niall and David. Although she and her parents had written to them several times, and she had written again after her parents were killed, there had been no reply. They had gone to France to fight, to join one of the mercenary bands there. Mora had the chilling feeling they were dead. She would not be surprised if, when her cousins learned where her brothers were going, they had made certain they would never return. If her brothers had joined with some mercenaries, she suspected it would not be difficult to get a few of those men to kill two of their own kind for the right coin.

Staring in the direction of the fire as she thought, Mora was slowly pulled out of her musings. The man stood with his hands on his hips staring into the fire and frowning. He was a fine-looking man from what little she could see. The flickering light from the fire made it difficult to see his face though. She was much more interested in his face. She had seen far too many men who had a fine, manly build that any woman would appreciate—only to discover they had a face that looked as if they had lost too many fights or a horse had sat on it.

She stared down at the ground fighting tears as a memory surfaced. She had said something similar to her mother once concerning her uncle's men-at-arms and had wondered aloud if her cousins chose such men purposefully so that no one of them would out-shine her cousins. Her father had laughed but had quickly smothered it as her mother had scolded her, telling her that a man's heart and soul were of more importance than his face.

Although she had never been unkind to any of the men, Mora had taken the scold to heart. After all, her cousins were all quite handsome, yet it was now clear their hearts and souls were dark as sin. She had had more proof of her mother's lesson many times and owed one homely, burly man for her cat as he had saved it from being drowned and asked her if she wanted it.

A sense that she was being watched drew her attention back to the man at the fire. He was staring right at her and she tensed. When he just shook his head, and turned to start walking into the woods, she sagged with relief. Waiting a few moments, she began to make her way, as swiftly and quietly as she could, toward the horse. When a branch snapped and she felt a tug on her braid, she cursed softly and waited a moment, fighting to untangle her hair from the branch, worrying that she was losing time to escape. Listening carefully for a moment, but hearing nothing, she hurried forward still struggling with the branch. She had reached the horse before she finally got free of it and started plucking out the bits and pieces it had left behind in her hair.

The animal stared at her but made no sound as she set her bag down and began to saddle him. She attached her bag securely and then swung up into the saddle. It was not a graceful mount because he was so tall, but she was soon settled nicely in the saddle, and was pleased he was such a placid beast.

She was reaching for the reins when the horse suddenly moved and Mora found herself flying through the air. The landing on the ground stole all breath from her body and she did not think she would recover fast enough to still get away. Then she groaned, for the small wound on her side that her cousin had inflicted stung badly. She wondered if it was not as insignificant as she had thought.

A big hand grabbed her by the wrist and she silently muttered every curse she knew. A tug on her arm turned her onto her back and for a little while she feigned unconsciousness, but then she opened her eyes. She stared at the man crouched beside her, still holding her wrist in a grip that did not hurt but which she knew she would not break free of.

She could see no weapon in his other hand as she felt her eyes grow wider and wider. She lost only a touch of the fear she felt when she saw that and it still hung on enough to keep her heart pounding so hard she was amazed he could not hear it. The man may not be holding a weapon, but that did not mean he had none or would be reluctant to use it on a woman. He would not be condemned if he struck her down since she had just tried to steal his horse. That was, after all, a hanging crime.

Then a deep voice asked, "Why are ye trying to steal my horse?"

Chapter Two

Sir Gybbon Murray heard the sharp, quick sound of a branch break and quickly finished his business. As he stepped around the tree he had just relieved himself against, he frowned at the shadowy figure struggling to free itself from a branch. He decided he was due a problem as most of his journey had been trouble free. When the figure finally straightened up, he recognized it firmly as a woman as she yanked pieces of the branch out of her hair.

Then she looked around and he pressed himself up against a tree so that he would not be visible. He cursed softly as she next hurried over to his horse, Jester. He had thought that by riding into the wood lining the road he had avoided the thieves who so often roamed the night. This woman obviously intended to take his horse. He looked around very carefully assuming she had to have some male compatriots, but could see nothing.

He smiled as he looked back at her. He did not have to rush over. Jester would take care of her, he thought, and had to smother a chuckle as he watched her saddle the animal and take the reins from the tree he had looped them around. He crossed his arms over his chest and waited as she attached her bag to the saddle and then mounted Jester in a particularly graceless way.

It did not take long for Jester to do what he did best. She was only just settling the reins in her hands when his horse moved. It took barely a moment, and little effort, for Jester to hurl her out of the saddle to the ground. Gybbon winced when she hit the ground hard. She sprawled face down and groaned softly, reaching for her side.

"Why are ye trying to steal my horse?" he asked.

He reached out and grabbed her wrist as she fumbled with her side, afraid she was about to get a weapon. Not finding the blade he expected, he looked down at her as she turned onto her back. She was pale but he did not know if that was just caused by the weak light from the fire he had built, or fear, or even pain. A long thick braid of hair had flipped up over her head and it was definitely pale in color. She did not open her eyes and he then wondered if she was unconscious or just in a swoon. He was ready to give her a light slap on the face to try and rouse her when she opened her eyes, brushing her braid off her face.

Gybbon wished the light from the fire was stronger so he could see her eyes clearly. He always felt more confident of his judgments when he could see someone's eyes. As she stared at him, her eyes grew wider and wider until he suspected they would soon sting. He just could not guess if it was because of fear or surprise.

Mora stared at the man crouched by her side. She could see no weapon in his hand and she lost a touch of the fear gripping her so tightly. It still hung in strong enough to keep her heart pounding so hard she thought he must be able to hear it. The man may not be holding a weapon but that did not mean he had none. He must also be incensed at what she had tried to do and knew he would not be condemned if he struck her down because of it. It was a hanging crime.

"I wasnae stealing him. I was just borrowing him for a wee while." She was not surprised when he gave her a look of annoyance as she knew it was a weak, senseless statement.

"I see. Just how was I expected to get him back when ye were done with him? Ye gave me no name nor a place to collect him at. Nay even a time when I could have him back. How is that nay stealing?" He frowned, cocked his head to the side, and looked toward his horse. "What is that sound?"

"I dinnae hear anything." She lied because she could hear Freya growling.

Still holding her, he stood up and walked toward Jester, dragging the woman with him. "It is coming from your bag." He reached toward it. "And now the bag is moving. Open it."

"Nay. They are just my belongings. Some clothes and such as that. Oh, and a few things I saved from the manor."

"Clothes that growl? Open it."

She sighed. His voice was hard and she sensed he was truly beginning to feel annoyed. In her experience, annoyed men struck out. Her father never had, but she had seen too many others who did. It seemed it did not take much for a woman to annoy a mon, either. She just hoped this man did not hate cats as much as her cousins did.

Carefully unlatching her bag, she took a deep, steadying breath. She could do nothing but hope she had not saved her pet once only to have another man kill her. The moment she opened the bag, Freya leapt out, landing on her shoulder and curling her tail around Mora's neck. The small, gray cat stared at the man.

"A cat? Ye have been toting around a cat?" He took the bag from her.

"I had to. The men I am fleeing almost killed her because she scratched one of them."

"Who would want to kill a kitten? The scratch couldnae have been a bad one."

Trying not to think on the long, bleeding gouges on Robert's face, several of them dangerously close to his eyes, she answered, "She isnae a kitten. She is two years old, probably as big as she ever will be."

"Ah. A runt." Still holding her by the wrist, he pulled her toward the campfire. "Sit."

"I should continue on my way," she protested, and reached for her bag.

He allowed her to grab it, then pulled her closer to the fire. "'Tis dark and nay a good time to travel. And where would ye go? I dinnae think there is another horse along the road for ye to steal. What is your name?"

"Mora Ogilvy." She had opened her mouth to protest the word "steal" and then sighed, knowing there was no point in it.

"Sit." He almost smiled at the way she narrowed her eyes as she stared at him, but she then sat down by the fire, setting her bag close by her side. The woman did not like to be ordered around.

Gybbon sat across from her and studied her. She

was small, almost as near to being called a runt as her cat. Her hair was blond, but the firelight glinted off some red strands as well. From what little he could see of her figure, she was temptingly curved in all the right places. Since it was difficult to see her figure as well as he would like in the firelight, he turned his study to her face.

Her eyes were wide and what appeared to be a dark blue, the light from the fire occasionally highlighting that color. Even though her mouth was turned down in a frown, he could see enough of its shape to guess she had invitingly full lips. Her cheekbones were high, and just under the right one was a large, dark bruise.

"Someone hit ye in the face?" he asked, wondering why that angered him so.

"One of the men I am running from." She sighed and tugged her cloak around herself as the cat walked down from her shoulders to settle on her lap, sitting within the folds of her cloak and staring at him. "Ye havenae told me who *ye* are."

"Sir Gybbon Murray. Who are these men ye are fleeing? And why do ye need to flee?"

Mora sighed, still frightened, and saddened by all that had happened, but seeing no reason not to tell him. "My cousins. All three of them. The fourth is, I believe, a reluctant partner and I do wonder about the other two. The eldest is definitely determined. The old laird gave his eldest son the castle but he also gave my father, his youngest son, a fine manor house and a few acres. The new laird's sons believe that was a mistake and that it should all go to their father, who would then hand it all down to one of them."

"Why didnae ye just go to the laird and tell him?"

"He is ill and I couldnae tell how badly ill he is. He

may nay have been able to understand what I told him and he certainly wouldnae be able to do anything to stop his sons. Also, telling him what his sons have done might weel make his illness worsen for he truly cared for my mother and father. For all of us." She shook her head. "And if I was right about all of that, I would then find myself too close to the ones trying to get rid of me and without an ally to fight for me. Every time I considered going to tell Uncle Tomas what was going on, I then saw all the ways it could go horribly bad for me."

He nodded. "True. Ye could have walked right into the lion's den. So, are ye just running until ye find somewhere to hide from them?"

"Nay. For one thing, they need to pay for the killing of my parents. I am headed to some kin of my mother's to ask for help."

"Who are they?"

She frowned and stroked her cat. "Why do ye need to ken who they are? Ye willnae be having to collect your horse," she added in a soft mutter.

"Weel, I may ken who they are. The Murrays ken a lot of folk in this land and are even connected to many through marriage. I may ken something ye need to learn to feel more certain that they will or can help ye."

The way she stared at him, her eyes narrowing slightly, told him she was not sure she should trust him with that information. Gybbon was not sure why that irritated him so much as it was a completely understandable doubt. It did not help ease his irritation when he noticed that her strange little cat still watched him closely as well, its eyes also narrowed.

"My mother was their kin. Surely they would aid

their kin, even if the connection isnae terribly close; 'tis, truthfully, a rather twisted, distant link. I cannae even recall the many steps it takes to make the link, but I have met them twice. Once when I was verra young and once when their clan suffered a fever that killed a lot of its people, mostly the adults. My mother felt he might need some help as there were a lot of them, so she and Da packed us all up and went to see them."

"But he didnae want her help?"

"He didnae really need it so Mother ne'er really offered, just said enough to let him ken the offer was there if he wished to call on it. She said there were some elder women still alive and helping. Also said she would probably end up being more of a thorn in his side than a help as she suspected she wouldnae agree with the things he did considering all his siblings. So, we left, but he and my mother often corresponded."

"It does sound like he would have no problem lending ye a hand. So, who is he and where do ye need to go?"

Mora sighed, seeing that he was just going to keep pressing her until he got an answer to that question. She thought about it and could see no real reason not to answer him. "I am headed to Dubheidland to request some aid from the laird there, Sir Sigimor Cameron." She was not sure the surprise he let show and the chuckle he let loose were a good thing.

"I ken where that is and I ken Sigimor. I will take ye there."

"Nay, I cannae pull ye into my troubles. . . ." She stuttered to a halt when he raised his hand.

"Greedy relatives trying to take what isnae theirs is a problem we have dealt with before. Money and land are the causes of a lot of family strife."

"How sad. I dinnae understand why my cousins are so determined to be rid of us. They have e'en dreamed up a few crimes to charge me with to help them. 'Tis a fine house we have, but nay that fine and only a few acres. They have a castle and a large swath of land. I cannae e'en see how it would help in splitting up the inheritance they'd get when the laird dies."

"When did the laird fall ill?"

Mora frowned. "The day my parents went to market and were killed on their way home. Robbed of the money they had as weel. Ye dinnae really think they would try to kill their own father, do ye?" She shook her head. "Nay, if naught else, Murdoch, the youngest, wouldnae have had any part of that. Although the murder they claim I did was done with Robert's sword, the item I am accused of stealing along with my own da's money."

"And your father was their uncle. Aye?" When she nodded he smiled faintly. "Nay a big leap from uncle to father." She was growing a bit pale, so he decided to leave that subject. "I will take ye to Dubheidland."

"I cannae take ye out of your way," she said as she fought to banish all thought of her cousins from her mind.

"'Tis nay really out of my way. I was actually thinking of stopping in there to beg a good meal and a proper bed for a night or two."

It was madness to go off with a man she did not know, Mora thought, but she was already caught fast in a kind of madness. What her cousins were doing had to be madness. Murdoch could not know the extent of his brother's crimes. She felt certain of it. He had not known they were responsible for her parents' death; she was sure of that. His expression as his brother taunted her with what they had done was one of horrified astonishment. He had definitely aided in hers and Andrew's escapes. And, she feared, it would eventually lead to his own death.

"Come, eat something," he coaxed as he held out a plate of rabbit and bread. "Then we can get some sleep and be on our way at the break of day."

Taking the plate, she nodded. She was not feeling particularly hungry, despite her stomach's interest in the rabbit earlier, but she knew she needed to eat. Strength was needed for what lay ahead. Staring down at her plate, she picked up a chunk of rabbit and nibbled on it, watching with calm amusement as Freya's small paw reached out and caught up a small chunk of meat. The faint smile that crossed Sir Gybbon's face did a lot to ease her mind about going off with him.

"It is always hard to discover one's kin are nay to be trusted," he consoled.

"Or just plain greedy and evil with the blood of one's own parents dripping from their hands?"

"Nay sure I would put it that way," he murmured, then glanced at her. "Ye did say one of the brothers didnae seem to be part of it all."

"Murdoch, aye. He is only eighteen and he really looked horrified, and then he tried to stop them from killing my goats. May be why some of them fled successfully. Then he said nothing when I helped my young brother escape out the window to run to Aunt Maggie. He also told me to run after Robert hit me and his other two brothers were trying to help Robert stop bleeding."

"Does sound innocent. Why was this Robert bleeding?"

"He grabbed me when I tried to get by him and I cried out. Freya leapt onto his face and slashed him. He threw her toward the fire, but she is an agile little girl"—she scratched her cat's ears—"and twisted while still in the air so she fell to the floor off to the side. I ran over and got her, and it was Murdoch who signaled me to run, to get out. So, I did, though Robert tried to stab me as I passed by him. And I have continued to run. I was surprised that they did not come by me while I was on the road. I then thought that they might have taken Robert to someone to tend to his wounds or even told the sheriff of the crimes they want to charge me with and got some of his men to help them."

Gybbon stared at the small cat, who was primly taking another piece of meat. "She really doesnae look so fierce."

"She always goes for the face." Mora smiled when he winced. "She is actually afraid of a lot of things. Think it is because she is so small. Even a hawk eyes her as a meal. Fortunately, it also eyes a small female with a broom as a threat. So, ye think Sigimor Cameron might help?"

"Aye, unless his own family is facing some threat. To Sigimor that would be the trouble he needed to deal with."

Mora nodded. "Of course it would be. Completely understandable."

"And your mother was right to not stay and mother everyone. She wouldnae have agreed with all the ways he did it. I am fair certain of it. A rough mon is Sigimor, but his brothers all turned out well and most of them are still at home."

"It is a shame she didnae live to see that. Every now and then she fretted over her decision. So Dubheidland is still a place filled with big men with red hair?"

"Aye. Often a lot of MacFingals, too, although that has lessened some as they get older and, I suspect, Sigimor doesnae appreciate any of them flirting with his wife."

Mora laughed. "Who are these MacFingals?"

As she finished her food she was thoroughly entertained by Sir Gybbon's talk of the MacFingals. Although the old laird was a scandal, she had to admire him for the care he took of all his children, legitimate or not. Few men would bother.

She was just setting her plate down when Freya stared at the road and then hopped into her bag. "I need to hide," said Mora as she grabbed her bag and tugged her hood up over her hair.

"Why?"

"Someone is coming down the road." She pointed to the woods just beyond the horse, and added, "I will only be hiding over there."

Gybbon watched her head into the woods and wondered if she meant to flee. Even as he thought he should make sure she did not, he heard the hoofbeats of a couple of horses coming. A man and a woman rode by, quietly talking to each other and taking no notice of him. As soon as they passed by, he stood up and walked to the edge of the woods. He stared into the shadowed area but caught no glimpse of Mora.

"Mora?"

Suddenly her head popped up and he was briefly

startled. Her hood had completely covered her hair. It appeared she had a true skill at hiding and he idly wondered why.

"It was just a couple riding by. Naught to worry about."

Mora climbed out of her hiding place. She wondered why she had not taken the chance to run. The man had said he knew Sigimor and knew how to get to Dubheidland, but she had no way to test the truth of that until she reached the gates and he was recognized by the Camerons. Then she shrugged and brushed the debris from her cloak. He was the best hope she had of getting where she needed to go before her cousins got to her, and he had a horse.

"I will come along in just a moment or two."

Gybbon started to ask why the wait and then clamped his mouth shut. Women needed a moment of privacy just like men. He walked back to the fire and began to clear up what small mess he had there. Just as he began to put some sand over the embers of the fire, she walked back into the campsite, that strange tiny cat at her side.

Mora stepped up to the fire and watched the man as he made certain it was fully out, no heat evident. He was a very handsome fellow, she mused. His hair was a gleaming black and a bit long, hanging a few inches past his shoulders. There were slender braids at the front and she recalled her father talking of warrior's braids when he would tell her stories about old battles, although she had gotten the feeling that was from a long time ago. It suited Gybbon, however. From the slightly elegant lines of his face, she would judge him well born.

When he stood up and looked at her, she had to

bite the inside of her cheek to keep from making any sound. His eyes were a beautiful clear green yet there appeared to be some blue in there as well. She wondered how she had missed that.

He walked off into the trees and she released a small sigh of relief. Now she had time to settle herself, calm the odd reaction she had to his looks. She had to admit she had never seen such a fine-looking man or had such a reaction to any man. Mora hoped that was not going to make the trip they would soon take together awkward. She would be humiliated if he caught her staring at him all cow-eyed.

When he returned he spread out a blanket for her, then spread another across the fire pit. "Sleep, lass."

"Is it safe to sleep out here?"

"Aye. Anything too mean and dangerous and Jester will alert us. I begin to think so would your cat. Would it help if I relit a fire?"

"Nay. I will be fine. An unwatched fire would make me nervous."

"Get some rest then. My sword is at the ready."

She smiled faintly as she settled on the blanket and tugged the rest of it over her. She also kept her cloak on. A moment later Freya nudged her way under the blanket and curled up by her chest. He was right. Freya would warn her if there was any danger. She just hoped her pet stayed close and did not give in to the rare temptation to wander.

Gybbon woke up and stared into the moonlit forest wondering what woke him before the sun rose. Jester was making no sounds to wake him. He turned and looked across the small fire pit at his companion. She was asleep, and right next to her, staring back at him, was her odd little cat.

The cat showed no sign of alarm, but he was surprised it stayed with her in the blanket. He had always thought that cats loved to roam the night. This one seemed perfectly content to stay curled up with the woman. Shaking his head, he decided he had been awakened simply by a need to make certain everything was quiet. He closed his eyes, determined to get a little more sleep, and hoped Sigimor would help her.

If Sigimor did not, or could not, then the Murrays would, he decided. Falsely accused and with a set of brothers close on her trail, she was going to need help. He began to go through the long, long list of his kinsmen and connections to think of which would be the best one to approach. It was enough to put him peacefully back to sleep.

Chapter Three

Someone was shaking her, Mora realized, as she became fully aware of a big hand gripping her by the shoulder. She swatted at it even as she felt sleep loosen its hold on her. Then a familiar furry head butted her and rubbed against her face. It was the loud purr that finally caused her to open her eyes. Freya sat tidily next to a pair of thick deer hide boots. She frowned as she slowly looked up long legs, over a kilt and a shirt, until her eyes finally rested upon a face.

Her sleep-clouded mind cleared abruptly as she stared into a pair of bright green eyes. Last night she had agreed to allow this man to take her to Dubheidland. In the clear light of day, she now questioned that decision. Freya leaned against his boot and Mora decided to trust in her pet. It was obvious that Freya trusted the man, or that fine boot she rubbed her head against would be shredded. Carefully, Mora sat up and rubbed her eyes.

A minute later she became acutely aware of needing a little privacy. She was just standing up when Freya spun to face the road and hissed. When the cat dashed to her side, still staring at the road and growling deep in her throat, Mora picked her up.

"What is wrong with her?" Gybbon asked.

"She hears someone riding our way. I need to hide again."

"How could she know?"

"I dinnae ken. The same way she can tell a wee mousie is running through the grass farther away than we can see, I think. She has been a great help. I always kenned when someone was riding our way and would hide." She put Freya in her bag, pulled her hood up to cover her hair, and darted into the trees.

Gybbon grabbed a branch, snapping it off the nearest tree, and brushed away all sign of her footprints. Tossing it back into the trees, he wondered why he was acting as if that cursed cat had just warned her of danger. He stared toward the wood she had run into, but could not see her.

Next, he looked toward the road as he folded up the blanket she had slept on. A moment later, four men came riding into view, pausing to stare at his campsite, which was much more visible in the daylight. When they cautiously turned off the road and rode toward him, he took his porridge pot off the fire, drew his sword, and faced them.

"We dinnae mean any harm, sir," said the one in the lead, looking almost apologetic with his blue eyes and blond hair tumbling around his face as he bent his head in greeting.

"Then why do four of ye approach a lone mon?"

"We are looking for someone."

"Who?"

He glanced at the man just to the right of the man he was speaking to. He was leaning forward in his saddle and looked as if he wanted to be the one to speak. He also had a badly scratched face. Looking at the ones close to his eyes, Gybbon was surprised the man still had eyes. Looking a little more closely, he decided they were also too red and swelling somewhat.

"Our young cousins. A woman and a boy of about six or seven. Their parents recently died and in their grief and fear, they saw danger everywhere, and finally fled."

Gybbon looked past the three men in front of him and saw the young bruised man at the back. He was slowly shaking his head and Gybbon chanced a nod of acknowledgment, rubbing his chin while he stared at the ground as if he was thinking. That young man, he was sure, was Murdoch, and Mora was right. The boy was not in league with his brothers. Sadly, she was also right to think he might not survive not joining with them wholeheartedly.

"I have seen neither a young boy nor a young woman. Anything that might help me ken they are the ones ye seek if and when I might espy them?"

"They are both fair-haired. The boy has a lot of red in his hair though. The woman carries a cat with her everywhere."

"A cat?"

"Aye, I fear so. It has caused some talk amongst the villagers, but she willnae give it up. But ye say ye have nay seen anyone like that?"

"Nay, and I have been on the road for nearly a week."

"She probably hid whene'er she saw ye," said the man Gybbon guessed was Robert. "She wouldnae trust any mon. Never did."

Gybbon could see why. Polite as the one talking to

him was, Gybbon knew he could not be trusted either. He did not wish these men anywhere close to Mora. It was going to take some hard thinking to figure out a way to leave this site without meeting up with these men.

"Then I willnae see her, will I? Now, it has been fine meeting ye, but I have somewhere I am trying to reach as soon as possible."

"Weel, if ye do happen to see her or her wee brother, just send word to the Ogilvys at Wasterburn. Just go down this road and ye will pass it. Ye will at least meet someone who can tell ye the right way to go."

"Got it. Wasterburn, just down this road. As ye wish." He glanced at Robert and said, "I would get those scratches seen to and cleaned out because they look to be starting to fester."

They all muttered something he suspected was supposed to be courteous thanks and rode off. Murdoch cast a quick look back at him and, after a glance at his brothers, gave Gybbon another nod. That boy was walking a very thin line, Gybbon thought, and shook his head. He turned back to place his porridge pot on the fire again and wait for Mora to return.

Mora slipped away from the spot she had chosen to hide in and took care of the business she needed to. As she used some of the water she carried to wash up, she watched Freya do the same. She had been scolding herself for taking the cat but began to think Freya would not have let her leave her behind. Mora had to accept that the animal was far too attached to her, but she would not do anything to end that, not even if it would stop the whispers about her in the town.

Freya came trotting back and got in the bag. Picking it up, Mora cautiously approached the campsite. The sight of her cousins facing Gybbon had chilled her blood. He had stood calmly holding his sword at the ready and Duncan had done the talking. She had winced as she had caught sight of Robert's face, not realizing how much damage Freya had done. He was going to be scarred and that was going to infuriate him as he was a bit vain. Mora scratched her cat's head and knew she could never leave the animal alone anywhere near Robert.

She had watched her cousins, afraid they might find some reason to strike out at Gybbon, but they finally just rode away. The way Murdoch nodded at Gybbon made her say a quick prayer for the boy. As Gybbon went to put a pot of something on the fire, she waited until she felt as certain as she could that her cousins would not come back, then stood up to go back to Gybbon and sit down next to him.

He handed her a plate of porridge and then set a small plate of chopped up rabbit meat in front of Freya. She idly wondered if he had had some experience with cats. Eating the porridge was a little difficult without the sweet cream she was used to putting on it, but it was good enough and she finished it. At some time, she would have to cook him a meal to make up for all the food he had supplied her with.

When she set her plate aside and looked at him, she caught him staring at Freya. "What is it?"

"I was just thinking on the scratches marring Robert's face. It is a bit difficult to believe such a tiny thing could do that much damage. She doesnae hunt her own meal?"

"Ah, weel, nay. Oh, she catches a mouse or bird now and then, but she rarely goes out alone. Every time she did something tried to kill her. Last time was the hawk. So, since I drove it off and it left her be, she considers a kindly person the safest armor to have and willnae go outside without one. Animals learn what to avoid when they are young, and she learned that being outside alone was bad and it stays with her." She took a deep breath and asked, "So did they wonder if ye had seen me?"

"Oh, aye. Ye and a small boy."

"I was hoping they were nay after Andrew as weel, but of course they are. He is still an heir, e'en if all the rest of us die."

"And, of course, ye are just seeing danger everywhere and need to be saved," he drawled.

Mora shook her head. "I am sure they will spread that tale as far as they can. Sadly for them, I am nay a person weel kenned in the area. My parents were because they went to the market each time it was held and kenned all the others who sold their goods there. Such a tale will serve them as weel as me. But I wonder why they didnae mention the crimes they seek to charge me with."

"Dinnae fret o'er it. I believe they took my word for it when I said I had seen neither a woman or a boy. They were nay pleased when I said I didnae ken who they sought, have never seen them, but they left me a description and rode away. I was just sitting here eating and wondering what would be the best and safest way to continue on to Dubheidland. Do they ken about that?"

"I cannae be sure. Mother made no secret of the connection, but I dinnae think it would have been much talked about. If they got their hands on Aunt Maggie though, they could have forced her to tell them." Just thinking of that possibility made Mora deeply afraid for the woman.

"They asked for Andrew and even gave me a brief description of him, so they dinnae ken where he went. Murdoch also shook his head when I looked at him, so even though I cannae be certain of what he was trying to say, I would guess part of the reason he did was to let me ken they had nay gotten any information from him."

"Good. He heard what I said to Andrew and could easily have led them to him and Aunt Maggie."

"Mayhap they have followed you."

"Andrew wouldnae be able to tell her how to get to Dubheidland. He kenned it was where we were going when we were packing up to leave before my cousins burst into the house, but he had no idea where that was. At least I dinnae think so. He may have overheard some of what my parents said and remembered it. Aunt Maggie might also ken, but I just cannae see her packing up my brother and leaving."

"She is probably worried about ye."

Mora sighed. "I expect so. She can be a worrier. I just hope she doesnae grieve or think she has somehow failed my mother. Andrew probably told her it was my cousins who killed our parents, and that is a concern. I cannae tell how she would react."

"Weel, 'tis best if ye dinnae worry on her as it did seem that your cousins dinnae ken where Andrew is so willnae be looking for the woman. I think ye have enough to worry about."

Mora laughed softly and rubbed her forehead. "Aye, I do. I ken Andrew is as safe as he can be, but I would prefer him to be with me."

"Mayhaps when we reach Dubheidland we can send someone after him."

"That would be nice. I am just nay sure if Aunt Maggie would let someone she didnae ken take him."

"Then ye give them a letter of introduction. Now it is time to leave."

"Ye dinnae think they will be just up the road or coming back?"

"We willnae be traveling right on the road. I mean to keep us within the trees for as long as I can," he said as he put out the fire and made sure it was out. "It means we will travel a wee bit slower than I like, but we willnae be in sight all the way." He glanced at the cat, which was carefully cleaning its face and paws. "And we have a nice alarm to let us ken if someone is coming."

"Oh, aye. I am nay sure how she learned to do that."

"Could be as simple as her noticing a rider approaching and how ye reacted to it. At least she is quieter than a dog when it is trying to warn ye of something. Some are clever enough to warn with a soft growl, but others start barking and let everyone ken where ye are." He cleaned off the plates they had used and packed them away. "We will head out soon."

Mora nodded and stood up. She carefully brushed off her skirts and took a few moments to tidy up her bag. Taking out the top cloth, she gave it a good shake and then spread it over the top of everything in her bag. The moment she was done, her cat leapt inside and settled down. She was surprised the man did not see this as odd as so many others did.

Gybbon went to his horse, saddled Jester, and put the blankets on the back. Mora walked up and held out her bag. He took a few moments deciding where best to put it, then looked at her. He was not sure where she should ride.

"Have ye done much riding?"

"Some," Mora replied, not really wanting to admit how little that was. "We had a few horses but I ne'er went far, just to Aunt Maggie or the village now and then."

"Then ye will sit in front of me."

"Why?"

"Easier to grab ye if ye start to slide off," he said, and ignored her outraged gasp as he swung her up into the saddle. "Also, ye are less visible to other riders this way."

The moment he mounted behind her, Mora decided it was not the best way to share a horse with him. His arms came around her to grasp the reins and she felt as if she was being embraced.

As they started out she tried to remain stiff and straight so that she did not end up leaning against him. She reached down to open her bag a little so that Freya could look around and would be better able to hear anything coming their way. Riding through the trees was a slow way to travel, but Mora had to admit it was much prettier and cooler. When her remark about that brought only a grunt from Sir Gybbon she fought the urge to sigh loudly. He might be one of the handsomest men she had ever seen, but he was obviously just a man. There would be no idle but pleasant conversation to fill the silence and make the time pass by faster.

Gybbon stared at her straight, slim back and almost grinned. She was trying so hard not to lean against him. That would not be a position she would be able to keep up for long. Soon her muscles would protest holding her so tensely upright.

He glanced down at her bag and saw the strange little cat resting her head on the edge as she stared around. It was the oddest little creature, he decided. Gybbon had never disliked cats, just never had much interest in them, although several of his female relations were quite fond of them. Jester was not bothered by the animal, so there was no need to worry about it.

Although he was more than willing to take her to Dubheidland, he was not all that certain Sigimor would or could help her. He knew his family would though, and that eased his mind save for one thing. He realized he was concerned that she might be hurt if Sigimor did not do as her mother felt sure he would. Shaking his head, he had to wonder if he was getting soft as he rapidly approached thirty years of age.

"My mother had heard that Sigimor had married," Mora said.

"Aye, he has," Gybbon replied, pleased to be pulled from his thoughts. "To an Englishwoman, a lady born and bred."

"He married an *Englishwoman*?!"

"Aye. She was running from a mon who wished to take hold of her nephew and all the boy had inherited. He killed her brother. He had even locked up Sigimor and his men, mostly his brothers, and she set them free. She surprised him when they wed with a nice dowry and some land in Scotland, which his twin now cares for."

"Are they weel suited?"

"I would ne'er have guessed that they were, but I have to say aye. She has nay problem getting openly angry with him and he actually seems to like that. He certainly tempts that anger with the things he says."

"My brother Niall was like that to my mother and me. Stirring the pot, my da used to say."

"Why didnae he come to help ye?"

"He and my other brother, David, went off to France about three years ago. They hoped to gain some coin by joining with one of the mercenary groups there and fighting some battles for France. We havenae heard from them and all attempts to reach them have failed for almost two years now."

"Ah, I see. I have kenned some men who have done the same as it appears there is always someone o'er there looking for some men to fight their battles for them. I dinnae ken how ye can find out anything for certain though."

"Weel, my thought was that Robert discovered where they were going and then paid some of those men to deal with it. I suspect it wouldnae have been difficult to do. Nay sure my brothers would have been able to sense the treachery. I doubt they would even have been expecting any."

"That too can be looked into. There are enough of our kin, mine and Sigimor's, who have been o'er there and ken people o'er there to hunt for some sign of them."

"I both dread the news and desperately want to ken the truth."

"That is how it is all too often, lass."

Mora just sighed and gazed up at the leafy trees as they rode. She had to wonder if she would ever learn the truth about her brothers' fate. It was easier, although sad, to just assume they were dead, especially since the chances of that were great, even without the aid of her cousins.

She blinked back the tears that stung her eyes. Now was not the time for a good cry. Later, when she found a chance to be alone, she would grieve for them. It would be a lot longer before she ceased to miss them.

Then Freya drew her attention. The cat was sitting up straight and staring back at the road. Then she hissed and ducked down into the bag. Before she could say a word, Gybbon rode deeper into the trees and draped one of the blankets over Jester's bright white tail. Mora leaned forward, tugged up the horse's mane and lay down, covering as much as she could with her cloak-shrouded body.

Gybbon was impressed. She had covered the other part of his horse that would have been easily seen even through the thick trees and done so without thought or direction. He had to admit she had learned the art of hiding very well. Then he heard the sound of horses approaching and idly wondered what his family would think if they knew he was accepting a cat's warning and acting on it. The laughter would probably deafen him.

He watched as her cousins rode by. They were not riding hard and fast nor looking around much. Gybbon wondered about their lack of urgency. He decided the men rode as if they knew exactly where they needed to go to find what they were looking for. Glancing at Mora, the look on her face made him think she already suspected that and could only wonder just how they had found out.

When the men halted just before they rode out of sight, Gybbon watched them closely. They were arguing about something and pointing in the direction he planned on traveling along in a short while. Cautiously, he nudged his horse along until he was close enough to hear the men, signaling to Mora to stay as she was and remain silent.

"Ye seem adamant that we dinnae travel to Dubheidland, Murdoch," Robert said as he looked at his brother. "I have to wonder why."

"I dinnae see anyone trying to go there, into a world of strangers, when they could travel straight on to a large town and disappear into a crowd."

"That would make a better place to hide," said the one who had given him the warning head shakes the last time Gybbon had spoken to them.

Despite how the scratches hid Robert's expression well, Gybbon was certain the man no longer trusted the young man. Gybbon hoped the boy had the wit to not give himself away. He had no doubt that Robert would kill the boy if he thought Murdoch a threat to his plans.

"I am nay sure we should just ride up to the Cameron keep anyway," said the fourth brother.

"We arenae going to fight them," snapped Robert as he turned his attention to another brother. "We are just going to inquire about our kinswoman, Lachlan."

"Nay sure he will be so trusting as to tell us anything."

"Why wouldnae he? She is naught to him. But now we will go to the town up the road a ways, wash up, and get our clothing cleaned so that we are at our best when we rap at his gates." Robert looked up at the sky as the first drops of rain began. "Find a damn bed to sleep in as we willnae be getting there this day. We may even be able to find out a few useful things about the Laird of Dubheidland that we can turn to our advantage."

"Are ye certain she would come all this way when she only met the mon twice, and her nay more than a child both times?"

"Aye, Lachlan, I am sure." Robert's building temper was clear to hear in his voice. "I was standing right outside the door when our dull-witted aunt told Da all about it. It was while he was still conscious enough to speak on occasion. I dinnae think he understood it all, but he did tell her to be careful. Now, let us ride on to the town," Robert ordered, and urged his horse to move on down the road, his brothers hurrying to trot along with him.

Mora did not move. As soon as her cousins were out of sight, Gybbon lightly rubbed her back. It had to be hard to hear the men speak so harshly of her mother, but he hoped the faint tremble he felt in her body was not because she was crying.

Moving deeper into the woods, he knew of a cottage nearby and hoped they could reach it before that one drop became hundreds. Grabbing the reins with both hands as Mora sat up straight, he made his way through the woods as fast as he dared.

Mora forced her eyes to open as the raindrops began to hit her faster. She pulled up her hood and did up her bag so Freya would not get wet. She was still fighting to calm the rage she had been seized by as she had listened to her cousins, but the sympathy Gybbon offered silently had helped. Mora suspected he had thought she was crying and was tempted to correct him. Then she decided it might not be a good idea to tell him of her murderous thoughts. She turned her energy to hoping they found shelter before the rain worsened. Her wound still bothered her and she decided she would try to find a moment of privacy to take a good look at it, so she silently prayed he would soon find the cottage he had spoken of.

Chapter Four

As they rode out of the trees Mora stared at the cottage they now approached. It looked sturdy and well tended to, yet showed no sign of habitation. She was surprised it had not been claimed by someone. When she finally saw Sigimor, she might try to gently suggest he go to some of the cities and hunt for tenants as she knew that was where he would find many ready to move and work for a decent home to live in.

Gybbon cautiously opened the stable doors, saw no animals, and led his horse inside. He quickly grabbed her by the waist and lifted her down. As he set down their bags and the blankets, Mora told herself it was the speed with which he lifted her down that left her a little breathless.

While he unsaddled Jester and then settled his mount in a stall and made sure he had something to eat, Mora opened her bag to let out Freya. When her pet escaped her and ran into an empty stall, she nearly ran after her knowing the animal was searching for a place to do her business, but then decided to just let her go. After all, she told herself, any animal stabled here would use the place the same way. A little buried cat mess would not bring any notice.

Freya had just gotten back in the bag when Gybbon came to her, collected the blankets and his own things, took her by the hand the moment she grabbed her bag, and went to look out the stable doors. It was now pouring and he sighed. Mora looked at the rain and sighed, too, resigning herself to getting wet.

"We are going to have to run for it, lass, and we will still get wet." He looked down at her as he draped a blanket over his head and around his shoulders. "Ready?" he asked as he stepped out, tugging her after him, and pulled the stable doors shut.

"Aye," she replied, glad for the slight overhang of the stable roof as it held off some of the rain if she pressed hard up against the wall. "Best to stay clear of me," she said as she pulled up the hood of her cloak, then grabbed tightly onto her bag and the cloak's front. "I cannae see too clearly with my hood up."

He released her hand and ran toward the cottage. Mora took a deep breath and then followed him as fast as she could. She used the temptation to get beneath the covered front step to keep going.

She bumped into Gybbon and quickly moved to stand beside him. He opened the door and, after looking around for a moment, grabbed her by the hand and tugged her inside. While he shut and secured the door, she took off her coat, then undid her bag to let Freya out. From the outside and in the rain it had not looked like a very big cottage, but from the inside it proved to be a lot bigger than she had thought. More important, she could not see any immediate sign of leaks.

She stood in a large room with an impressive stone

hearth in the middle of one wall. As she hung her cloak on a hook to the side of the fireplace, Gybbon piled some wood in the hearth and worked to get a fire started. Mora glanced at the narrow steps that led up to the loft, then over at the far wall where a kitchen and eating area had been set apart just a little. There was one shuttered window on each wall and Mora welcomed the light thrown off by the fire almost as much as she did the heat.

Glancing at the neatly stacked wood by the hearth, she said, "'Tis weel supplied for a deserted home."

Gybbon stood and hung the blanket he had worn on another hook. "Sigimor made it clear to any who visit regularly that they must leave something to help the next visitor and was verra firm on the need of leaving some wood at the ready to start a fire. He kens that the occasional stranger makes use of the cottage when the weather turns against them on the road but, as long as they dinnae stay too long or destroy anything, he lets it be. Many of my clan have used the cottage when traveling."

"Do ye think he hopes someone useful to him might come along and be convinced to stay?"

"I wouldnae be surprised. He has invited any Murray or MacFingal to settle if they feel inclined to."

"But no one has yet?"

"I think he may get a few of the MacFingals before long if only because there are so many of them. The men in my clan seem to marry weel or will inherit something, but one cannae tell if some of the younger sons might be tempted if they are nay so fortunate." He looked toward the kitchen and frowned. "I am nay sure we have much hope for a decent meal. The rain will keep most of the game away, e'en the small game.

I have a wee bit of rabbit but saved it for the cat. And, of course, I have the fixings for porridge."

"That will serve weel enough. I have a few pippens in my bag and a small number of berries. We can at least dress it up a bit." She went to her bag and dug out a box, then handed it to Gybbon.

Gybbon stared at the fine carving on the lid of the wooden box. "Nice work." He traced the shape of the thistle with one finger.

"My da did it." She reached out to touch the horse standing next to the thistle. "He liked to do that. He said it gave him some peace and made him happy. I brought three different ones from the house. I feared they might be taken or destroyed and they are the one thing that was unmistakably his."

"Aye. Someone who does such work puts a wee bit of himself in the thing he makes." He smiled faintly and set the box aside. "Then porridge and berries it is."

Mora moved back to her bag. She reached down to stroke the tops of the other boxes, holding the bottom of the bag firm. Gybbon was right. She could almost feel her father's presence as she touched his carving. Mora wished she could have brought along some of her mother's pottery, but it was simply too fragile for the trip she had needed to take. All she could do was hope it would still be there when she could finally go home.

Looking back at Gybbon, she saw him begin preparing some porridge. Mora sighed, but did so quietly so as not to insult the man. She liked porridge but suspected she would be desperate for something, anything, else by the time they reached Dubheidland.

"Do ye think my cousins are also sheltering from the rain?" she asked.

"Aye. I dinnae ken the men, but I would be willing to bet they tucked themselves up in a warm inn as fast as they could and are now enjoying a nice hot meal and an ale."

"Bastards," Mora muttered softly.

Gybbon laughed, revealing he had heard her, and Mora blushed.

"Exactly so."

Murdoch watched Robert guzzle from his tankard of ale and tried to maintain his expression of calm with a touch of disinterest. His brother's great plan was nothing less than madness, but he knew if he said as much he would die. What he could not think of was how he could get free of the plan and maybe even aid poor Mora.

He had liked Mora's parents and had been stunned when Robert had confessed that he had killed them. Lachlan had later whispered the tale to him of how Robert had struck them down even as they smiled and greeted them cheerfully. It was fortunate he had not been there and had been too stunned to say anything when Robert had boasted of the killing, he decided. If he did not remain as completely in agreement with Robert's plan as his eldest brother insisted all his brothers be, he would pay dearly. His brother had always held him firmly in place with a hard hand, and a part of Murdoch was growing very tired of it, especially now that he did not have his father to stand between them.

"Where do ye think our cousin has gone?" he asked Robert, and nearly winced at the fury on his brother's face.

"She may already be at that damned Cameron's keep with him and his horde of brothers. Her mother was so damned proud of her connection to that arrogant fool."

"Then we have lost her." Murdoch was proud of how he kept the hope he felt out of his voice.

"For a wee while, mayhap, but she willnae be able to resist going home. She also will need to get the boy if he isnae with her or want him to ken what she thinks is his now."

Murdoch kept his eyes lowered to his plate as he forced himself to eat a little food. The land and house did belong to her and Andrew. Their grandfather had left it to David. He had left that in his last will and testament. It would still be in their uncle's hands if their father was not so ill.

As he glanced toward one of the young maids scurrying through the room serving food and ale, he thought about his father's sudden illness, one that looked certain to kill him. It had come on so suddenly, and no matter what healer they brought him, it clung to him tenaciously. A sudden thought as to how that might have happened made Murdoch feel color rush to his cheeks, a flush born of fury and shock, and he was glad he was staring at a buxom brunette so that Robert would not think anything of it.

"Ye cannae handle a lass like that, boy," taunted Robert.

Murdoch gave his brother an angry look, then went back to staring at his plate. He could not banish the thought that Robert might have had a hand in their father's illness. It would explain why he had killed poor Old William. From what little he had heard of their argument, it was possible the man had been about to accuse Robert of poisoning his father.

Murdoch's brother was mad. He was now certain of it. A subtle look at Lachlan and Duncan told him they either knew it or had begun to suspect it, too. All Murdoch could do was try to keep all such suspicions to himself, not even hint at them by expression or word, and pray he could keep all blood off his own hands. It was cowardly, he thought, but he did not wish to be just another victim for his mad brother.

Robert reached out and curled his arm around the brunette's waist, tugging her down onto his lap. He then nuzzled her neck and the girl laughed, although Murdoch could see fear and disgust on her face. Murdoch wanted to say something and must have been too obvious about it, because Lachlan kicked his leg under the table. He went back to studying the food he tried to choke down and wondered just how deep into Robert's crimes Lachlan and Duncan were.

Robert soon dragged the girl off to his bedchamber and Murdoch looked at Lachlan. "Why did ye kick me?" he asked Lachlan quietly.

Lachlan studied him and said solemnly, "I wasnae in the mood to watch one brother kill another."

Murdoch heard Duncan grunt and said, "He is mad, ye ken."

"Just keep that thought to yourself, fool," snapped Duncan.

"If ye ken it, why are ye nay stopping him?" Murdoch could not understand their loyalty to Robert.

"He will kill us without blinking," replied Lachlan.

"Without hesitation and, I suspicion, without warning," added Duncan.

Murdoch dragged his fingers through his hair. "But . . . there are three of us and only one of him."

"And, as ye said in a too loud voice, he is mad. He can also wield a sword with far more skill than any one of us can." Lachlan pushed aside his empty plate and picked up his tankard to have a deep drink of ale. "Ye are younger than the lot of us by many a year, so ye dinnae ken much of how he has always been a fierce and deadly fighter with a blade. Sword or knife."

"Or both. The mon has a lot of blood on his hands. Tried to stop him from running off to kill some poor farmer whom he claimed had been insulting once and he cut up both of us," said Duncan. "Stopped only because Da and Old William ran out and made him. That was when I understood why Da ne'er left ye without a guard when ye were small, e'en if it was only a woman who could send up a loud scream and alert everyone."

"Yet he didnae protect himself weel, did he," muttered Murdoch.

"I would say nay, yet I cannae believe Robert would have aught to do with what ails our father." Lachlan shook his head. "'Tis a mortal sin, a heavy one, to set at his feet with nay proof."

Murdoch finished his ale and stood up. "Weel, if we dinnae do anything, wee Mora and Andrew will be dead soon. I ken I will ne'er be able to stomach it. Mayhap ye should decide if ye can."

Lachlan watched as Murdoch went to his bed-chamber and then sighed. "I hate that I share his suspicions."

Duncan gave a short, harsh laugh. "Weel, dinnae bother donning a hair shirt o'er it. It isnae needed."

"What do ye mean?"

"I mean he has probably done just what the lad suspects. I saw the lad listening at the door when Robert and Old William were quarreling. 'Tis why Old William is dead. He was arguing with Robert about what ailed our father, about how he was damned to hell's fires for trying to kill his own father. He demanded Robert tell him what poison he used and how he was getting it into the mon. That was when Robert killed him. Foolish old mon. William should have seen that coming," he said softly, and shook his head.

"Why didnae ye tell me? Tell someone?"

"It seems I have a verra strong will to live and to sleep at night. Our brother would slip in and cut my throat if he thought I kenned it." Duncan stared hard at Lachlan. "And heed this warning, Lachlan. If he e'er tries to get ye to go off alone with him, find a way to nay go. Always study the danger if he tries to get ye to do something for him."

Lachlan sat quietly for a moment. "We cannae do this. I thought if we rode with him we could keep it bloodless or stop something. We didnae stop a thing. Poor Rona and David were smiling at us one moment, Robert was smiling back, and then, with just a few swipes of his sword, they were both dead and our cursed brother was still smiling."

"I ken it. See it when I try to sleep, but we cannae run from it either. That would be a sure way to die. And watch Murdoch closely. When he tried to stop Robert from killing the lassie's goats, ye saw what he did to the boy, and trust me in this, he hasnae forgotten and will ne'er forgive Murdoch for interfering. He has always had a hate for the boy."

"Ye are saying that the best we can do is try to stay alive."

"Aye, and to keep that fool boy alive as he is the best of us. Robert has always been jealous of how our da treated the boy."

Lachlan signaled one of the girls to fill their tankards and then just drank quietly with his brother, his mind so full of troubled thoughts he suspected it would ache in the morning, if he got any sleep at all.

Mora finished scrubbing the pot Gybbon had made the porridge in as he walked around exploring what was in the house. There was not much to explore. It was ample comfort for a traveler and she was very glad of a roof over her head, but she desperately wanted a bath and there was also nothing to do as the night settled in.

As she wiped her hands dry she thought of how she should look at her wound. She had bandaged it while on the road and it had not looked like much more than a scratch. Yet now it ached all the time and she knew it was because of the walking, the riding, and the horse throwing her to the ground. She also suspected it was bleeding again.

"Do ye play chess?" Gybbon asked.

She looked at him where he stood, next to a set of shelves and holding a board in his hand. "Aye. Why would there be a chessboard here?"

"I wouldnae doubt it was left by one of my kin or a MacFingal." He searched through all the shelves and sighed. "I cannae see any of the pieces needed to play, so 'tis only good for kindling or something to cut cheese on."

She hurried to his side and took the board. It was a plain one, yet perfectly done. "Nay, I have something we can use." She hurried over to her bag and dug out the small box she had packed her father's chess pieces in. "My fither loved the game," she said as she returned to his side and handed him the box while fighting back a wave of sadness.

"Did ye even pack any clothes?" he teased, and then opened the box.

"Of course. There were so many things I had to choose carefully. If I had brought all I wished to save, I would have needed a wagon."

"These are magnificent," he said quietly as he studied a pawn. "Shall we play then?"

"Ye can set it up and I wish to go up to the loft for a few moments."

"The pot is in the far corner," he said as he continued to look over the chess pieces.

Mora knew that she was blushing slightly as she hurried up the stairs, and told herself that was silly since everyone had to use one at some time. Once done with the pot, she sat on the bed, relieved to see there were two narrow ones. There would be no awkward discussion on how to share the bed, just a simple decision about who sleeps near the window and who sleeps near the stairs.

She sat on the edge of the bed nearest the stairs and undid her gown, pulling it down to her waist. That did not give her access to the wound at her waist so she stood up and allowed it to fall further down. She then grabbed the bottom of her shift and rolled that up until she could see what was happening with her injury.

Untying the torn piece of her shift she had used as a bandage, one she noticed nervously was wet with blood, she tossed it aside and looked carefully at the wound. It looked to be a wider cut than it had and she wondered if that was because she had fallen on it. It was possible that she had erred by not stitching it, but her stomach had turned at the thought of stitching herself up. She had enough trouble just seeing her own blood leaving her body. Ripping another strip of cloth off her shift, she carefully tied it over the wound and then dressed.

When she stood up she swayed for a moment and feared she was about to swoon, but the feeling passed. Grabbing up the bloody rag, she intended to slip it into her bag as she went by it. It would probably be a good idea to mention her wound to Gybbon, but she feared he would insist they stop and tend it, perhaps even make her take to a bed for a few days. She had no time for that. When she was safe somewhere and had her young brother safe beside her, then she would see to her own hurts.

She sat down across from Gybbon at the table, the chessboard between them. He won the chance to make the first move, so she focused all her thoughts on each move to make after that, determined to win. He was one of those players who had to carefully think over every move while making soft sounds to indicate all his deep thoughts. She was tempted to throw the pawn he lingered so long over right at his head, but she was closing in on him until he finally made the next move and won.

Mora did not like losing but had to admit he had

earned the win. He was as good as her father and she had only beaten her father once. It would have delighted her father to match himself against another good player, she thought, as she picked up the pieces and carefully put them back in the box.

Gybbon watched her and could see the shadow of grief touch her face again. He suspected she had played against her father and thought of him. Such moments would come often, he thought, but he hoped she would soon reach the time when such fleeting thoughts warmed her heart instead of stinging her eyes with tears.

As soon as she finished putting the chess pieces away, he took her by the arm and helped her up the stairs. She was looking very pale and he suspected that loss of color had nothing to do with grief. He wondered if the small wound she had mentioned was worse than she had led him to believe. The moment they reached Sigimor and his wife, he would have her looked at. He would do it himself but suspected that would be bluntly refused. The only way he would be able to tend her wound would be if she collapsed from it.

Once in the room, he chose the bed by the stairs and left her to the window bed. He was somewhat disappointed that there would not be any sharing of a bed, but this was easier. And the bed by the stairs was the best one to take if one was concerned about intruders, he reminded himself. He went to pull the blanket down, then frowned at it for a moment. It had blood on it. Only a few spots, but a light touch told him it was fresh, for it was still damp. Her wound was troubling her and, if she did not say something soon, he would demand a few honest answers.

"I dinnae wear clothes when I sleep in a proper bed, so ye may wish to turn away now." He grinned when she did so with impressive speed.

Once in the bed, he tugged up the covers and settled into a surprisingly comfortable mattress. Someone had made sure the bed was well kept. If he ever found out whom, he would have to thank them. Hearing nothing, he glanced over his shoulder and saw only a bundle of blond curls over the top of the blankets on the other bed. Turning back to face the stairs, he closed his eyes and hoped they would have a trouble-free day on the morrow.

Chapter Five

"How long do ye think it will take us to get to Dubheidland from here?" Mora asked as he helped her mount behind him this time. She tried to take her mind off how it made her feel to sit so close to the man, her arms around his waist.

"Weel, it may take near an hour to reach the place where we have to turn off and take a new path. At the pace we have been setting it could be another day and a half until we reach the keep. But I ken this path and there will be another cottage to shelter in. 'Tis also why I have set ye behind me this time. We may be able to set a better pace this way."

"Would it be safe to use them? What if the ones who own them come round and find us there?"

"It will be safe."

"Who owns them?"

"The Camerons. As soon as we take the new path we will be on their land. There used to be a lot more people, but the fever took so many and, sadly, many of the ones left behind arenae ready or willing to live in them."

"Are there no drovers or shepherds or farmers to take them and work?"

"Oh, aye. A few have been placed, sworn loyalty to the clan and all, and carry on the work of the ones who used to live there, but when ye lose so many people and dinnae really trust some of the other clans' men, it takes a long while to get back all that was lost. Travelers to Dubheidland use them and occasionally some of those damned MacFingals when they come round."

She laughed. Every time he spoke of those men he got grumpy. Mora found herself looking forward to meeting them and rather hoped some of them were visiting when she arrived.

"I am surprised he doesnae have others just slipping in and taking the cottages over."

"That rarely happens, and when ye meet Sigimor ye will understand why. He has allowed one or two to stay, but he is training others in what is needed so he can fill the houses with his own people as quickly as possible. It hasnae been all that quick, really, near on twenty years, but he wants to be absolutely sure of any person he allows to live on Cameron land."

Mora shook her head. "I cannae imagine losing so much of one's clan. 'Tis a miracle he didnae lose his entire family, only his parents and some of the other elder people. My mother was verra concerned as Sigimor was nay so verra old himself and had a lot of siblings to care for. As I told ye, after meeting him, she decided he could deal with it."

"Och, aye, he dealt with it weel, though I suspicion his brothers might argue that. I will warn ye, Sigimor is no courtier. He is a mon who says just what he thinks e'en when he shouldnae. Just a wee warning so ye are prepared."

"Weel, thank ye for that, but I believe my mother said much the same. My da thought he was a wonderful mon." She could not stop the sigh that escaped her as she missed her parents more than she could say.

He felt her rest her head against his back and wished she was seated in front of him again so that he could pat her on the back. Instead he patted her on her hands, which rested on his belly. Her words carried the weight of the grief she suffered and he doubted a pat on her hand, no matter how well meant, would do anything to ease it. Gybbon suspected she would have done well enough if her cousins were not so determined to grab hold of all her parents had left behind and kill her and her only surviving brother, a child.

Gybbon could understand a man wanting to better himself. He could easily understand a man wanting a fine house and some land to bring his bride to. What he found difficult to comprehend was the ones who cheated or killed their own kin to gain such things.

"Weel, I wouldnae say wonderful"—he chuckled—"but I do like the mon and I trust him."

"Since he is the one my parents wanted me and Andrew to run to, I must assume they trusted him as weel."

"Aye, and your fither probably saw Sigimor's ability to protect ye and the boy."

"Are they truly all redheads? I remember a lot of boys and a lot of red hair."

"Every shade of red and, aye, they are mostly boys, only having one sister. She wed a mon from the MacEnroy clan."

"Connections all over."

"Och, aye. Our families' lassies have done us proud with their marriages. As have a fair number of the lads. We e'en keep a presence at the king's court, and it has been clear that there are those who see our good fortune with a jealous eye and it can rouse some bad feelings. We send our smartest lads, sometimes our prettiest, too, but they are also the ones who can be diplomatic, even courteous, nay matter how badly he may wish to punch someone in the face."

She laughed softly, thought briefly of pulling away, but decided she liked where she was. The strength she could feel in him and the warmth of him were both comforting. It was hard to imagine a family as vast as his sounded, the connections to other clans so various and, from the way he talked, strong and friendly. As for keeping a person in the king's court to watch out for any possible enemies, it was difficult to imagine. Her parents had never appeared to even think of such things.

When he abruptly rode Jester into the midst of a clump of trees, she sat up and looked around. "What is it?" she asked as he draped the blankets over his horse to hide the white mane and tail.

"Someone comes." He pointed at her bag to show her Freya sitting up and scowling at the road, her ears flattened and the fur on her back slightly bristled.

"My cousins?"

"I think it may be as the cat only reacts so fiercely when it is them coming our way. Dinnae ken how she can tell though, yet it appears she can. Several men riding our way. They dinnae sound as if they are in much of a hurry." He stared down the road and whispered a curse when he recognized the four men riding their way. "Aye,'tis your cursed cousins."

Mora quickly pulled up her hood to hide her pale hair, which could easily be a beacon telling her cousins where she was. "They didnae linger at the inn."

"Nay, and obviously didnae hear anything to deter them from riding straight for Dubheidland."

"So, what do we do now?" She tried to talk as softly as he did.

"We wait. E'en if they get there and are let in, they willnae get what they want, so will soon be headed back this way," Gybbon said as he bent forward until he was flat against his horse's strong neck.

After settling herself flat against Gybbon, Mora waited for her cousins to ride by. She had hoped they would stay at the inn, enjoying proper beds and hot food for a few days. But they had not, and thus she and Gybbon would not have at least one day without trouble. It was evident that Robert was determined to be rid of her as soon as possible. She prayed Maggie was hiding Andrew well.

Then Gybbon began to sit up, but continued to frown in the direction her cousins had gone. "What is wrong?" she asked.

"I am nay sure. Robert looked his usual sullen self. Yet, I noticed that his brothers all stayed behind him as they rode and rarely took their eyes off him. He would look back at them now and then, but it wasnae a friendly or brotherly glance."

"Mayhaps they just grow weary of the chase."

"Possible, but I begin to wonder if they now all think as we do. Robert isnae quite sane and, I believe, none of what he is doing is for the benefit of his brothers. Cannae be sure because we dinnae ken what reason he told them for all of this."

"So what do we do now?"

"Might as weel ride closer to the cottage. We cannae ride to Dubheidland with them straight between us and the keep. But at least when they finally leave the place, we will be close to where we can take our rest for the night."

"Good idea. And mayhap we can overhear something important when they go by again."

"That would certainly be helpful."

"I just wish I could understand what he thinks he can gain with all this. Aye, the house is a good one and the land is fertile, but there isnae all that much of it, not compared to what his father still holds. The keep is far grander with a great deal more land, fertile land and good grazing land. It just doesnae make any sense."

"Greed often doesnae. It would shock ye to discover how many of those who seek out more and more actually have a lot already. 'Tis as if they get a wee taste of the riches and grow gluttonous."

She sighed. "Nay, it wouldnae shock me, I fear. One just hopes for something better from one's own kin."

"Weel, we shall ride on within the trees and hope they come back this way and leave before we find a cottage or that small manor house that is out this way. If they dinnae show, then it will be another night on the ground."

Mora could not completely hide a grimace. Her wound would not like that at all. She needed it looked at and then pampered for a short while. It needed to be cleaned, closed, and have healing cream put on. A night on what would be cold, damp ground could easily bring on a fever. As they wound their way through the trees, she prayed they would reach Sigimor's soon. She needed to tend the wound properly or it would become very troublesome indeed, dangerously so.

She hung onto him as they continued to meander through the trees. Mora was beginning to get sleepy as the day drew near an end when Gybbon suddenly stopped and moved up nearer to the road. He tossed blankets over Jester's tail and mane again and she struggled to wake herself up so she could hear whatever her cousins might speak of.

"Is it them again?" she asked softly.

Gybbon looked around at her, thinking she sounded very groggy, but the light was too dim under the trees now that the sun was setting to see what ailed her. "Aye, and Robert looks furious," he answered just as softly. "Didnae ye hear your cat sound her alarm?"

She just shrugged. "I felt ye change direction and when I saw ye draw nearer to the road, I just assumed it was them." She reached down to scratch her cat's head. "Good lass," she murmured.

Finally awake enough to see the road they watched more clearly, she saw the four men slowly approach. Robert led them, his three brothers still staying as far out of his reach as possible yet close enough to hear any orders he might direct at them. Gybbon was right. Robert looked furious. Since he was still alive, she had to assume he had not openly displayed his temper to the Camerons.

"So what do we do now, Robert?" asked Duncan.

"About what? Those fool Camerons?"

"The fact that Mora wasnae there, nor was Andrew."

"We go and hunt for Andrew. He cannae be any harder to find than she is."

"Robert," said Murdoch, and he swallowed visibly, "Andrew is just a boy. Only seven."

"Aye, and with no male about to raise him."

Mora could feel all the blood drain from her cheeks for she now knew what he had planned. If she was right, and both her heart and mind screamed that she was, the man just might win if she could not get Andrew to someplace safe where Robert could not find him. Andrew would never survive if Robert got the care of him.

"I dinnae ken what ye mean."

"He is a boy child and heir to a fine house and a goodly amount of land. He should have an older, higher ranked male guardian."

"Ye want to take care of the boy?"

"God, nay. I just want to get my hands on him and that will help me do so. Who is that fool woman Aunt Rona liked so much? She lives in the town."

"Maggie," Lachlan said quietly. "She lives in a cottage just down the street from the butcher's. What do ye think she can do for ye?"

"Give me the boy."

"Ye think she has him? If ye thought that, why have we been riding all over the countryside?" Duncan demanded.

"If Mora doesnae have him, he is with Maggie. Thus far we have nay proof that he is with his sister, do we? The Camerons arenae going to let us look for Mora on their land; the laird made that verra clear as did the ones at the keep, so we will take the time to go have a look for the boy and start to get the papers needed to take him into our care. We are his closest male relatives. It shouldnae be hard to get whomever has a say in such things to hand him over to us."

Mora felt as horrified as Duncan, Lachlan, and Murdoch looked, although they did their best to quickly wipe those expressions from their faces. She knew Robert meant to kill her brother, neatly ridding himself of the last heir to what he coveted, but she also knew he would make life a living hell for the boy before he found a way to kill him without being blamed for it. As soon as possible, she had to find Andrew and get him tucked away safely before Robert got his murderous hands on him.

Then she thought of Aunt Maggie. That woman's life was now also in danger. Robert would not tolerate any defiance from a woman and Maggie would give him plenty as she protected her dearest friend's child. Somehow Mora had to find a way to get to Maggie and help her.

Her cousins rode out of range and she could hear no more. Gybbon began to ride back into the trees, stripping off the blankets that hid his mount's startling color. He knew she needed to get someplace where her wound could be seen to before she could even attempt to think of a way to help Aunt Maggie.

Once away from where her cousins had slowed their pace to talk, she said, "I have to get my brother before he does."

"Aye, ye do, but we can decide how that will be done when we stop winding our way through the woods." Gybbon glanced back at her. "Do ye think they mean to ride fast to town and catch her or that she is fool enough to stay where they ken she should be?"

Aunt Maggie was neither brave nor terribly clever,

but she was not completely witless. She knew who had killed her friend and her husband. She would expect them to come looking for the boy. Mora was just not sure where she would, or could, go. Maggie had never spoken much of her family, save for one elder sister, or her life before the old laird had taken her for his leman. She did have one friend near her, Morag Sinclair, who would take her in and hide her, but that would then put two older women in danger.

"Nay, she isnae. Oh, she can be verra silly at times and she isnae the bravest woman, but she will ken that they will come looking for the boy. Of that I feel certain. She and my mother were as close as any sisters and adored each other. Aunt Maggie will do what she must to try and protect Andrew."

"Then let her do what she must for a wee while as we come up with a sound plan to go and get her and Andrew."

"I will." Mora just hoped she could hold to that and not let fear and worry make her break that vow.

"Damn. Someone is staying in the manor." Gybbon rode a little closer, almost out of the trees. "I guess we will have to go on and find the cottage and hope it is empty."

"Wait," Mora said as the door opened and some man stepped out. "Who is that? He has red hair. Could he be a Cameron?"

"Not only Camerons have red hair, ye ken, but aye, that is Sigimor." Gybbon nudged his horse forward and the man turned to stare at him.

"What are ye doing lurking about in my woods?" asked Sigimor as Gybbon rode up.

"Keeping this lass from being killed by her greed-maddened cousin."

Mora leaned around Gybbon and smiled at Sigimor. Now she understood why her own family had so much red hair. He looked big and strong and was frowning at her.

"Weel, come on in and tell us what the trouble is."

Gybbon put his horse away, then led Mora into the manor. He entered the hall where Sigimor and his wife sat at the table and a maid was finishing the laying out of food and drink. After greeting Jolene, and introducing Mora to both of them, he urged Mora to sit on the bench and then sat beside her. She set her bag down under the table and a moment later Freya appeared at her side.

"Ye brought a cat?" Sigimor said.

"This is Freya," Mora said. "She is my cat. Do ye wish her away from here?"

"No, of course not," said Jolene, ignoring her husband's frown. "I love cats, especially little ones."

"So why are ye running about my woods, Gybbon?" asked Sigimor. "I shouldnae have Murrays skipping through my woods."

"I was bringing Mora here. Her parents told her to come to ye if there was trouble, and there was. Someone killed her parents as they were coming home from the market."

Sigimor looked at Mora and asked, "Who were your parents, lass?"

"They were Rona and David Ogilvy." She saw a brief flash of sadness touch his face and was both saddened

by the news she had just given him and pleased he
had remembered her parents.

"A shame, lass. Your mother was very prompt in re-
plying to any question I wrote her about when I was
raising my brothers and sister. She would have stayed
to help me if I had asked even though she ne'er
mentioned it, but there was great comfort in kenning
I had someone I could ask who would answer
promptly."

"I think she knew that."

"Who killed them?"

"My cousin Robert. His brothers ride with him, but
I begin to think they havenae had anything to do with
killing anyone."

"Then why are they riding with him?"

"I think they ken he is mad and wish to keep him
from doing something even a nearly dead laird's son
cannae escape harsh punishment for."

"Is he mad?" Sigimor asked Gybbon, and Mora
used the chance to help herself to some food, carefully cutting up a bit of meat for Freya.

"Such a pretty little cat," said Jolene as she sat on
the other side of the animal and gently stroked her fur.

"And the best warning bell I have e'er had," said
Gybbon.

"Warning bell?" asked Jolene, staring at the cat,
who calmly kept eating.

"Aye, she lets us ken when anyone is approaching
on horseback. She growls or hisses when someone is
coming, looks in the direction they are coming from,
too. We now ken she hisses when it is Mora's cousins."

"Why would she do that?" asked Sigimor as he
watched the cat his wife was cooing over.

"She is verra little for a grown cat and everything

frightens her. She kens what is a danger and avoids it. In truth, she stays with me all the time, ever since I beat off a hawk that thought she looked tasty. I suspicion she also senses my alarm."

"Smart cat, and those are words I would ne'er have thought to say. Why are your cousins trying to kill ye? And why did they kill your parents?"

"They want what was left to my father. I fear they also killed my brothers, Niall and David."

"Ye dinnae ken for certain?"

"Nay, they were in France to fight and gain some coin, but they have nay returned and ne'er wrote to my mother and father. Verra unlike them."

Sigimor kept asking questions and Mora did her best to answer though she was feeling deeply tired, fighting to keep her eyes open even as her head ached and her wound throbbed. When he turned his questions on Gybbon, she turned to Jolene. She hoped the woman knew something about healing as she knew she needed something done soon.

"Do ye ken anything about healing?" she asked softly.

"Aye. Do ye need something?"

"I got a wee wound when running from Robert and I begin to think it needs something."

"Oh." Jolene felt her forehead and frowned. "Yes, I believe ye do."

"Has she got a fever?" Sigimor asked.

Jolene sighed. "Nay. She just needs a little woman's aid. 'Tis just habit to feel for a fever. There is nothing I can catch here, so you can just go back to pummeling Gybbon for information."

Gybbon watched Mora collect her bag, let Freya in it, and then follow Jolene up the stairs. "Why are ye fretting about fever? It hasnae struck here again, has it?"

"Nay, but I admit, I fret o'er illness," Sigimor answered.

"No one has better reason. Is that why ye are here? There is illness at the keep?"

"Aye, and I am certain Jolene is right, that it is nothing of any great consequence, but I rushed her and the bairns here as fast as I could. Fergus will come to tell me when it is gone."

"Good. It is that time of the year, Sigimor. I doubt it is anything truly bad."

"I ken it. Annoys me as I didnae ken I was worried so about such things until I had my bairns and a wife. Now, we can talk more plainly about this trouble the lass has. I am saddened by her parents' death as her mother was a great help, yet wise enough to wait until asked and nay pushing herself into the family. And now I am here to talk of these murderous cousins and sort them out. 'Tis the least I can do for how she helped me and mine."

Gybbon grinned, helped himself to some more cider, and proceeded to tell Sigimor everything he knew. He also told him all he and Mora had guessed at from overhearing the cousins' conversations. The questions Sigimor asked and some of the ideas he threw out told Gybbon that Mora's parents had chosen well when considering their daughter's safety.

Chapter Six

"Oh, my dear," said Jolene when Mora disrobed enough to show her the wound. "You are very close to being badly infected by this wound. Lie down. I fear the first thing I must do is close it."

"I ken it." Mora lay down on the bed and winced as she looked at the wound; it looked redder than it had, was still open, and there was a little swelling around it. "I thought that it might need a stitch or two, but I just couldnae sew my own skin shut."

"No, I can fully understand that. This will all hurt," Jolene said as she began to gather the things she needed to work.

"Ye dinnae have any soothing words?"

"No, and if I tried them on any of these mad Camerons, I would be laughed at or seriously lectured about lying. I do have to cleanse this as much as I can and that will hurt. Mayhap that will make the rest seem less unpleasant. Myself? I will cry like a tiny bairn if I am even told a wound on me needs stitching."

"I have ne'er been stitched up but all my brothers

have been, and they tried to make me believe it was naught, just a wee pinch."

Setting down a bowl of hot, soapy water, Jolene wet the clean rag she had and then placed a cloth beneath Mora in the area of the wound. She then grabbed a couple of long strips of cloth to tie around Mora's wrists, tying the other ends to the small posts that were at the head of the bed. She met Mora's very wide eyes and suddenly laughed.

"I should have warned you. I do that so I do not get punched in the face when something I do hurts the one I am working on."

"People have punched *you*?" Mora worried about what she was about to suffer.

"Oh my, yes, and when you get punched by a Cameron, it really hurts, and then I must act as if it doesnae hurt much to keep Sigimor from hurting them for hurting me." She wet the cloth, wrung it out, and without another word, she started to wash Mora's wound. "Try not to scream or curse or I will have the men in here and I think you would like to avoid that."

Her teeth clamped tightly together against the urge to do just that, Mora nodded. She would laugh later over her thought that she could have done this herself. No one could inflict such pain on themselves. By the time Jolene was done cleaning the wound and had begun to thread a needle, Mora was panting and could feel the sweat dripping down her face. After the pain of having her wound cleaned, however, the pinch of the needle was nothing. When Jolene finished, spread some surprisingly nice-smelling cream on her, and began to bind her wound, Mora could feel that her face was still wet with sweat and she was panting.

After untying her hands, Jolene held Mora steady

as she slowly sat up enough to drink some cool cider. "I truly hate the pain caused by so much of healing work. Telling myself I have helped does not always work to rid me of that."

"Ye helped," Mora said in a soft, hoarse voice. "I ken it will feel better once the pain of tending it eases away."

Getting the cloth wet with cool water, Jolene wiped off Mora's face. "It was bad. Mora. Ye were very close to it spreading the poison all through you. I will warn you, you may fall under a bit of a fever for a few days. Hope it is not too bad."

"I dinnae have a few days."

"What do you mean?"

"My cousins are going hunting for my youngest brother. He is just seven. We heard how Robert plans to get his hands on poor Andrew. He plans to get himself named guardian of the boy. I ken he will torment the boy until he can find a way to kill him without anyone kenning he was the one who did it."

"Sad to say, I know just the sort of men you speak of. It reminds one of when a cat corners a mouse. Poor thing tries to flee, but the cat keeps it cornered and toys with it a while more before killing it. I believe it is one of the reasons some people truly hate cats, that moment of what appears to people to be naught but a deep mean. Your cat is lovely. I want a small one like that. I dinnae suppose she has kittens often."

Mora almost laughed. "That would mean she would have to go out and find a strange cat, a male cat. Nay. She never goes out unless I can go with her. Or some other person she sees as safe. Doesnae mean she willnae be caught some day."

"Get some rest. I will fetch you a clean shift and

then you can sleep. I have a potion to help you if you cannot sleep."

"Nay, I believe I will have little trouble sleeping."

"I will fetch the shift now."

The moment Jolene left, Mora had to grip her hands tightly together to keep herself from massaging, or worse, digging at the pain in her side. At the moment, there was little comfort to find in the knowledge that what Jolene had done would help her. She closed her eyes and sucked in a sharp breath as she tried to fight the pain.

When Jolene returned, Mora snapped out of a light doze and knew she had been close to going to sleep. Right next to the woman marched Freya. Her cat showed no hint of unease around the woman, and even though Mora told herself it was foolish to trust in an animal's opinion, she did.

She sat up with help from Jolene and hissed with the pain of the movement. Once the shift was on though, and she was able to lie back down, she quickly recovered. Freya leapt up on the bed, avoiding her wounded side, and curled up next to her.

"Do you need a box of dirt for her?"

"Oh, aye, if it is nay too much trouble."

"Well, from all you said, I realized you will not be able to be her guard outside, so it might be best. We had one for Old George when winter came as he loathed the cold, and I quickly got weary of cleaning up messes by the kitchen door. Be right back," she said even as she hurried out the door.

Soon she had all she needed, Jolene even placing a tankard of cider on the table by the bed. The woman promised to let Gybbon know where Mora was and explain that she would not be coming down the stairs soon. Mora curled her arm around her cat, holding her closer to her uninjured side, and closed her eyes.

Gybbon frowned at Jolene when she returned alone. "Where is Mora?"

"She is resting."

"Was it that wound she tried to tell me was just a scratch?"

Jolene sighed and nodded. "Aye, and she will have to rest for a few days if she wants it to heal."

"It was no scratch, was it?"

"No. To be fair, it may have looked like one when she first bandaged it, but something made the small cut widen. She thinks it was when Jester tossed her off. I have cleaned it, stitched it, and put a clean bandage on as well as some healing cream. She will be fine soon. We just have to keep a close watch for a fever but e'en that may not be serious."

"At least she had something to break her fast."

"A full belly can be very helpful in healing. The cat is with her. I did worry it might hurt her wound in some way, but it carefully avoided it. I had Jeannette bring in a box of dirt for the cat as Mora said the animal does not go out unless she has a guard."

"Ye wouldnae either if ye had to fret about even what flies in the air seeing ye as a quick mcal."

"Might be why it is so hard for me to find a runt," Jolene murmured.

"That and the fact that many a mama cat allows the runty ones to be pushed aside by the others," said Sigimor. "One of those ugly, hard facts of life."

"Of which there are far too many," said Jolene.

"True, but at least we are in a quiet time, no battles

or wars. Havenae e'en had a raid. Men are getting soft," he said with a hint of sadness, but he glanced at his wife as he spoke, and his eyes were full of amusement.

Gybbon decided it was time to talk about something that would draw Sigimor from his game of irritating his wife into yelling at him. "So, what do ye think should be done about her cousin?"

"Kill the murdering bastard," Sigimor replied. "Aye, and as quickly as ye can."

"Sigimor," Jolene said in such a mildly scolding tone Gybbon suspected she agreed with her husband. "Killing is not always the answer."

"Sometimes, lass, it is the only answer. Dinnae forget, the mon now seeks to get his well-bloodied hands on a lad of only seven and make sure he isnae alive long enough to inherit what his poor murdered parents have left him."

"True. I just find it hard to believe anyone would murder a whole family just to have their house and lands, especially when there is a big inheritance coming his way anyway."

"That reasoning is what troubles Mora now and then," Gybbon said. "She cannae understand it, either. In truth, it does make little sense. They are killing people for what is but a small piece of the estate their da holds, and I dinnae believe Robert intends to share any of that with his brothers, either."

Gybbon shook his head over the senselessness of it all and asked Sigimor, "So where is this son ye are so puffed up about? And, come to think of it, where are your lassies?"

"My son is asleep as all smart bairns should be, and my beautiful girls are visiting Ilsa. They do that now and then, so when the illness came I sent them right off to her."

"I hope ye sent her some help to deal with them as weel," Gybbon teased.

"Seven maids," said Jolene. "The ones that often help care for them so they know all their tricks."

Gybbon laughed but then grew serious. "Mora's uncle, the laird and the father to her cousins, had fallen ill. It was soon after that happened that the trouble began."

"She thinks they had a hand in that, does she?" asked Sigimor.

"Aye. It fits, doesnae it? The laird liked her parents a lot. Her father was his youngest brother even though they had a break that ended the closeness they used to have, and the mon never had a problem with what the mon had been given."

"Then Robert decided he wants that piece back and suddenly the laird is near to dying. The mon who was caring for him has also been killed and Robert is blaming Mora. He is claiming she stole his sword and cut the mon down."

"That wee lass?"

"Men are all too quick to believe women are murderous liars." Jolene shook her head. "And if they are led to believe she did it because the mon kenned she was poisoning the laird, something else all men believe women commonly do, then she has to also worry about the sheriff or his men."

"Aye, sadly true. I just wish I kenned a way to find out the fate of her other two brothers. There is nary a male to stand for her now and it would help a great deal if she had one."

"She has you, and a Murray on your side is not a bad thing to have."

"Nay, it isnae," said Sigimor, "and I would stand at her side if it was needed as weel. Mayhap ye ought to get her to Gormfeurach."

"Her parents told her to come shelter with you."

"I ken it, and she is most welcome if that is what she chooses, but right now my keep and, sadly, a lot of my men in it are too sick to be much help."

"The sickness spread so far?"

"Aye. 'Tis why I decided to get the three of us out of there. I was slower to act than I really liked but have been keeping a watch on things. It appears to be passing but they are all weak as babes."

"Then, aye, I will take her to Gormfeurach as soon as we can find the boy."

"That I can help ye with. We will set to it in the morning."

"I will tell Mora."

"Do ye mean to take her with ye?"

"I dinnae really want to, but the boy might come faster if we do take her."

"True. We will see how she fares in the morning." Sigimor stood and grabbed his wife by the hand, tugging her out of her seat.

Gybbon watched them go and a few moments later two women hurried in to clear away the last of the food. He rose and made his way up the stairs. He was just thinking that Sigimor had not told him where he was to sleep when he noticed a door open and, as he looked into the room, saw his belongings dumped on the bed. He was just about to go inside when he heard a soft scratching.

Walking down the hall, he stopped when he saw a

tiny gray paw slide out under the door. He opened the
door and found Mora whispering to her cat to come
back. Once he stepped inside, the cat ran to the bed.
Gybbon walked to the side of Mora's bed and looked
down at her, then sighed. She would not be going
with them in the morning. She was pale but there were
hints that she was feeling a bit feverish. There were flags
of red in her cheeks and her eyes were half shut and
far too bright.

"A scratch?" he drawled as he sat on the edge of
her bed.

"Well, that was all it felt like and it wasnae so bad
when I looked at it and bandaged it. I blame Jester."

"Why not? I often do. Of course, it wouldnae have
been made worse if ye had tended it properly in the
beginning."

Mora just rolled her eyes. "It has been weel tended
now. Washed, wrapped, and sewn up neatly and had
cream put on it."

He peeked into the tankard set on her table but
saw only a tiny bit of cider. "Did she leave ye a potion
to help ye sleep?"

"Nay, I didnae want one." She glanced at the
tankard. "I drank all the cider."

"I will fetch ye more."

"Thank ye. When I wake up, I wake up verra thirsty."

"No need to try and look pleading and pathetic;
I said I would fetch ye some."

"I didnae look either."

He laughed and bent to kiss her forehead, taking
note of how hot it was. "I will bring ye two."

Mora smiled at his back as he walked away, then
lightly touched the place he had kissed. She knew it
had just been a friendly brush of his lips, but it had

made her heart race. Then again, she thought with a grimace, that could just be the fever she could feel building in her. She closed her eyes, then opened them again fast as she did not wish to be asleep when he returned.

When Gybbon walked in with two tankards of cider he found Mora sitting up against her pillows. She looked asleep but her eyes opened the moment he set the tankards down. Cautiously he sat down on the edge of the bed again.

"Sigimor and I are going to ride out tomorrow and search for your wee brother. So mayhap before ye sink deep into a fever and cannae say anything of sense, ye could tell me where this Aunt Maggie lives and what your wee brother looks like."

"Weel, Aunt Maggie lives in a wee cottage near the butcher shop. Its door is painted blue and there are flowers all around. Andrew is a bit tall for his age, thin, has hair that is an odd mix of brown, red, and gold, and big blue eyes. He also is ne'er without his soldier."

"His soldier?"

"Aye. Our da carved him one with a big broadsword and Andrew always has it with him. If ye think the boy ye find is Andrew, just ask to see his soldier. He will have it on him somewhere. Says it is his protector, which is what Da said, I think. He is a painfully shy child and my da thought it might give him the courage to be a little less so. He calls it the Bruce."

"That will do. Anything we can use to convince this Aunt Maggie we are safe?"

"Ah, that is a bit harder. Ye could say something about Freya, I think. Oh!" She sat up a little straighter.

"Ye can say something my father said a lot. Check-mate! Time for another game."

"I can remember that. It could be that she may have an idea of what Sigimor looks like."

"My mother most assuredly told her about him, but I think just his name, size, and red hair will be enough."

"Then we should be successful." He reached out and held her hand because what he had to say next might prove hard for her to hear. "If we cannae find your Aunt Maggie and the boy has been left alone, where would be a likely place for him to hide?" He felt her hand clench on his but could see she was think-ing hard.

"There is an old oak at the back of the rear garden at the manor, looks half dead. It is hollow inside and Andrew can climb way, way up into that hollow part and stay there. All of us had to swear on his soldier that we wouldnae ever tell anyone about that as he needed a safe place and that was it. But I might be better in the morning and ye can take me with ye."

"Ye ken ye are a little feverish, right?"

"Aye. Just a wee bit though."

"Weel, having suffered a few wounds in my time, I believe it will get worse before it starts to get better."

"Oh. Damn."

"Exactly." He stood up and lightly brushed a kiss over her mouth. "Get a lot of rest. Sigimor and I ken how to hunt someone."

"Good night," she said as he walked to the door, and he just waved back at her.

Mora sighed and closed her eyes as she settled her-self flat on the bed. The moment her pet curled up next to her she put her arm around the animal and closed her eyes. She prayed Andrew had no need to go to his secret safe place. That would mean Aunt Maggie had been killed.

Despite her best efforts to stop them, a few tears slid down Mora's cheeks. She was losing too many of her loved ones. If she lost little Andrew, too, she was not sure how she could bear it.

But ye will, a voice whispered in her mind, and it sounded so much like her father she actually looked around the room expecting to see him. The fever was clearly disordering her mind, she decided, and closed her eyes. They would find Andrew, she told herself firmly. The boy would have at least two strong knights hunting for him and protecting him.

She wished hard for her fever to fade so she could go with them, but her heart did not really believe that would happen, so she prayed. A rough tongue went over her cheek and she knew she was still crying a bit, which always upset Freya. She fumbled a bit before she could scratch her pet's ears, and the animal's purring was enough to help her sleep.

Chapter Seven

Gybbon stretched, then reached for his clothes. It had been good to sleep in a bed again. It had taken so long to be free of Mora's cousins that he had feared he would be making himself a bed on the hard ground again, and it would probably have been damp as well after all the rain they had gotten. He was not fond of that.

He had been spoiled, he thought, and grinned as he pinned his kilt. Too much of the soft life, he decided as he stepped out of his room. Hearing Sigimor talking, he headed down the small hall to the stairs. He frowned as he passed the room Mora had been given. He heard a faint scratching and quietly opened the door to find Freya staring at him. Glancing toward the bed, he saw that Mora still slept soundly.

Freya stepped out to sit by his feet and he quietly shut the door. By the time he reached the dining hall he became all too aware that he still had the little cat at his side. This is what comes of feeding an animal, he scolded himself. Sighing with resignation, he walked

in and took the seat on Sigimor's left when the man
pointed to it. The cat hopped up to sit beside him.

"I see ye have brought your cat," Sigimor drawled,
making no attempt to hide his amusement.

"Mora still sleeps and this isnae my cat."

"Oh, hush, you two," said Jolene. "She is a sweet
cat. And so dainty and small."

"A runt. If ye like a runt, sort through the next litter
or three. Ye will find one."

"I tried that before and I picked out one you
thought was a runt, but it grew. And grew some more
until it was nearly as big as a dog. It also did not wish
to sit with me but go out and kill things."

"Aye, George was a fine rat killer," Sigimor agreed.

"He was, but he did not need to parade around
with his kill as he so often did."

Sigimor just grinned and Gybbon nearly laughed,
but Freya distracted him. She sat up, put her paws on
the table, and started looking over the food there. He
tugged her back down onto the bench beside him.
He glanced at Sigimor's wife but she just grinned.
Gybbon thought she might be spending too much
time around Sigimor.

"I will make her up a plate of food," Jolene said.

"Ye intend to feed that cat *our* food at *our* table?"

"'Tis clear she is accustomed to sitting at the table,"
Jolene replied to her husband as she cut up some meat
and put it on a plate. "Does Mora allow it?"

"Aye. Freya is a verra tidy eater, tidier than many
men I ken."

"And I suspicion you cut up the meal for the wee
thing?"

Gybbon sighed and nodded. "I put aside some of a

rabbit I caught to use it as her food as we traveled." He shook his head and poured himself some cider as Sigimor laughed.

Jolene set a plate in front of the cat and then slapped Sigimor on the arm. "Hush."

"Where is this son of yours?" Gybbon asked. "He was sleeping when we arrived, but I thought for certain a child that young would be up at this time of the day."

"And then we would not have a very comfortable breakfast, would we?" said Jolene. "He is awake and has broken his fast, but his nurse is with him."

"Ah." He frowned toward the door. "I wonder why Mora is late to rise."

"She was very tired when you arrived."

"Is that what she wanted your healing skills for?" Gybbon asked, wanting to be certain Mora had told him exactly what ailed her.

Jolene winced. "I got the feeling she did not want you to know and, perhaps, worry."

"So, it was her wound? The one she always claimed was nay more than a scratch?"

"I told ye last night. Aye, it was as though her fall worsened it. It was far more than a scratch. It looked as if some fool tried to gut her."

Gybbon growled and Freya rubbed her head against his arm. "Robert. She told me of that incident but said the point of his knife just scratched her a bit, although I could tell it pained her from time to time."

"That does not surprise me. It should have been stitched up immediately, and when your ill-tempered horse tossed her to the ground the wound opened wider than it had been, but I can certainly understand her reluctance to stitch up herself. The bleeding had ne'er really stopped."

"I wondered. When we stopped at the cottage I found a few small spots of blood on the blanket. I dinnae understand why she just suffered and didnae tell me."

"Weel, the wound can only be reached and treated if she sheds her clothing," Jolene said as she sat on the edge of the bench and shook her head.

"Ah, of course." Gybbon grimaced. "Modesty."

"Silly thinking, I know, but I am no good at suffering with pain. I would shed my clothing before a whole army if it meant someone could stop my pain."

"And I would wear myself out killing all those men who looked at ye, so we best hope ye are ne'er pushed to that point," drawled Sigimor. "Come to me if ye feel a pain."

Gybbon shook his head and laughed softly. "And what would ye do?"

"I would do a lot of patting her on the back and saying 'There, there, stiffen your wee backbone and grit your tiny teeth.'"

Grinning at the way Jolene rolled her eyes, Gybbon looked at Sigimor as Jolene said, "Aye, and that worked so very well when I had the girls."

Something in Sigimor's eyes told Gybbon that his friend had suffered every moment his wife was in pain during a birth but that he loved the results of it so deeply he would not stop fathering more.

"Weel, it stopped your screaming."

"Because I was stunned! I could not believe you thought it would help." Jolene looked at Gybbon, as she ignored the way Sigimor fed Freya a little meat even though her lips twitched with the need to laugh.

"Now, Gybbon, she may have just been denying that she was hurt or it simply was not a serious hurt at first."

"That sounds like foolishness," Gybbon said. "She just didnae want me demanding to see the wound. That could have gone on for quite a while longer, but the moment she swooned from pain, fever, or the constant slow loss of blood, I would have tended the damned wound. She was just being stubborn or hiding behind needless modesty." He glanced toward the door again. "I think I should check on her before Sigimor and I leave. She just wouldnae sleep so long. She had a touch of fever last night, ye ken. Do ye think it got worse?"

"It could have. I will go have a look at her."

"Ye dinnae have to go up. I ken how to tell if she is feverish or nay."

"I did the patching. My job now is to make sure it is working," Jolene said as she walked toward the door.

Gybbon thought about that reasoning for a moment, caught Sigimor grinning at him, and hurried to follow her. When he reached Mora's room, Jolene was already sending one of the maids for a pan of cool water and collecting up what she would need to change the bandage.

"The fever has worsened," he said as he walked up to the bed and stroked Mora's hair. Freya leapt up on the bed as the maid returned with the water.

"Aye. I feared it might." Jolene set the bowl of water on the bedside table. "I want you to bathe her face to try and cool her down while I take a peek at her wound, mayhap even change the bandage. Ye are also to try very hard not to look at her."

"Jolene, I have seen a few women without their clothes on. I *am* nine and twenty."

"She would be embarrassed and, if she asks, I want to be able to say no without guilt or the need to hide my expression."

"That bad a liar, are ye?"

"Abysmal."

He wrung out the rag in the pan of water as Jolene arranged the bedcovers to hide as much as possible while still giving her access to the wound. With as soft a touch as he could manage, he wiped Mora's face and neck. Despite his best efforts to do as Jolene had asked, he glanced down at Mora. There was little to see and her wound grabbed his attention.

Her skin was pale and the wound with its stitches, and lingering redness, was glaringly obvious. It was ugly, marring what looked to be unmarked skin. It also looked like far more than a scratch, and probably had been even before Jester had tossed her to the ground. Jolene was right. Robert had attempted to gut her as she fled him.

Thinking of all the ways he could kill the man, he washed down her arms, then wiped the skin showing above the edge of the blanket. She had also been unarmed. He suddenly grinned and thought, Unless you count Freya. Seeing the seriousness of the wound also convinced him it was very necessary to hunt down the boy. A man who would try to kill a small, unarmed, and fleeing female in such a way would not hesitate to cut down a small boy.

"Has the wound improved at all?" Gybbon asked as Jolene tied off the new bandage.

"Aye," she said as she washed her hands. "The fever

is probably just because she was so long without the care it needed, acting as if she did not have a gash in her side."

"But she probably shouldnae ride a horse for a while, aye?" he asked as they left the room.

"Oh, nay, she should not do that until the wound is tightly closed, and even then, she will have to go gently for some time. It would be best if ye could take her in a cart or wagon."

He softly cursed as he turned to walk into the hall, not waiting for Jolene as she had darted into her bedchamber saying something about washing and changing her clothes. Sigimor was no longer alone. There were his brothers, Fergus and Tait, and three MacFingals as well. He had to wonder just how close the clans had become since Sigimor had recognized the connection between the families.

"Do ye ever stay at your home?" he asked the three young MacFingals as he sat down on Sigimor's left.

"A lot, but we are nay missed much when we do leave. Too many of us," replied Nathan.

Geordie MacFingal nodded. "Aye, and 'tis probably for the best if some go for a wee wander now and then. Thin the herd," he added, and grinned.

Gybbon looked at Sigimor. "Jolene feels Mora's fever is just because she didnae get the wound tended to fast enough. She shouldnae ride a horse for a while though, nay until the wound is closed up tight."

"Ach, then we will need a cart for ye to get to your brother at Gormfeurach, and that could make the journey more dangerous than it need be if for no other reason than it will be slower and thus longer." Sigimor shook his head. "Ye can take some of these fools with ye though as, for the moment, we are on good terms with most all the clans and lairds for a fair distance."

"And ye think I should leave as soon as I get my hands on her brother and aunt, dinnae ye?"

"I do." He looked at his brothers and cousins. "Ye lads ready to travel to a wee village up the road?"

"What are we looking for?" asked Fergus.

"A wee lad of about seven and a woman who was caring for him."

"Someone wants them dead?"

"Aye, e'en though they are cousins. They want what was given them by their father's father."

"Reason enough for some." Nathan helped himself to some of the bread still on the table.

"Why do they think they should have it?" asked Fergus.

"Because it used to be part of the keep and its lands and their father is dying. They dinnae like that their grand-da took a piece out of the estate, e'en if it was for his own son."

Fergus shook his head and took a long drink of cider. "Madness."

"Happens all too often," murmured Nathan.

"Still doesnae make sense," said Fergus. "Ye are supposed to be able to trust kin. Ye are blood and there can nay be anything as close as that. It isnae e'en a fair battle as family kens all your secrets and all your weaknesses."

"I dinnae have any secrets," said Sigimor, and frowned when Fergus just shook his head and laughed before shoving some eggs into his mouth. "Why is that funny?"

Wiping his mouth, Fergus looked at his big brother, who was also his laird. "Because ye simply cannae keep them inside."

Sigimor looked thoughtful for a moment, then said, "That may be true. Ne'er really done anything I felt I had to hide."

"Because ye are so weel behaved?" Gybbon just laughed when Sigimor spared a moment of glaring at Fergus to glare at him.

"The only reason to be quiet is if ye did something wrong or something ye are ashamed of."

"Then you must be fair to bursting with secrets," said Jolene as she walked into the hall and sat on Sigimor's right.

Sigimor gave a sharp tug on a lock of her hair, then grinned as she fussed to put it back in place. "So, the lass will be abed for a wee while, aye?"

"Aye," she answered, "although I cannot say for how long. Could be as little as a day or two or could be a week or more. I do not know how fast she can throw it off."

"What is the longest ye think it may take?"

"A fortnight, and if it is not gone by then, then something else is wrong."

Sigimor nodded. "Then we will figure we have that long but hope it is much less, and definitely no riding a horse for a week or more."

"Aye, definitely none of that."

"The cart is already here, so we dinnae need to sneak it over here, so that is done. We just need to come up with a way to hide her in it and how to get it to Gormfeurach with as little trouble as possible." He looked at Gybbon. "And get as much information as we can along with the boy."

"Do ye think he is still there with that woman?" Jolene asked.

"I *hope* he is. But all we can do is hope he was taken somewhere safe before the cousins rooted him out."

"Do ye think they have gone to do that?" asked Gybbon.

"I think they went to do that as soon as they failed to get into my keep."

Gybbon sighed and nodded. He thought the same, feared the same. The town was very small, so he doubted the boy would go unseen for long. He did not have any strong, armed men to watch out for him either. Only a woman that even Mora said could be silly now and then. There was very little to hang a hope on.

"Then we best work hard to dig out as much information as we can."

"Aye." Gybbon nodded and then took a deep drink of his cider to hide his sigh and worry. "The moment we start poking about they will start watching us much more closely."

"Ye think they ken ye are with her?"

"Nay certain of it, but they did use time to speak with me once on the road where they were looking for her. Somehow, they kenned about ye and that her mother would have sent her to ye. So, it wouldnae be much of a leap for them to quickly put that all together and decide I was helping her. I brought Mora and ye more trouble than I thought."

"Nay, it wouldnae be a big leap at all. But cowards who try to kill and steal from their own kin are nay ones who will come at me in the open. They dinnae have an army with them."

"They do have the sheriff, I fear, and his men."

Sigimor shrugged. "Dealt with that mon before and some of his men are kin to mine. Just worry about the lad.

"And when you go to the village remember all the ones those idiots may see as useless so do not question them, but they are just the ones you wish to speak with. The ones who run the shops and the women who hold the houses together. To ones who Robert thinks are not worth troubling himself with. He will see them as no better than dumb animals."

"Ye are right about that," Gybbon said. "The mon is arrogant, blindly certain of how important he is. Ye should see how he treats his own brothers. I think they are all afraid of him."

"Yet they follow him."

"They do, but nay out of brotherly love or family honor. Out of fear. The youngest is tempting his brother as he actually tried to stop him from killing off all of Mora's goats."

Jolene gasped. "What was the reason for that?"

"She could still have a living if she had her goats."

"Oh. But he did not kill them because his brother stopped it."

"Only for a moment and he got a good beating for it. Nay, e'en if Robert is successful in getting hold of the boy, Murdoch's life will be verra short. E'en the other two have warned him. I only saw the looks of warning, but I suspicion they have said something, too."

"So, what happened to the goats that lived?" Jolene asked.

"Murdoch's interference allowed some of them to leap the fence and run. Robert decided it was enough, that she wouldnae be able to gather them all up, I suppose."

"Which shows he has little knowledge of animals. I suspect those goats were well fed, sheltered, and pampered even. Of course they would wander back home."

"Or to one of the people who cared for them. That may help us find the boy," said Gybbon.

"Aye, it might. Will have to keep it in mind," Sigimor said, then frowned. "Nay such a good thing though, as it may help Robert get to the lad, too." He stood up and then bent to quickly kiss his wife. "We best be on our way. Ye keep watch, Jo. They may come here."

"We have big, burly men with swords here," she said, and patted his hand where it lay on the table. "We will be fine. You just watch your back."

"Always do."

Gybbon got up, said his thanks and farewells to Jolene, and hurried out after Sigimor and his men. Sigimor paused to give some orders to the men lurking around outside, and Gybbon watched them station themselves more precisely around the manor. Jolene was right. She had big, burly men with swords to protect her, and he wondered if Sigimor had purposely chosen his biggest men.

Once mounted, Gybbon felt a touch more confident about what they had to do. It was a small but impressive little force of men and he doubted anyone would hesitate to answer their questions. He hoped he would have as much when he had to take Mora to Gormfeurach. He prayed they would not be needed, but he was not foolish enough to think Robert would not prove to be a problem. He was eager to get to Gormfeurach.

Chapter Eight

"Nay sure the eight of us riding into the village like this is good. Could make folk wary or e'en nervous," murmured Gybbon as he glanced at Sigimor.

"Nay, they have seen us before. The bigger town in the other direction sees us more often as it has an excellent alewife and an inn I dinnae mind taking my wife to."

"There is the butcher's shop," said Fergus as he moved up on Sigimor's other side.

They all stopped to look around but did not immediately see a blue door. Sigimor stared hard at a burned-out cottage, his expression growing darker with each moment he looked at it. Gybbon then noticed the flowers in front of the still smoldering pile, some burned, some stomped down by the ones who had come to fight the fire.

Gybbon cursed. "They have already come after her."

Sigimor nodded. "Appears they have, but did they start the fire just to kill her and the boy or because they were angry that they couldnae find them? We will inquire of the butcher first."

Following him, Gybbon left his horse under the

watchful eyes of Fergus and the MacFingal lads as he, Sigimor, and the others walked into the butcher shop. It was clean and well set up. One could smell the blood but only if one breathed deeply, yet there was no scent of rot.

"What can I be doing for ye lads and m'laird?" asked the plump, aging man at the counter, nodding respectfully at Sigimor. "'Tis usually your wee lady who comes by. Mayhap ye could tell her that I will have fresh pig on the morrow."

"I will do that," Sigimor said. "We were wondering if ye kenned what happened to the cottage across the road, the one that has burned down and that should still be being soaked as it smolders? Did it have a blue door?"

"That it did, aye. A wee bit of fancy done by the woman who lived there."

"Did she get out?"

"Cannae say and, if any can, they are nay talking. She had a wee lad with her for a wee while and no one will say what has happened to him, either. A sad thing."

"And no idea of who did it?"

"Nay that any are speaking of. That poor woman ne'er did anyone harm. She used to bring me flowers for my shop. To keep away the smell of death, she would say."

"Was anyone verra close to her?" asked Gybbon.

"Lady in the house two doors down from it—has a green door." He pointed in the direction they had just ridden in from. "The two of them often came in here together chattering like magpies and looking o'er what I had. I would often hear them talk of meals they had shared. So, aye, Morag Sinclair would have been close to her, I am thinking. Sheriff talked to her though and he didnae look happy, so I be thinking she didnae tell him much. 'Course those Ogilvy men were with the sheriff, too, and he didnae look too happy about that either."

"Thank ye," said Sigimor. "I will be certain to tell my wife about the pig."

Gybbon looked at Sigimor once they were back outside. "Do ye think we ought to talk to the sheriff?"

Sigimor frowned and rubbed his chin. "Let us speak to this Morag Sinclair first. She might already ken what he thinks about the house or what he may plan to do about it."

"I hope she has some information as I would like to be able to give Mora some news."

"E'en if it is bad?" asked Fergus.

"Aye, e'en then. Kenning something is usually better than kenning nothing."

Leaving the youngest to watch over the horses again and keep an eye on the smoldering cottage, Sigimor, Gybbon, Nait, and Nanty walked up to the door of the tidy little cottage. Gybbon wondered why the man who owned the land was so tight-fisted about the land he allowed the cottages to be put on. None of the ones in this row had much at all, not even enough for a proper kitchen garden. He had seen ones like this in the smoky, bustling towns that he thought had far too many people crowded into them.

"This is all Ogilvy land," said Sigimor. "Old mon clung to every patch of land he had. Mayhap that is where his grandsons got their idea that it should all be theirs again." He looked up and down the road. "They are rather, weel, fancy for field workers though."

"Because they were built to hold his lemans," said a woman's voice.

They all looked at the black-haired woman standing inside the now open door. Gybbon was relieved that he was not the only one who had not heard her open the door. Even Sigimor looked surprised. Quickly counting the buildings in the row of cottages, he decided the old laird had been a randy old goat. There was a dozen, if one included the burned out one. Looking at the older woman's still very pretty face surrounded by a thick fall of curly black hair, he also decided the mon had had very good taste.

"The old laird?" Sigimor asked.

"Aye. The son is a bit of a pious fool. *His* sons, though, are nay so good. Eldest is pure evil. I willnae let him cross my thresh stone." She looked them all over and grinned. "What can I do for all ye fine lads then?"

"We were told that ye might ken something about Maggie, the woman who lived in the cottage. The butcher said ye were her friend."

"Aye." Tears glistened in her eyes and Gybbon felt his heart sink as she shook her head and waved them inside. "Take a seat and I will fetch some cider for us. Dinnae sit on my dog," she called out as she disappeared into another room.

Sigimor stood in front of one of the settees and glared down at a mottled gray ball of curls. "That isnae a dog. 'Tis a furry rat."

"I heard that!" the woman said as she came into the room with a tray of tankards. "Impudent boy."

"Boy? Havenae been called that in a long while." Sigimor nudged the dog out of the way and sat down right after the woman did.

"When ye are my age near every mon who isnae gray and bent is a boy. Do the lads with your horses want anything?"

"Nay, they are fine. Ye dinnae need to serve them."

"I wasnae going to. I was going to make ye do it."

Gybbon saw her mischievous grin, then looked over to see Sigimor's surprise quickly change to a narrow-eyed look with a strong hint of laughter behind it. "Ye stayed with the old laird the longest."

"I did indeed. How do ye ken that?"

"Ye picked up some of his bite."

The woman's laugh carried a strong hint of bawdiness. She shook her head and retorted, "Och, nay. Nay. He got that from me. I will fetch ye some tankards and the jug for the other boys." When she stood up, so did all the men. "Ye dinnae need to do that or ye will be bouncing up and down all the time. I am nay one who can sit still for long. Come along," she said, signaling Sigimor to follow her.

Sigimor did and then went to serve some cider to each of the men watching their horses. Watching closely, Gybbon saw Sigimor give Fergus a rap on the head, then hand him some cider. When Sigimor stepped back inside, the woman rushed to meet him and hand him a tray with four little tarts on it.

"Go on. Give them to the boys." She nudged him outside and dashed off again.

With a heavy sigh, he walked over to give each of the men a tart, then paused to glare at the smoldering pile that used to be Maggie's home. "Hate to reward that brat Fergus for whining about food," he said as he came in and sat down.

"He is fore'er hungry. Dinnae ken why he isnae so

fat ye could roll him along the road to spare the horse," said Nait. "Fire still smoldering?"

"Aye, and it troubles me that no one has done a thing about it."

"Well, there are four men out there," said Nanty.

"True enough, but we dinnae have any water."

"Ye need water for something?" asked Morag as she came back in the room with a tray of tarts.

"That fire is still smoldering under the wreckage and it troubles me. Could just go out but could also flare up of a sudden."

"Aye, it could. Could take down this whole row if it did. If ye have the men, I have barrels of water at the side of the house. I collect the rain when it falls. Use it to water the horses and all."

"I have men." He stood up and walked toward the door and then strode back to grab a tart, wink at Morag, and go out.

"Oh, that is most certainly a Cameron."

"I apologize, ma'am," Gybbon said. "I cannae believe we ne'er told ye our names. Aye, that was Sigimor Cameron, Laird of Dubheidland. Those men outside are his brother Fergus and three MacFingals of Scarglas. Here we have Nait Cameron and Nanty, Sigimor's brother by marriage. I am Sir Gybbon Murray."

"Oh, I once met a Murray at the king's court. Lovely man. All the lassies sighed after him."

"I would wager that would have been Payton Murray."

"Aye, that was his name. Had a bit of trouble, but it must have been sorted out as he married. Many a lass wept over that, I can tell ye."

Gybbon sighed. "I imagine so." The door opened

and Sigimor started to walk in, but the man with him hesitated. "Sigimor?"

Looking at the man behind him, Sigimor grabbed his arm and started to tug him into the house. "I got the lads to toss some more water on the fire and met this mon. Think he might have a few things to tell us, Gybbon."

"Hello, Iain!" Morag leaned forward, waved and smiled at the mon.

"Ma'am," Iain said, and nodded at her.

"Ye ken what happened to Maggie and the boy?"

"I do, ma'am."

"Did ye tell the sheriff?" asked Gybbon.

"I wasnae about when he came, so nay, havenae told him anything. I hadnae told my wife what I saw, either. Maggie was in the house, ye ken. Ran back in after she made the boy wait outside. He was watching her through the door, but then the ceiling fell in and he ran. Maggie came out after he fled and looked for him, then got in the cart. I ran up to toss some water on her skirts because they were burning a bit. She told me to nay say a word, but if the Laird of Dubheidland asked questions, I should answer and be sure I tell ye she was headed for her sister's."

"Good. Dinnae tell him," said Sigimor.

"I willnae. Is Maggie in trouble?"

"The sheriff has been told she stole and is hiding a child, and also a killer. Those fool Ogilvy brothers are trying to make him believe little Mora killed Old William and has tried to kill their father with poison. 'Tis the excuse they use to justify the way they are hunting the lass."

"Little Mora? The one who totes around that cat most others would just drown? And to think of Maggie stealing anything is laughable." Iain suddenly stood up straighter. "They did it, didnae they? They want that bit of land taken out of the estate for David."

"They do. They killed David and Rona for it," Morag said.

"Nay. I willnae say a word to the sheriff. Doubt he will recall me anyway, or he will think because he talked with my woman, I have nothing to say to help him. Thinking we should ask for a new sheriff if he can be made to listen to such lies. Bribed, I suspect."

"Most likely," Gybbon said. "Do a lot of folk in the town ken anything or think like ye do?"

"Most of them, I suspect, and if they kenned it was those Ogilvy brothers who killed David and Rona, they would hang them themselves. Those two were verra good to the people in this village." Iain glanced back at Sigimor and smiled faintly as he said, "He would heed the Laird of Dubheidland."

"And so he should," Sigimor said as he walked to the settee and sat down.

Iain looked at Gybbon, his eyes a little wide, and Gybbon just shrugged. "We will have to go hunt down the lad," he said to Sigimor.

When Sigimor reached for a tart, Morag slapped his hand, then held the tray out to Iain. When he chose one and thanked her she held the tray out to Sigimor. He was watching her with that narrow-eyed look that held a hearty laugh in its depths.

Sigimor pointed at himself. "Laird."

"Not of this place." She smiled sweetly as he took a tart and she settled the tray on the table.

"Oh, ye really must meet my wife."

"Arenae ye afraid I will teach her all manner of naughty things being that I was a leman?"

"Nay, hoping perhaps." He grinned when both Iain and Gybbon laughed.

"Rogue."

"I do my best."

"Weel, if ye are done flirting with our hostess, Sigimor, I think we should try to hunt down the laddie. If he thinks he saw Maggie burn up in the cottage he will be terrified."

"I was just making certain I gave the lads enough time to put out the last of the fire," Sigimor said as he stood up. "We will go find the lad now. Ye ken where this safe place is, aye?"

"Do ye want me to go with ye?" said Morag. "The boy kens me as a friend of Maggie's."

"That would be good, but then we would have to bring ye back and we need to get him away from here as fast as we can," said Sigimor. "Ye could help by delaying the sheriff if he and his men come looking. I had the understanding that the boy doesnae tell many about his safe place, but ye can ne'er be sure of that when 'tis only a child."

"And I will keep a close watch on the fire," said Iain. "Cannae believe the fools left it smoldering as they did."

"Thank ye."

Sigimor strode to the door, the other three men followed, and Gybbon moved to follow them. "Sir Murray?" Morag smiled when he turned to look at her. "When ye see wee Mora again, tell her Morag says hello and to ne'er forget to reach for the fruit that is highest on the tree or vine. It is often the sweetest."

"Aye, I will tell her," he said, even as he wondered what she meant.

He nodded a farewell to them both and hurried after Sigimor. All of them were on their mounts and ready, so he quickly mounted Jester and started toward Mora's home. It was not very far from the town and he got angry when he got there and had to sit tensely, hiding in the trees with the others as they watched the sheriff, his men, and the Ogilvy brothers search all around. He leaned forward on his horse a little as he watched the sheriff argue with Robert, but then they all went to their horses and left.

"Wait a bit," Sigimor said quietly as they all tensed to move.

"It looked as if the sheriff is getting weary of Robert," said Gybbon in an equally quiet voice.

"Aye. Fool boy is too arrogant to understand that the sheriff sees his place as one who only answers to the laird and Robert isnae sitting in that chair yet."

It was several minutes later before Nanty suddenly slipped into their group. Gybbon was annoyed that he had not even realized the younger man was gone. All Nanty did was nod at Sigimor and that was enough to tell the man they could ride to the manor house. Gybbon tried hard to keep the slower pace the other men did until they reached the rear yard. He then dismounted and raced to the old oak that was hollow inside.

Sigimor came to stand beside him. "Why are ye looking at a rotting tree?"

"It is hollow inside and the lad can tuck himself up inside that hollow. Mora said he insisted it was his safe place and they should never tell anyone."

Sigimor stuck his head inside and looked up into

the darkness. "Cannae see a thing but I can hear something," he said as he backed out.

"What?"

"Breathing. Lad," he called up the tree, "your sister sent us to collect ye."

When no one came down, Sigimor stood back a little and frowned. "Mayhap we should have brought Morag."

"Nay, what I told her still holds. Nay matter how fast we get her back to her cottage, we would be seen. And then we would run the chance of meeting with the Ogilvy brothers or the sheriff and his men."

"Ah, right. So how do we get the lad out of there? None of us could wriggle up there to bring him down."

"Weel, she told me a few things to talk to him about that may help." He went to the tree and looked up. "Mora sent us to get you, lad. She is with us at Laird Sigimor's place."

"Is she all right?" a small voice asked.

"Oh, she is good enough but cannae go riding about for a wee bit, so she is abed with her silly cat, Freya."

"Ye let her take Freya with her?"

"She wouldnae come without the animal, would she?"

"Nay. Maggie is dead. I saw the roof fall on her and it was burning. She was going to take me to her sister's."

"I will take ye to the place your mother and father wanted ye to go."

"My mother and father are dead, too. Robert killed them."

"And he will pay for that. But they cannae get ye, can they? Ye still have the soldier with the broadsword your da made, aye?"

"Aye. He protects me."

"We wouldnae mind a wee bit of added protection, too. It will help us care for your sister and ye as was agreed." He could hear a soft scrambling noise and hoped it was the boy coming down.

Glancing back at Sigimor, he nodded, letting him know they would soon have the boy, and the man went to don his large cloak, which he planned to hide the boy under as they rode. He looked back into the tree and came face to face with a handsomely carved soldier, sword in hand. The small, pale hand holding it out was shaking a little.

"Come on, lad, almost there."

"Could ye please hold the Bruce for me? I need both hands to finish getting down."

"The Bruce?" he said as he took the finely made soldier. "Very fine name for him."

He looked up as the boy dropped to the ground. His clothes were dirty and Gybbon could see a few torn spots, but no wounds were visible. The dirt on his face was well smeared by tears, and Gybbon caught the boy by the hand to pull him outside the tree. Sigimor returned and studied the child, then looked at the wooden soldier. Gybbon almost grinned as the child looked up at Sigimor and his eyes widened.

Sigimor wrapped his arm around the boy's waist and hefted him up while the wide-eyed Andrew snatched back his soldier and held it in front of him. "Now, lad, while we ride to my home I will have to keep ye covered by my cloak but dinnae be afraid. Ye have the Bruce."

"Aye. My da gave it to me. Are Mora and Freya really at your house?"

"Och, aye. That cat has even eaten at my table like a wee, furry princess."

The boy giggled and Gybbon shook his head. Say what one would about the many things that might be wrong with the man, he had a gift of making children feel safe. Andrew did not even protest as he was set up on Sigimor's large horse, then Sigimor mounted and wrapped his cloak around the boy.

"Sit hard up against me, lad, so there is no part of ye to see, nay even the shape of ye, and we will go to join your sister."

Chapter Nine

Jolene met them at the door. "Oh, thank God, ye found him," she said as Sigimor set the boy on his feet and then shed his own cloak.

Andrew pressed himself hard up against Gybbon's legs and stared up at Jolene. "She is English!"

"Aye, laddie." Sigimor walked over to stand next to Jolene, who was trying hard to hide her irritation, and he put his arm around her, tugging her close to him. "We noticed that but I wed her anyway." He grunted when she elbowed him in the side.

"Are the English hunting me, too?"

"Nay, laddie," said Gybbon, and he ruffled the boy's curly hair. "As Sigimor said, she is wed to him."

Then Andrew stepped away from Gybbon and gave Jolene a nice bow. "Thank ye, m'lady, for sending your husband to help me. They told me that Mora is here."

"She is." Jolene suddenly gasped and stared wide-eyed at Gybbon. "And she was just awake. If she hears him . . ."

"She might attempt to do something foolish like try to come hurrying down the stairs," Gybbon said, even as he ran up the stairs to grab hold of Mora, who stood there clutching the top post. "Easy, lad," he cautioned Andrew, when the boy ran up to her. "I fear a good hug right now could hurt her."

Andrew frowned but grasped her by the hand instead. "They found me, Mora. I was in my safe place."

"Good lad. Ye did right. I think that I had best get back on my bed now though," she murmured, feeling a bit shaky.

She squeaked when Gybbon scooped her up in his arms and Andrew kept his grip on her hand, running along with them as Gybbon strode back to her room. He set her down on her bed and frowned down at her. Mora sensed a lecture coming on, but Jolene hurried over and pushed both Andrew and Gybbon away from the bed.

"Are you sure you did not open the wound again?" Jolene asked Mora.

"Aye, verra sure. I just had no strength left after the short walk to the stairs."

"No surprise. I will have a look later, though; mayhaps change the bandage."

"Thank ye. The cream does seem to still the sting and itch of it."

A moment later Mora found herself alone with Gybbon and Andrew. "Maggie?" she whispered.

"We cannae be certain. The cottage was burned, but one mon, a fellow named Iain, said he saw her run out and he helped to put the fire out where her skirts had caught alight. Then she looked around, probably for Andrew, who had run off to hide by then, and then she got in her wagon, which was packed with a lot of her things. Iain said she told him not to tell anyone but Mora that she was going to her sister's, and then she rode off. No one else has seen her. We e'en talked with Morag Sinclair."

"Maggie went to her sister's?"

"Aye, she did," said Andrew. "I thought she had died in the fire. She ran into the house while it was burning fierce and the roof started falling down. I heard her scream and could see a bit of dress catch on fire, so I believed she had died. I should have waited."

Mora reached out to ruffle his hair. "Then Gybbon and the men wouldnae have found you."

"Oh, is that true?" Andrew looked up at Gybbon and Gybbon nodded. "Can I get up on the bed now?"

"Weel, I think ye need to get washed up and change your clothes. Ye smell strongly of smoke."

Andrew sniffed the sleeve of his shirt and grimaced. "Aye, I do."

"Go ask the lady we met at the door when we arrived here. She will help."

The moment the boy was gone, Gybbon frowned down at Mora. Her eyes were already closing and he guessed the small burst of strength she had found when hearing Andrew's voice had faded away. There would have to be some time spent for her to get a lot of rest until she could hold on to that strength before they headed to Gormfuerach. He reached out to brush strands of hair from her face.

"Thank ye so verra much," she said softly. "I feared he was lost."

"I think it may have been close. Maggie had been packing to leave. She made Andrew stay out by the wagon so that the men wouldnae see him when they came. Maggie's only mistake was thinking they were done after they had knocked her around some. They set fire to her house as they left. Andrew saw her come out but then run back inside. When he saw the ceilings fall he was so certain she had died, he ran to his tree. The mon named Iain came by then and saw her stagger out, coughing and with her skirts alight. He threw some water on her skirts, she looked about but didnae see any sign of Andrew, so she left."

"And then ye went to his safe place. His wee keep as my mother called it." She smiled faintly.

"We did. Sigimor was impressed. Took some coaxing to get him out, but talk of his soldier, you, and Freya did the trick. Get some rest, Mora. And, aye, before ye ask, ye are still too weak to move about much or travel, but that will pass quickly. As soon as Jolene believes ye are weel enough, we will go to Gormfeurach."

She nodded, only the faintest of movements, but he knew she was still more asleep than awake. He bent down and kissed her on the mouth, lingering for a minute and savoring the warm softness of her lips. Then he stood up straight, could not resist running his fingers through her hair once more, and walked away.

Mora opened her eyes enough to watch him leave, then sighed and touched her lips. She had to wonder what a proper kiss, one where they were both awake, would feel like. Considering how the small kisses he gave her made her heart pound, she was not sure she could survive a proper one.

"How does she fare?" asked Sigimor when Gybbon sat down next to him and poured himself some ale.

"Weak but no fever and clear of thought. There isnae any way to tell how long it will take her to be able to move about freely enough for even a ride in a wagon. Especially for the two, mayhap e'en three days it will take to get to Gormfeurach."

"But it may give us time to stare down the sheriff and get him to cease sniffing around and find out how he can keep believing in the lies those brothers tell him."

"Mayhap we should take the time to go visit the mon and see just what lies he has believed."

"I dinnae have much say in getting a mon that post for 'tis Ogilvy land, but my opinion is nay ignored."

Gybbon grinned. "Does anyone manage to ignore your opinion on something?"

"My wife."

Gybbon just laughed for Sigimor sounded truly impressed and proud of that fact. He was satisfied with the meager plan. It would be good to be home, to have his brother at his side as he attempted to help Mora. He also wanted to take this trouble away from Sigimor. The man would stand firm for the ones he called friend or family in front of anything, but he had to live here, near the Ogilvy clan. He also had a wife, a son, and two little daughters who needed an army of nurses to keep them out of trouble. There was also the matter of so many of his people being ill. It was going to be better if he took this trouble with him when he left.

It was late the next day before they got a chance to ride back to the village. This time only Sigimor, Gybbon, and Tait went. As they rode past the house with the green door, Morag was out cleaning her thresh stone. She paused, looked at them and smiled, then waved. All three men waved back.

The place that held the jail and the sheriff was impressively tidy but the men standing outside looked sullen. Gybbon wondered if the men the sheriff had hired knew the Ogilvy brothers were spouting lies. They all dismounted, tied up the horses to the post, and went inside.

The first thing one saw upon entering the building was the sheriff. The man sat behind a big, heavy table covered in a rather ornate cloth. Even though where it was set made it clear to anyone coming in that this man was the leader, Gybbon thought such a huge wooden table made the man look small. It was more suited to a man like Sigimor.

"What can I do for ye, sirs?" the man asked, but did not get up.

"We want to ken what the Ogilvy brothers have told ye," said Sigimor.

"Ye mean about that lass with the cat?"

"Aye, about the lass. What have ye been told that has ye hunting her?"

"She murdered Old William, who was caring for our laird, and she stole Robert's sword to do it. We are wondering if it was she who also killed David and his wife."

Sigimor laughed. "And ye considered that a possibility? Fool. The lad is using ye to get what they want. They want the estate back to what it was in their grandfather's time and will kill anyone who stands in the way."

"David was their uncle," the man said angrily, and shifted around in his chair.

Sigimor sighed and stood up straight, using his size

as an unspoken threat. "And a mon as honorable as any I have met." He walked up to the sheriff, yanked him and his chair back, reached under the desk, and yanked out a buxom blond Gybbon had once seen in the tavern. "Go on, lass, and I would suggest ye keep as far away from those Ogilvy boys and this mon as ye can until this mess is all over." He looked back at the sheriff as the girl ran out of the office. "Now, mayhap, we will have your full attention." He glanced at Gybbon as he walked back to stand beside him. "That was the cause of those sullen looks outside, I am thinking."

"Aye, he wasnae sharing." Gybbon was fighting back the urge to laugh heartily.

"Look, the laird . . ." sputtered the sheriff, but he shut up when Sigimor raised his hand.

"The laird is dying. Have ye even looked into why? He gets worse every day. Old William was killed because he accused Robert of poisoning the laird and, surprise, Old William then dies by Robert's sword. Now, Old William was a tall, burly mon, but the lass, Mora Ogilvy, is near as small as my wife. Ye truly think she could swing a blade that size and kill a man? And what crime have they said the seven-year-old lad is guilty of that warrants trying to kill him? Nay, ye are nay thinking on any of this."

"I have been thinking on it. Ye look for who gains. 'Tis the lass."

"'Tis Robert as the firstborn. His da dies, he becomes laird. That family of David's ends, then that land comes back to the laird."

"She still has twa brothers."

"Does she?" asked Gybbon. "They havenae sent any word and nay come home. I suspect David came and spoke to ye of it." Gybbon nodded when a faint color hit the man's cheeks. "Didnae help him either, did ye? Come on, Sigimor. There is nay point to this visit."

"True. I liked David," Sigimor said in a low, quiet voice that even made Gybbon feel like shivering. "Since ye seem incapable of doing the job, I may start looking for his and his poor wife's killers myself."

Gybbon followed Sigimor outside. "Are ye sure threatening the mon was a good idea?"

"He would have talked us to death trying to convince us the lies he was told are fact and then I would have had to kill him. Aye, a nice threat was better for the moment. At the next meeting of the lairds round here I will make my opinion of the fool clear. He is getting a nice sum from us all to bumble around and be bribed by pretty little blonds under the desk."

Gybbon released the hearty laugh he had held back while with the sheriff. He and Sigimor mounted their horses and slowly rode out of the village. He noticed Morag still by her front door, but she was talking to Iain and another man. It was possible Morag could get people in the village thinking more on what was happening. Gybbon wished her luck if that was what she was trying to do.

"How are the people of Dubheidland doing? Still sick?" he asked.

"Improving slowly. As ye said, 'tis that time of year."

"Good. It will pass and everyone will be back in fighting shape. But we cannae ask it of them now. My brother's men are now all trained, weel and hard, and they are eager to practice their skills."

"Ye think those fools will hunt her down there?"

"Robert is killing his own father with poison, he killed two innocent, well-liked, generous people and one of them his own uncle, and maybe e'en two brothers who had ne'er done him any wrong that we have heard of. So, aye, I think he will see her hunted to the edges of the earth."

"Ye are probably right. That poor laddie, too."

"He is just another male heir so, aye, the boy, too."

"I wonder what the people at the keep are thinking."

"They probably ken the truth, but what power do they have to do anything about it? The laird is useless yet nay dead and would he e'en listen to accusations against his own sons? Nay, I suspect they are all scurrying about, tending to their chores, and keeping their heads down."

"I wouldnae mind getting a look at the old mon though, with Jolene. She could tell if it was poison or nay."

"I am nay sure it would be safe for either of us to go to the keep. We cannae be sure if Robert is there and he would recognize us as the ones who are getting in his way."

"Mayhap, but I dinnae think he would chance acting against any laird round here when his father is only ill, nay dead. 'Tis hard to judge the mon's greed, true enough, but 'tis clear to see he has a good idea of what is needed to protect himself." Sigimor frowned. "He was probably one of those children who delighted in beating down the children of those he considered less important than himself."

"I doubt ye would get much protest from his brothers as I am growing more certain that this is his idea, his plan. The others go along out of fear."

Sigimor looked at Gybbon and cocked his head. "Ye think they would just stand by and allow him to be accused?"

"I do, yet cannae say they would do so if he cried out for their help or if they felt sure he would get out of the trap and then come looking for them. I have ne'er seen brothers like them. 'Tis as if he is their lord and master and one who would probably kill them if they disobeyed. Aye, brothers ken which one of them will be the laird when the father is gone, but they still act as equals until it happens."

"Weel, your family is a strong one. And I suspicion your father would have interfered with a strong hand if one brother tried to rule the others. Seems the old laird may have played favorites and gave Robert too high an opinion of himself, or he was just born mean." Sigimor reined in in front of his manor. "I think we will go to see this ailing laird and offer my wife's skills if needed."

"Are we taking any men with us?" asked Gybbon as he hurried to follow Sigimor.

"Of course. I am a laird. Need some men when I ride about distributing my largesse." He grinned when Gybbon laughed.

Although Jolene was not sure it was a good idea, she gathered up her things for healing, making certain she had what was needed to treat a poisoning, and had her mount readied. Five men rode with them as they traveled to the Ogilvy keep. Sigimor just sighed when they had to go through a careful examination of who they were and what they wanted before the gates were opened.

When they were allowed inside the keep they were met by the head of the guard and the woman who ran the household. Sigimor knew the head of the guard and Gybbon watched in amazement as Jolene charmed the housekeeper so well the two linked arms as they went up to the laird's chamber. The shock of her being English had not lasted long.

The laird's room smelled of sickness and approaching death to Gybbon. The man in the bed looked gray and he kept moaning, a low, soft noise that made the housekeeper teary eyed. Jolene patted the woman's arm and walked closer to the bed.

"What is she doing?" he asked, as Jolene carefully looked at the laird's hands.

"Checking him for signs of poisoning. I occasionally wonder if I should worry that she kens so much about them." He exchanged a grin with Gybbon. "There is one that is used so often ye have to wonder why all healers dinnae ken what to look for."

Jolene then spent a long time talking with the housekeeper, who grew more and more upset. She took the woman to a bench under the window and calmed her, talking quietly and seriously until the woman was nodding her head. The head of the guard walked over to Sigimor.

"Your wife thinks someone is poisoning our laird," said the guard.

"Then someone probably is. When it comes to healing I ne'er question my wife."

"Unless she tells you that you have to stay abed," Jolene said, and went right back to talking with the housekeeper.

Gybbon laughed and noticed even the head of the guard was fighting a grin. "It was Robert, wasnae it?" the man softly asked.

"Aye," replied Sigimor. "He also saw to the killing

of David and his wife, may have seen to the killing of David's older sons, and is now after the boy, Colin."

"Jesu. There always was a meanness in the lad, but I ne'er would have thought he would do all this."

"Watch your step, Colin. Ye can do nay good if he kills ye, too."

"Och, I ken it, but I am verra good at looking like I am doing what I am told without actually doing it, and I can keep a secret."

"Can the housekeeper?"

"None better. She just has to worry about getting the laird better without telling how she kenned who made him sick. I will watch her as I suspect the cure will be slow."

"Aye. It all depends on how much the lad has given the mon."

"He can clean out his system slowly and it will be messy and ugly," said Jolene.

"So somehow they have to keep Robert from 'aiding' his da until there is proof of Robert's guilt he will believe."

"That willnae be easy. The other lads? Young Murdoch?" asked Colin.

"It looks as if Robert leads and the others are too afraid nay to follow," replied Gybbon.

"That feels right. It has always been that way, but the old laird wouldnae listen if ye tried to tell him that Robert needed some reining in. He was a mean, often vicious boy." Colin shook his head.

"We will be busy trying to keep the lass and the wee lad safe," said Sigimor.

"Ye shouldnae put yourself in the way, m'laird. Ye have to live here."

"Oh, I ken it. 'Tis why we are handing that job over

to the Murrays." Sigimor clapped Gybbon on the back. "But if ye think there needs to be someone other than a clan member to do something, ye ken where I am most days, Colin."

"I certainly do. Thank ye."

"We best go now. Housekeeper is about to give the laird the first of the cleansing tonics he must drink," Jolene said softly, and started for the door.

"This is going to be bad, aye," said Colin, and cast a longing look at the door. "It always is when a healer says cleansing."

"Just verra messy, I fear."

Sigimor said their farewells to Colin and got out of the room. Just as Sigimor was shutting the door behind them they heard that the ordeal had begun. He slammed it shut and hurried down the steps. At the bottom stood Robert and his brothers. Murdoch looked wretched even though his bruises appeared to be healing. Robert looked furious, whereas Lachlan and Duncan moved carefully until they flanked Murdoch.

"What are ye doing here?" Robert barked.

"We came to see your father," Sigimor said as he kept moving forward, until Robert stepped out of the way. "Ye do ken that we make an effort to keep the three clans around here close and friendly so all is peaceful. I thought that this time my wife's skills at healing might be helpful."

A woman went racing up the stairs with a bucket and two others followed with mops and rags. "What have ye done?" Robert demanded, foolishly glaring at Jolene.

"His system is being cleansed as he appears to have eaten or drunk something poisonous. He should get better now with the housekeeper tending all he eats and drinks. Colin will oversee it all." Ignoring the man before her, she slipped her arm through Sigimor's and said sweetly, "Shall we go now, m'love?"

Sigimor just nodded and led her out the door. Gybbon followed and saw Murdoch slip out after him. He turned to face the youth and felt badly for him. It was not a trap he would like to be in. If Murdoch angered Robert he would pay, but his loyalty was to his father in the end.

"Do ye want something?" Gybbon asked.

"It was poison, was it?"

"Oh, aye. Lady Jolene kens her healing arts and she says so."

"Thank ye, and get the lass and the boy away from here." He turned and went back into the keep.

"What was that about?" asked Sigimor as they started the ride back to the manor.

"Murdoch just wished to be certain it was poison," Gybbon replied. "Then he told me to get the lass and the boy away from here."

Jolene sighed. "He is afraid his brother will increase his efforts to be rid of them now that the laird is being watched."

"And so ye shall do as he asks, as soon as possible," Sigimor said.

"Aye. To Gormfeurach and shut the gates on her as soon as I can."

Chapter Ten

Mora woke up slowly and stretched. It felt good to be able to do so, even tentatively, yet not feel the pull and pinch of stitching. Jolene had removed the stitching last night and declared her wound healed with a caution: she could still not ride a horse for a while. Mora was not pleased by that but knew she would do everything the woman told her to.

She turned onto her unwounded side to look out the window and found herself staring into Gybbon's eyes. They were mostly green this morning. Mora had not yet made up her mind about why or how they changed at times. Then she became fully aware of the fact that he was lying in her bed. She squealed softly and pushed away, catching herself just in time to save herself from the humiliation of falling out of bed.

"What are ye doing in my bed?"

"Waiting for ye to wake up. We leave today for Gormfeurach, ye ken."

She found the thought of him watching her sleep a little alarming and hoped she had not done anything too unappealing. "But 'tis barely sunrise."

"Sun has already cleared the horizon. It is a bit of a long journey to my home."

"How long?"

"Twa days, mayhap three. Ne'er made the journey with a cart before."

"We could wait until I can ride a horse."

"Nay. 'Tis best if we can slip away from here as soon as we can. The sheriff and his men are looking hard for ye and Andrew. Sigimor rebuffed Robert, too, who now leads more than just his brothers. I say ten men, but Sigimor said twelve."

"They still hunt for me and Andrew?"

"Aye, I believe his brothers do as he says, but they are afraid of him. Others only see that he is their laird's firstborn son and should be obeyed. I have ne'er understood why, but a lot of people seem to think a firstborn son is just like his da."

"Do ye ken if Colin and the housekeeper are still weel?"

"Och, aye, they are, and they remain close by the laird. I think some of the men protect them as weel, and as much as they can, but the place is ne'er going to be verra safe for them until Robert is gone. Seems they have tried to warn the laird about his son, but he isnae heeding them. They stopped because they didnae wished to be pushed away and leave the old mon unprotected."

"There is naught we can do?" She tensed a little when he reached out to toy with a lock of her hair.

"Nay. We did all we can and he is getting better. What needs to be done now is getting ye and Andrew far away from Robert and here, where the sheriff can reach ye, too."

"Weel, if we are to be traveling soon, ye best get out

of here so that I can get ready." She shivered as he slowly stroked her neck.

"I could help," he said as he shifted close enough to wrap his arm around her waist. "I am verra good with laces."

"So am I. I believe I can manage without aid despite my infirmity," she said as she placed her hands on his chest, intending to give him a little shove. "And that may be something ye shouldnae say to women as they then wonder why and where ye got such skill."

He grinned. "Your *infirmity*? And the skill can be picked up easily enough if one has a family that includes a lot of women and girls, unlike the Camerons or the MacFingals." He laughed softly as he tugged her closer.

Mora had the feeling that she should stop him as he lowered his mouth to hers and held her close. Instead she let him kiss her, and this time it was not an innocent, light brush of the lips. This time he put some urgency into it. Slowly, making very certain she caused herself no pain, she reached up to put her arms around his neck and hold him close, savoring the feel of his strength and warmth. When he lightly nipped at her bottom lip, she gasped, and suddenly his tongue was in her mouth. He stroked the inside of her mouth and she began to warily mimic his actions as a strange fever began to grow deep inside her.

This is desire, she thought, and was both fascinated and tempted. The embrace he held her in tightened and he pulled her even closer until their bodies were hard up against each other. She was just sinking into the pleasure of another kiss when a sharp pain caused her to cry out.

Gybbon pulled away from her and cursed himself

for being so impatient. He had wanted her from the moment he had set eyes on her, but her wound, as well as all her other troubles, had worked to hold him back. Knowing that her stitches were out had loosened the reins on that control. Kissing her had snapped them completely.

"I am so sorry," he said as he tried to lift the hand she had clapped over the wound. "I wasnae thinking. . . ."

Mora pushed his hand away. "'Tis all right. Truly," she reassured him when he looked doubtful. "'Twas mostly surprise that it could still hurt."

"And so it should when some braw laddie is clutching you tight and tossing you round the bed."

Covering her face with her hands so that she hid what she knew was a fierce blush stinging her cheeks, Mora wondered why they had not heard Jolene enter the room. Now she could add the embarrassment she felt at crying out like a child over what had only been a brief, if painful, twinge to the humiliation of being caught abed with a man by the lady of the manor.

"How do ye keep sneaking up on people?" asked Gybbon as he hastily checked his clothes to make certain they were not too badly disordered and stood to frown at Jolene as she walked to the side of the bed. "Ye have a true skill for suddenly appearing to make your opinion known."

"And it is a skill I do not wish to share with anyone. I get too much pleasure out of stating my opinion. Now, shoo. I have come to help Mora dress for her journey."

"I could probably do it myself," Mora said quietly, trying hard not to laugh at the way Jolene had told Gybbon to "shoo."

"Aye, but the less you twist and turn and lift your arms, the better it will be for you on your journey."

Gybbon walked to the door and ignored the way Freya trotted in as if he had opened the door just for her. Then he frowned at Jolene's back. "Did ye just tell me to shoo?"

Jolene's lips twitched into a quick, faint smile and then she raised a hand to make a shooing gesture at Gybbon. "Aye, so shoo," she repeated, then grinned widely when she heard the door shut behind him. "They hate when I do that. Now, are you really all right?"

"Aye, I really am. It just startled me. Ye had taken out the stitches and removed the bandage. Despite the fact that I had dutifully noted all ye said about being careful, I still just thought that I was healed, so when there was a sudden small pain, I think it shocked me a bit."

"I suspect it did." Jolene held out a hand. "Best you get dressed now. Time to break your fast."

"Oh, I do find myself really hungry," said Mora as she took Jolene's hand and let the woman tug her to her feet.

"That is good. You did not have the fever for long, but it is good if you eat as well as you can for a while."

"Thank ye kindly for the use of the shift."

"Keep it. I am pleased it served and I fear yours is now gone. I used it for bandages."

"That was what I was doing," said Mora as she unlaced the shift.

"I will send the last two home with you. I was just thinking it might be a good idea if I put a loose one on you for the journey. 'Twill help keep the area clean and keep the healing salve off your gown."

"Are ye giving me some of the salve?"

"Aye. It will help the wound and I think it also may ease a bit of the scarring that will be left."

"I am trying nay to think about scarring." Mora walked over to the bowl and, grabbing a cloth, gave herself a quick wash. "When do ye think it would be safe to have a bath?"

Jolene laughed. "You could have one now save I dinnae think you would then have time to break your fast. Have one when you reach Gormfeurach. They are verra efficient at it and have lovely baths to lounge in. 'Tis one of the many improvements Lady Annys has put in and I fully approve of it."

"Ye have been there?" After drying herself she accepted the shift Jolene held out for her and pulled it on.

"Aye. Sigimor likes to keep on good terms with the Murrays. They are a large clan with a lot of allies from the Armstrongs, near the border to England, to Sir Simon Innes, who used to be called the King's Hound. I swear, there must be dozens between there. E'en if Sigimor didnae like Gybbon and his brothers Harcourt and Brett so much, he would still make certain that alliance stood."

"Oh my." She had just been kissing a very important man.

As she tugged on her hose and tied the ribbons to hold them up, she had to wonder what her parents would think about a flirtation with such a well-placed man. Her mother would have danced around making plans to bring him to the altar, and her father would worry. He had been happy with just what he was. A younger son with few duties who did not have to bother with allies, alliances, or even hordes of relations that you were expected to keep on your side. Her father had just wanted to raise his family and carve his wood.

Jolene walked up and held out her gown. "We cleaned and mended it. 'Tis not too rough now and will suit to riding in a wagon all the way to Gormfuerach."

"Ye didnae have to do that. I could have just bundled it into my bag and dealt with it later."

"It would have been utterly ruined by then. Getting to the dirt and the blood fast is why it looks as good as it does. It also looks verra comfortable and worth saving."

"Aye, 'tis a country woman's gown. They are nay such slaves to fashion quirks. And they usually have to work in the gown unlike a titled lady. My mither made it for me."

"Another good reason to save it." Jolene helped Mora get dressed.

"How is Andrew?"

"He is just fine. He slept in with Fergus and the MacFingal boys. That has left him feeling quite full of himself. Boy thinks he has slept with the men like a warrior would. He still clutches his soldier though."

"I would nay be surprised if he always does. His da made it. He did love Da." She sighed, releasing a little more of the sorrow that clung to her. "I wouldnae be surprised if, when he is a grown mon and I go to see him, his wife, and his bairns, if I ask about the Bruce, he will pull it out."

"'Tis a lovely thought. I think he is looking for you, as well."

"Then I best get down there to eat."

Mora hurriedly put some things in her bag. Her injury had kept her from unpacking much, so it was quick. Then she walked down the stairs with Jolene. The moment she entered the hall, Andrew ran over to her.

"I was starting to worry about you," the boy said as he gently hugged her.

"Why? Gybbon was here."

"But Gybbon wasnae hurt."

"True, but now I am nearly completely healed, so you can cease worrying about me."

She started to make her way to the table, Andrew clutching her hand. Gybbon waved her over and indicated room on the bench for her and Andrew to sit with him. Mora helped Andrew sit next to Gybbon and then she sat next to Andrew. She saw Gybbon look at the boy and then at her, his mouth twitching into a smile briefly.

"Why is everyone so big?" Andrew asked softly as she served him some porridge and apples.

"Because they are full grown. Our da was tall."

"Aye, that is what Maman said. But *ye* are full grown, too."

"Ah, aye, I am. I took after Maman." She reached around the boy and pinched Gybbon on the arm when she saw he was laughing.

"But I am almost as tall as ye are already and I am only seven."

"I suspect ye will grow even taller and be bigger than me."

"Like David and Niall?"

"Aye, like David and Niall."

"Did Robert kill them, too?" he asked softly, stirring his porridge instead of eating it.

"I dinnae ken, Andrew."

"Eat your porridge, laddie," said Sigimor in a gentle

yet firm voice. "Ye have a long trip ahead of ye. No need to chew over sad things by asking questions no one has an answer for."

"Where are we going?"

"I told ye," said Mora. "We are going to ride to Sir Gybbon's brother's keep."

"'Tis a fine keep, too," said Gybbon.

Mora smiled faintly as Gybbon told Andrew all about Gormfeurach and her brother ate his porridge, even accepting a small added serving. He kept Andrew fascinated with his talk of big gates, high walls, and a dungeon. Mora heard most of it and had to admit she was eager to see it.

Something bumped her arm and she looked down to see Freya at her side. She scratched her cat's ears and cut up some of her meat to put it on a small plate for the animal. Mora hoped a three-day journey hidden in the back of a wagon would not cause the animal too much distress. She was not so certain how she would endure it, either.

As they left the table and collected up what they needed for their journey, Mora felt a touch of sadness. This was her family's land, where her parents had grown up and where she had spent her whole childhood. She could not help but hope she would be able to return sometimes without worrying about her cousins.

She stared at the cart Gybbon put her bag in. It would be a crowded ride, but they had so well padded the bed of it that she suspected it would not be too uncomfortable. She and Andrew stayed inside the door as Gybbon and Sigimor told them to and waited.

The way the man was so carefully making sure they were not seen as they left woke a fear within Mora. It strengthened what she already felt about her cousins by telling her just how hard they were hunting her and Andrew. He had even come up with a clever way to sneak both of them into the cart without much risk of them being seen.

"My Sigimor is a very careful planner," said Jolene as she stepped up beside Mora. "Before he even takes a step he has plotted out every one of those steps and all that could go wrong so he can be prepared for that, too."

"Oh, I wasnae doubting that. It was just how all of this made it so sharply clear that I am in a fight for Andrew's life. And my own."

Jolene patted her on the back. "A hard thing to look straight in the eye. I was faced with such a dark sight when we fought to keep my nephew alive. And for much the same reasons. Greedy relations."

"If David and Niall should come back and come here to ask after us . . ."

"Oh, Sigimor will ken what to say and tell them how to find you. As well as giving them a fine escort. Do you think they might appear?"

Mora shrugged. "Who can say? They were going to meet up with some friends who had gone to France for the same reason, so I can only hope they had others on their side if Robert went after them there. Since I have heard naught from them, any of them, and I ken little about France and its wars, I simply cannae say."

"And so, a tiny spark of hope flares now and then. Aye, I would not wish to believe the worst without proof, good hard proof, even if it would make me sad beyond words. But, not to fret, if they do happen to come and speak to Sigimor, or if he e'en hears word that they have returned, he will take care of them if it is needed."

Jolene looked closely at Mora. "You have not really taken time to grieve for your parents, have you?"

"A bit, but there is Andrew to worry o'er. He grieves and is afraid and I have to appear strong. Da adored him and was teaching him about the wood and how to see what could be made in it, what it wanted to be made into. Andrew actually understood what he was talking about. I see a lump of wood as nothing more than something ye put on the fire." She smiled when Jolene laughed. "My older brothers were much like I am. I think David understood what Da was talking about but simply could not see it as he did."

"Did the laird get sick long before your da died?"

"Nay, 'twas shortly after. 'Tis why I have nay seen much of him. I would go with my mother, but he was rambling and near senseless each time we went. Then my parents were killed. And, aye, I think that was all planned out that way."

"I think so, too, and so does Sigimor. We just say Robert is mad, and he most certainly is, but he can plan carefully and that makes him even more dangerous. And you are mucking about with his plan. Sad to say, even if he believed Andrew was no longer a problem, Robert would still come after you."

"The day he burst into our home and tried to kill me, I could see that. He was furious and then in pain, but the hate still gleamed in his eyes."

"Men do hate it when women muck about with their plans."

"As they should," said Sigimor as he kissed his wife on the cheek. "Especially if it is a good plan."

Mora laughed when Jolene just rolled her eyes

as she slid her arm around Sigimor's waist. As she watched them she realized no one would have ever tried to match them. They would have looked at the small, somewhat delicate, raven-haired Englishwoman and the big, rough-mannered, and red-haired Scot and never thought of them as the perfect pair, and yet they were.

Sigimor suddenly left to direct the placement of some barrels of cider and ale at the rear of the cart. Mora realized she and her brother would not only be covered by a blanket but have a solid wall of casks behind them. This was going to be a very long journey.

Sigimor and Gybbon appeared to be having an argument as they walked around the side of the manor, the cart slowly following them, so Mora asked, "Is there a problem?"

"Aside from the fact that Gybbon insists he should pay Sigimor for the cider and ale, no." Jolene took her by the hand and caught Andrew by his to lead them into the somewhat fancy little sitting room Jolene had set up for herself and any ladies who happened to come by. "Sigimor decided to slip you two into the cart out this way as it can be brought closer to the door, so if you are in sight, it will only be for a very short time if at all."

"He has really planned this out," Mora whispered in amazement.

"Aye." Jolene picked up a crate but shook her head when Mora reached for the other one. "You are not to lift anything heavy for a while. Your wound has closed and looks fine, but the skin is fragile there, so you must play the invalid for a while. A very annoying pose to hold but, trust me, just reminding yourself that if you ruin my work you will have to go through all the mending steps you have done already all over again can be enough to make you behave."

Sigimor stepped up to the door, leaned against the frame, and held his cloak out a bit. "Tuck yourself up in here, lad," he said to Andrew, and the boy hurried to do so. "Feet on my foot and hold on to my leg. Good lad," he said, and walked back to the cart after taking the crate from Jolene.

Mora watched as he went to the rear of the cart, talked to Gybbon, and Andrew quietly slipped into the back of the cart. Even she barely caught a glimpse of the child and she knew where to look. Sigimor then slid the crate in place.

He came back to the door, stood in the same position, half inside, half outside, and took the second crate from Jolene. "Now, lass, under the cloak, feet on my foot and arms about my waist. I tested this out with Jolene so ken I can walk fair normal when ye do."

"I am more weight than Andrew."

"Nay by much, I suspect."

Taking a deep breath, Mora did as he asked. She found it odd to be hugging another man but fascinated by the way it did not affect her at all. If it had been Gybbon she was sure it would have. When Sigimor stopped, she scrambled into the back of the cart as quickly as she could and watched the crate be slid in behind her. She sat next to Andrew and, for once in her life, was very pleased that she was rather small for a grown woman.

A moment later, Gybbon slid his arm in and reached into the crate. That was when Mora realized that was where they had put her bag. She watched with a little smile as Gybbon scratched her cat's ears before he pulled his arm away. Freya climbed out to sit on Mora's lap. She doubted Robert would have recognized her bag, but Sigimor had even thought about that possibility. Jolene was right. Her husband was a very careful planner.

"It is like we are in a cave or my safe place," said Andrew.

"Aye, it is," she said, and hoped she would not give in to her small fear of such places.

The bright sun shone through the blanket enough to lighten where they were, but it was still a small place to spend three days in. There were enough small gaps in the arrangement to let air in, so they probably would not get too short of fresh air. Nevertheless, Mora knew it was going to be a very long journey.

She idly stroked her cat and wondered what they could do to pass the hours they would be stuck in this place. There was only so much one could talk about to a boy who was barely seven. Mora tried to think of what stories she could recall and was sad to admit she knew very few. She had listened to ones her parents told but had to confess she had made no real effort to recall them later. Looking all around, she noticed the blanket was tied down on the top, but where the ties were there were a few gaps so they might be able to spend a little time just watching what went by.

"What do ye do when ye are up in your safe place by yourself for a while?" she asked Andrew.

"I tell myself stories."

"I thought of that, but I dinnae recall many."

"I can tell ye some stories."

"That would be nice and might pass some time."

"Niall and David often told me some, although David sometimes smacked Niall on the head because he said that he shouldnae be telling a small boy that." Andrew heaved a sigh that Mora felt was too big and filled with sadness for a small boy. "They were funny though. I miss Niall and David," he added softly.

"So do I, Andrew. So do I."

"It is only ye and me left in our family."

"I ken it, which is why we must do everything these men tell us to do, even if it means we have to stay in this small place for a few days."

"Aye. Then when I get big and Gybbon or Sigimor trains me, I can kill cousin Robert."

Mora nearly wept. He was too young to have thoughts of a bloody revenge. At his age, his thoughts should be of wondrous tales and playing with other boys. Yet, she could think of nothing to say. She wanted that, too, only in her thoughts it was she who would strike the blow.

She leaned back against the pillows Jolene had insisted be put in and tried to think. There was a hard fight ahead as Robert would not give up. The only thing she was sure of was that she did not want anyone else hurt or killed because of her relations.

It was true that she could not fight a battle with a man with fist or weapon, but she had the wit to figure out some way that would make it so Robert had to cease his mad attempt to take all her father had gotten as an inheritance. The laird needed to be told the truth. It would hurt her uncle, but far better his feelings were savaged than men who had no part in this argument got hurt or killed. All she had to decide was the best way to get the truth to her uncle.

Sighing, she closed her eyes. When said, it sounded so simple, so easy, but she knew it was a dangerous thought. Robert could well have allies within his father's guard. How could she get the truth to him through what could prove a large force of armed men on Robert's side? It was a trouble that needed a great deal of thought and planning.

Chapter Eleven

Staring up at Gybbon as he lifted the blanket to hand her something to drink, Mora tried to hide the foul mood she was in. He did not deserve anger from her, he was just trying to help her. She just wished that help would have come in a nice open wagon or on a horse and with something to make the time pass. Mora took a long drink of water and handed the water skin to Andrew.

"No pain or return of the fever?" Gybbon asked.

"Nay," she said, and decided it was not a lie, that she felt warm simply because she had been enclosed inside a blanket-covered cart bed for two days. "Do ye ken, I ne'er went much beyond the village. Yet, the first journey of any distance I take, I do so under a blanket and see naught."

She decided not to mention all the times she and Andrew had lifted the blanket at the sides and peeked out like children spying on their parents. It had also allowed in more fresh air, which was welcome. The fact that a few times one of the men riding alongside of the cart had waved at them told her Gybbon probably already knew about those peeks.

"I promise to take ye for a good ride once ye are healed and ye can look at all ye want."

"Any sign of Robert?"

"The MacFingals say he is following us, but he stays far away, and now that we are actually on the land of Gormfeurach, they appear to be slowing down even more. I expect to see some of my brother's men soon."

"Ye mean we are getting that close?"

"Weel, 'tis still a few hours but, aye, we are close."

"Good. Have ye seen Freya?" she asked, worried because her pet had leapt out of the cart the last time they had stopped and had not returned.

"She is sitting up on the seat between two MacFingals. Jumped up there the last time we stopped."

"But Robert will surely recognize her."

"By the time he gets close enough to even see her there, he is close enough for us to see and reach. They have already checked on that. She will be fine. I am nay so certain Nanty will be though, if he doesnae stop teasing them about how they talk to her."

Mora laughed. "She must be enjoying herself, although she is rude to go out there when we cannae."

"I am nay sure she kens a way back in."

"Oh. Nay, I suppose she doesnae."

"I could grab her and hand her in."

"Nay, she is outside and surrounded by people. I willnae deprive her of that just because I feel comforted when I can pet her. She will let ye ken somehow when she wants back in here."

"Keep the water skin then, and the journey is almost over. Ye have been a verra good lad, Andrew."

"Thank ye. I have to be sure to stay alive for Mora," he said.

"Aye, that ye do."

Gybbon saw a sadness cross Mora's face, but then she smiled at the boy and gave him a brief hug. Gybbon tugged the blanket back in place and rode up beside the MacFingals, the cat sitting up happily between them. Andrew was carrying too much worry and sorrow for a young boy, but he could think of nothing that would ease it save, perhaps, the return of the brothers lost to France and an end to Robert. Gybbon promised himself that he would do what he could to find out what had happened to their brothers. His family had connections in France and it might be time to make use of them.

"Who comes this way now?" asked Ciaran as he shifted forward on the cart seat so Freya could tuck herself behind him.

Looking at the group of men riding out of the trees far ahead of them, Gybbon laughed briefly. "Some of my brother's men."

"How can ye tell?"

"I am fair sure that is Nicolas at the fore." He raised his hand in greeting and the man he thought was Nicolas waved back. "Aye, it is."

"Can we now let the lass and the boy out of their cage?"

"Nay just yet. I am sure they are my brother's men, but even if they are not, they show no inclination for battle."

"Shall I just sit here then or move forward?"

"Just wait."

Ciaran nodded and waited. Gybbon sat on his horse with his hand on his sword. He did not see Harcourt, but was not really disappointed by that. The man had a family and a keep to run. He would see him at

Gormfeurach when he got there. So, he sat and watched the men ride up to them.

"Ye couldnae ride out to meet us?" said Nicolas as he reined in right in front of Gybbon.

"Resting the horses," Gybbon drawled, and grinned when Nicolas chuckled and shook his head.

"Ciaran, why is there a cat hiding behind you?"

"She didnae ken whether ye were friend or foe." He grinned when Nicolas frowned in confusion.

"Since ye are here and so we now have a goodly force of men to protect us, I will free our passengers." Gybbon rode around the cart, undoing all the ties that held the blanket over its back. "Harcourt's men are here, Mora," he said as he tossed aside the covering. "Ye two can be free to be seen now. Plenty of eyes to keep a sharp watch for your cousins," he assured her as he dismounted and walked up to the side of the cart.

Although she was sorely tempted to immediately leap out of the cart, Mora stayed seated and frowned up at Gybbon. "But that will let them ken that I came here with you, aye? Ye cannae want that."

"Lass, I believe they already ken it. They were fair certain Sigimor was hiding ye, but they didnae have the courage, or the men they needed to face him and his clan. We were just fortunate that they didnae realize how many of Sigimor's men were laid down with an illness."

"If ye are sure," she said, and when he nodded, she steered Andrew to him.

Gybbon swung Andrew out of the cart and set him down, but the boy stayed close to him and studied Nicolas and his men. "Now ye," Gybbon said, and grabbed her around the waist, careful to put his hands above her newly healed wound, and grinning when she squealed softly as he swung her out of the cart. Then, after he set her on the ground, she slapped his arm.

Mora clasped his arm after slapping it and smoothed down her clothing with her other hand. The dizziness that had seized her when he had picked her up was not fading as fast as it should. When she was steady again, she shook off that worry. Her wound was healed. Her fever from that had passed and she would not worry about her health like some old woman. Feeling more at ease, she watched Gybbon introduce all his brother's men to her and Andrew.

The moment that was done, she turned her attention to her cat, who was rubbing her head against Ciaran's arm and purring. "Are ye going to come to me or nay, ye shameless, unfaithful wretch?" Freya left a chuckling Ciaran and leapt onto her shoulder.

"What has Sigimor sent us then?" asked Nicolas as he dismounted, then walked over to the cart.

"Cider, a bit of ale, and some fruit. Apples and some berry things. They had a very good season and reaped a hearty harvest."

"And he still insists his ale and cider are better than ours," drawled Nicolas.

"Of course. He feels ye just need more taste comparisons." Gybbon laughed along with Nicolas.

"Berry things?" Mora asked in confusion as she stepped closer and looked at the many covered jars that were in the crates. "Oh, lovely." She looked at Andrew, who was also studying the things packed in the crates. "Ye can put some on your porridge when ye break your fast in the morning."

"Mora? We are going to ride out now. Do ye want to get back in the cart or do ye wish to ride?" asked Gybbon.

"I would love to ride, if it willnae be a trouble."

"Nay, no trouble."

"I think ye need to remove Freya first."

"Oh. Aye, that would be best."

She reached up to pat her cat, then went to put her pet in her bag. When Freya immediately leapt out to go sit by Ciaran she just laughed and returned to Gybbon's side. He swung her up into the saddle, but this time she suffered no overwhelming dizziness so cast aside her small concerns about her health.

It was nice to look around as they traveled. It was lovely land and the sparkle of water she could see off to the left told her it was well watered. She idly wondered if they did more grazing of animals than they did planting.

"'Tis verra pretty here," she said.

"This is the end of Glencullaich land. The land for Gormfeurach starts just inside those trees. We share water from that burn but Glencullaich has the best land of the two keeps."

"'Tis why a lot of folk call them sister keeps now," added Nicolas. "We are verra intertwined now. A lot of our people are related to each other. A sister in one, the brothers in another. Parents in one, grown children at the other. If we ever fought each other it would be hard on both sides and a lot of people could weel just leave."

"That is rather unusual, isnae it?"

"Verra unusual, but it works for the moment. The lairds are close friends and that helps."

"'Tis a shame there is nay more of that."

"Our swords would dull," teased Nicolas.

Mora just shook her head as the two men laughed. It was still nice that, for the moment, there was at least one spot where it was peaceful. It was probably a good thing that Sigimor and his clan were three days away, she thought, and laughed softly.

"What has ye laughing?" Gybbon asked.

"It was an unkind thought."

"Then I must hear it."

"It was just that I thought how nice it was that it was such a peaceful moment. I then thought suddenly that it was probably good that Sir Sigimor and his clan are about three days away." She smiled when both men laughed heartily.

"He does love to poke and poke until something bursts open," said Nicolas, and then looked at Gybbon. "Harcourt would have come with us, but he injured his foot and has been told, most firmly, that he best nay mount a horse for a while. And he had no wish to greet ye while in a cart."

Gybbon laughed again and shook his head. "How did he hurt it so bad?"

"Fell off the stable roof." Nicolas looked behind them and frowned. "Some of your men rode off a while ago."

"Aye, I sent them to look for Robert."

"Weel, they are coming back at a good speed. Might just be hungry for a gallop after plodding along with a cart for a few days."

Gybbon hoped that was the case, but the minute

Ned reined in near him, he knew it was not. "What is wrong?"

"Weel, Robert hasnae left. He got far behind us because he was waiting. He was just joined by a force of armed men and it appeared by the greetings that they were from his clan. Mayhap a dozen but, e'en as we left, a few more rode up. Robert and the head of that wee group started having an argument."

As they all began to ride on toward Gormfuerach, Gybbon grimaced. "Probably the sheriff and a few of his men."

"I am sorry," murmured Mora, knowing she was the reason the men were there.

"Ye have naught to be sorry about," said Gybbon firmly. "Ye did naught to the mon. 'Tis his greed bringing him here."

"I ken it. I am nay e'en sure just handing him the house and land would stop him."

"Nay, because she refused to give him what he wanted."

"Like a spoiled child," she murmured, and she felt Gybbon nod before turning his attention to riding with the other men.

Gybbon signaled some of his men to keep a close watch on Robert and turned his full attention to getting to Gormfeurach. The mon was going to keep pushing for what he wanted until he got himself killed. Gybbon began to think over what he needed to say to Harcourt to make him understand that.

Just as she grew weary of riding the horse, despite the pleasure of being so close to Gybbon, Mora saw the walls of Gormfeurach. She could see the men high up on the walls and felt her fear of what she might be bringing to the keep ease a little. Once behind those walls, it would be nearly impossible for Robert to get to anyone since she did not believe he had gained the power to order his whole clan into the field to fight.

They rode in through the gates once they were opened. For a while there was an organized confusion as everyone dismounted, the horses were led away, and the cart unpacked. Mora hurried to grab her bag and make sure Freya was secure. As they walked toward the steps she saw that a small woman stood waiting for them, her blood-red hair in a long, thick braid pulled forward over her shoulder. When Mora got closer she realized the woman had dark green eyes.

"Greetings," the woman said, and held out her hand. "I am the Lady of Gormfeurach, Lady Annys Murray. Welcome to our home."

Mora shook the woman's hand and smiled. "'Tis a fine keep, m'lady."

"Oh, please, call me Annys. I have ne'er gotten used to all the 'm'lady this and that.' Come in. Ye too, Gybbon. We have baths ready for ye and there will be a meal soon."

The promise of a bath got Mora moving right along with Lady Annys. She desperately wanted to wash away the dust of her travels. Although she was listening carefully to what Lady Annys said as they went up the stairs, a lot of her mind was fixed firmly on getting her dusty gown off and sitting in a bath. Then she suddenly realized Andrew was not at her side.

"Where did Andrew go?" she asked Gybbon.

"Oh," replied Annys, "the boy has gone off with my son Benet and my maid's boys so that they can show him where he can clean up. Is that all right?"

"Of course. I was just startled as we have been kept close for the whole journey and then he was gone."

Annys nodded and pointed to the room for Gybbon, who thanked her and hurried inside. To Mora's surprise the woman then led her into the room right next to his. A slightly older, more buxom woman was just setting down a bucket of water next to a large wooden tub.

"Joan, this is Lady Mora Ogilvy, just arrived from Sigimor's manor with Gybbon."

"Greetings, m'lady. Your bath awaits."

Before Mora could say much more than thank you, the two women left and a young girl entered to help her get out of her clothing. Mora gladly accepted the offer to clean the clothes, but then shooed the girl away and stepped into the tub. A sigh of pure pleasure escaped her as she sank into the water. She cleared her mind of all thoughts of her troubles and decided to simply enjoy her bath. Sadly, the troubles would still be there when her bath was done.

She sniffed the soap she scooped out of the dish and smiled at the soft scent of lavender. Her mother had loved that scent, she thought with a pang of sorrow as she washed herself. Freya came to stand with her paws on the edge of the tub and Mora suddenly recalled that she had brought in her bag.

"How did ye get out?" she asked the animal as she began to wash her hair. "I thought I had secured the bag closed."

Freya reached a paw out and touched the water, then shook her paw dry. Mora laughed, only to have the cat do it again. Then she crossed her arms over her breasts when her door opened, but it was just the young maid.

"Oh, m'lady, I am so sorry." The girl started to move toward Freya. "I dinnae ken how it got in here. I will just toss it outside."

"Nay! 'Tis fine. The cat is mine. Is having it inside with me a problem?"

"Nay! I just thought it was one of the stable cats and it had somehow wandered in here. I came to see if ye needed your hair rinsed."

"Aye, now that I think on it, I believe I do."

She allowed the girl to finish the washing of her hair and then the rinsing of it. When the girl started to dry it for her, Mora wondered how she had managed without such luxury for so many years. She then sternly reminded herself she was not some grand lady who lived in a walled keep.

"I will lay out your clothes, shall I?" the girl said even as she started toward Mora's bag.

"If Freya will allow it." She stepped out of the tub and began to dry herself off, watching as the girl cautiously approached the bag, which Freya sprawled on top of.

Freya moved and Mora almost smiled at how the girl sighed with relief. She wrapped her hair and then walked over to where the girl had picked out her clothes before she picked up her shift and put it on. The girl hurried to do up her laces. In no time at all Mora was fully dressed in a gown she did not recognize and suspected her hostess had brought her in one. Mora thought how very easy it would be to become thoroughly spoiled by having servants to flutter around.

"Thank ye," she said to the girl, then reached for

the drying cloth that had been wrapped around her head. "What is your name?"

"Mary. I was the first here, so it is just Mary." The girl took off the drying cloth and started to dry Mora's hair even more. "There is Red Mary because of her hair color, Old Mary, and Big Mary. Being just Mary isnae such a bad thing."

"Nay, I would have to agree with that."

She allowed Mary to lead her to the fireplace and sit her on a stool while the girl slowly combed out her hair before the warmth of the fire that dried it even more. As Mary braided her hair, Mora decided she was getting too warm and hoped the girl worked quickly. She moved away from the heat as fast as she could when the girl said she was done.

Leaving Mary to deal with emptying the bath and forcing herself not to feel guilty about that, Mora stepped out of the room. Freya quickly trotted out to join her, and Mora sighed. Eating with her had obviously been a big mistake as she was not sure she could keep the cat away now. When she walked into the hall, she saw Gybbon near the head of the table and wondered where she should sit. Then he gestured to her to come and sit by him. Freya beat her to the place right next to him on the bench and Mora tried to ignore how both he and the man he was speaking with grinned at her.

"If it troubles ye, I will remove her," Mora said.

"Nay, I have been warned. Cats dinnae bother me. My son walks around with one all the time. 'Tis why I am stuck in a chair much of the day at the moment." He waved at his bandaged foot, which he had rested on the bench set near to him. "I am Harcourt Murray, Laird of Gormfeurach."

"Ye just love saying that, dinnae ye?" teased Gybbon.

"I worked hard for it. Pleased to meet ye, Mora Ogilvy. I believe I met your father once when I visited Payton at court. Nice mon. Verra sorry for what happened to him and your mother."

"Thank ye. He must have been young then as I can ne'er recall him mentioning that he had actually gone to the court."

"He hated it nearly as much as I. Ah, food. The one thing I am allowed to do," he muttered as he frowned at Annys, who just ignored him.

Mora hid her smile and watched as Gybbon put some meat on her plate. It troubled her that she felt no great urge to eat for she knew she should. As Harcourt and Gybbon taunted each other, she picked away at her food and thought that it was too warm in the hall. By the time the sweets were served, she could barely keep her eyes open and decided she needed to excuse herself. Saying all that was expected, she rose and walked slowly to the door. Taking a deep breath, she was only two steps into the hall and turned toward the steps leading to the next floor, when blackness swept over her so quickly she had no chance to make a sound, even when she hit the hard stone floor.

Gybbon heard the soft thud and stared in horror at Mora sprawled on the hard floor. He leapt up and ran out with Annys hurrying after him, but to his annoyance, the foolish cat got to Mora before any of them. He resisted the urge to shove it out of the way and picked Mora up, standing as Annys checked her head for any wound caused by the fall to the floor.

"Fool animal," he muttered while he stared at the small cat sitting on Mora's chest as he carried her up the stairs.

"Nay, Gybbon. The cat is worried. I think Mora has spoiled it a bit."

"A bit? Nay, dinnae frown, Annys. I actually like the animal. Now, I just wonder where Andrew is."

"He is eating in the room where we feed the children, but I think he may have heard something because someone is running this way fast."

"And we ken it isnae Harcourt," he said, and Annys laughed.

"Mora!" Andrew cried out, and Gybbon thanked Annys for catching the boy before he slammed into him. "Easy, laddie," he said to Andrew.

"She just fainted, Andrew. That is all," Annys said as she stroked back the boy's curls. "We just need to wake her and find out what made her swoon." She looked at Gybbon with narrowed eyes and he shook his head, knowing she suspected he may have bedded down with Mora.

Gybbon set Mora on the bed and stared down at her, then frowned. She looked pale, but on her cheeks were two growing flags of red. She had shaken off the fever, he thought, as he felt her forehead and found it hot.

Annys also felt her forehead and frowned. "She has a fever, mayhap even a bad one. Is she ill?"

"Nay. She got a bad wound and became a little feverish, but it passed and the wound healed. Jolene just said she shouldnae ride for a week or so."

"Good advice. Weel it has come back. Out." She gently pushed both Gybbon and Andrew out of the room, then hurried to the head of the stairs to bellow for Mary and Joan. The two women came running up the stairs and then all three disappeared into Mora's room. The door was shut firmly behind them.

Gybbon looked at Andrew and patted the boy's back before leading him down the stairs. "She is in good hands, laddie."

"What happened?" asked Harcourt when Gybbon sat back down beside him.

"Her fever has come back."

"Annys will fix that and, if she cannae, we will send for Jolene or one of our own healers."

That eased Gybbon's worry and he turned his attention to an anxious Andrew. He had to do a lot of talking to the boy before he calmed down and finally went back to be with the other children. Gybbon stayed long enough to finish his meal with an outward calm. It was strange that she had gone down with a fever again, and Gybbon realized that he faced strange with little calm at all.

Chapter Twelve

Gybbon stepped into Mora's bedchamber and watched Annys bathe her face with cool water. "Annys, go to bed," he said quietly as he walked up to her. "Your husband wants company."

"He just wants someone to complain to," she said, but stood up and dried her hands. "She is a bit cooler now, and I had a good look at her healing wound thinking I may have missed something. There was no sign of infection, but I wouldnae expect any since it was Jolene who took care of it." She shook her head. "So, I have nary an answer for why this fever came on."

"It may be as simple as the journey she took to get here."

"Aye. Mayhap it was too much too soon as I heard she spent the whole time stuck in the back of that cart and covered over."

"Needed to keep her out of sight for her murderous cousin was following us."

"Aye. She did too much too soon, that is all. Just

because someone feels better or their fever fades doesnae mean they are truly ready and hale enough to make a journey, especially nay one where they must sit and hide in a cart. Do ye ken, it could even be just the constant worry and fear she must have been feeling for a long time now. I ken I had a lot of it when I was dealing with Adam and the possibility that he would win the battle for my home. It hasnae been so verra long since she had to bury her parents. She also must believe her brothers are dead as weel. Then there is a mad cousin doing all he can to kill her and her last surviving brother. A body can only take so many blows."

He nodded but said nothing for he was still uneasy, but her words had worked to calm him a little. "How did Harcourt hurt his foot?"

Annys stopped just as she reached the door and looked back at him, smiling faintly. "Didnae he tell you?"

"Nay." He could see her lips trembling as she fought what he suspected was hearty laughter. "Since there were so many of us round the table and everyone was talking, I let him mutter something about how he shouldnae have been on the stable roof anyway."

"He was on the cursed roof because Roban was up there and Benet was afraid he would fall. A few little tears and Papa is getting up on the roof."

"It is a cat and has more weight and more everything than even this one," he said, and pointed at Freya, who was curled up at Mora's side. "Animal could probably have nimbly leapt to safety all by itself. What harm could come to it?"

"Verra little I suspect, but Benet was scared. And,

aye, the cat took care of itself once Harcourt got up there. Made a beautiful leap from the stable roof to the bathhouse roof and then to the ground. Unfortunately, Harcourt lunged after the cat and lost his footing. He was nay so graceful as he flailed around trying to grab anything that might stop or slow his fall. I had to get Benet to go away because the boy was so pleased with his cat he was boasting of how it had jumped, then wondering why his papa couldnae do that." She grinned when Gybbon laughed. "Harcourt is verra lucky he didnae break more than his foot."

"It is broken then, is it?"

"I think it might be, so I have treated it as a broken limb, but it was definitely twisted and badly wrenched."

"Go on," he said, laughing softly. "Big bairn was whining about a lonely bed."

Annys giggled and hurried out the door. The image of his older brother climbing up something to get a cat because Benet shed a few tears was amusing. But he could understand why Harcourt did it. Looking down at Mora, Gybbon had to admit that he would probably do something similar if her cat looked to be in danger, but at least he would have the excuse that the cat was a runt that needed such protection.

He stroked Mora's forehead, finding it only faintly warm. Then he noticed that the red in her cheeks was gone. This time if she roused free of the fever, she would be sternly instructed to go very carefully until she had been free of it for at least a fortnight. Or longer, he decided. He wet the cloth and gently bathed her face, hoping she could throw off this fever as easily as she had the other one.

"Is she going to be all right?"

Gybbon started in surprise at the small voice

speaking up beside him. He looked down at Andrew and wondered how he had missed the sound of the boy entering the room. The child looked terrified and Gybbon could understand. Mora was all the boy had left of what had sounded like a very decent family.

"I believe so. She has already lost most of the burn of the fever."

"Then why did she get it again?"

"Lady Murray thinks that your sister just had too much sadness, and then there was all the trouble caused by Robert, a wound, worry, and even fear, and it proved to just be too much."

"Mora is little but she is strong. My da said so." He sat down on the edge of the bed and leaned over to lightly hug his sister. "She e'en beat him at chess once and Maman said she was stunned for few grown men could do that."

"She *is* good at the game."

Andrew stood up and tilted his head to the side as he asked, "Are ye staying here with her?"

"Weel, I think someone should, aye?"

"Aye, someone should. Good night, Sir Gybbon."

"Good night, lad. Just where are ye sleeping?"

"With Benet and Joan's lads at the end of the hall, so I willnae be verra far away if ye need to call me."

"I will remember that. Sleep weel."

He let the boy out and watched him run down to Benet's door. To his surprise Benet and Joan's two boys poked their heads out the door, grabbed hold of Andrew, and tugged him into the room. Gybbon hoped the boys suited each other well. Andrew could find himself with more brothers even if they were not blood connected. Bonds formed at their age could last a lifetime. Young as they were, all three could understand the fear, sorrow, and anger Andrew had bubbling inside him.

Stepping back into the bedroom and shutting the door, Gybbon returned to Mora's bedside. He reached down to brush her hair back and froze. She was shivering, shivering hard, like some poor, naked beggar caught out in the snow. Despite telling himself it did not mean anything truly bad, he felt the touch of panic.

When Annys tended someone, he remembered that she always left a bell for the one who would sit with the sick person, one they could ring and Annys would come. He told himself to let the poor woman sleep, but then Mora hissed out the words "so cold" between tightly clenched teeth. Going to the door, he found the bell. He could still hear Mora mumbling behind him as he stepped out into the hall and rang the bell, before hurrying back to her side.

In just a few minutes Annys rushed in and hurried over to the bed. Deciding he would not mention that her voluminous night shift was on inside out and backward, Gybbon had to fight a grin. She looked at Mora, then dashed over to the chest set near the fire, opened it, and pulled out another blanket. He took it from her and spread it over a still shivering Mora. They did that twice more in the next hour, but Mora continued to shiver slightly.

"I have ne'er understood why this happens, but it often does," said Annys. "I have ne'er had anyone appear to have suffered badly from it though. Dinnae look. I am just going to take another quick peek at her wound."

Gybbon just shook his head. As soon as she had Mora's night shift tugged up, he glanced at the wound himself. It looked healthy to him, still sealed and no hint of the poison that could too easily grow in such injuries, making even the smallest one become deadly. It was just an ugly reminder of how someone wished her dead and did not belong on such smooth, pale skin.

Annys stood up, put the night shift back in place, and pulled up the covers. "Just keep her warm and, if anything else changes, ring the bell."

Gybbon looked at the door Annys had shut and decided it would have to be a big change and a worrisome one before he rang that bell again or he would never hear the end of it from Harcourt. He stood by the bed and wondered what he should do. The blankets had not solved the problem. Then he recalled what he had done from time to time when a boy forced to sleep in a cold room with other boys.

Smiling, he started to shed his clothes. When he was naked, he crawled under the covers, tugged her into his arms, and waited until her shivering stopped. Not long after, he decided that as soon as he could he would pull down a few of the blankets as it was too hot for him.

He lightly rubbed her back and she snuggled closer, putting her arms around him and laying her cheek against his chest. He could grow to like this, he thought, and smiled. Her night shift hid little of her shape when he held her so close. Curious if her skin felt as soft as it looked, he slipped his hand just under the hem and stroked her leg. Then he pulled his hand away with reluctance, knowing it was a grave trespass and not wishing to get caught and then have to try and explain what he had been doing. He had proven his suspicion. Her skin was as soft and smooth as it looked.

Moving just enough to reach out and turn down the added covers, he then held her close and closed his eyes. He would have a short rest, then return to just watching her for any sign of some new turn in her illness. Briefly peeking at Freya, who sprawled on the pillow near her head, he caught the cat watching him.

"Wake me when the sun starts to rise," he said, and chuckled as he closed his eyes again.

Mora woke up slowly. She was so nice and warm when she could faintly recall being so very cold, the kind of cold that sank right down into your bones. Snuggling closer to the warmth, she suddenly realized that it was not a blanket wrapped around her legs. It was a leg. She shifted her legs a little. It was a big leg, too.

Cautiously, she opened her eyes and found herself staring at a big arm wrapped around her shoulders. Mora knew she should not be having so much trouble figuring this out, but it was as if her brain was wrapped in a fog. She turned her head and felt the slight tickle of hair against her nose.

It was hard, but she resisted the strong urge to leap out of bed. She felt no fear, which was odd, she thought. Leaning back a little, she looked up and saw Gybbon's sleeping face. He looked years younger with his face relaxed in sleep.

That was why she had no fear, she decided. She also had no idea why he was in her bed and—she lifted the covers, then quickly put them back down—why he was naked. Glancing around, she saw no one else in the room and rested against him again.

Gybbon was why that cold she recalled was gone. A glance at the window told her it was just dawn, and still early dawn for the sun was down by the horizon. Despite the hilly land around them she could still see a bit of the sun. So, too early to be awake, she decided, but she felt no strong need to go back to sleep.

After lying there for a while trying to decide what she should do and enjoying being held close by Gybbon more than she probably should, she noticed a sore spot on her head, one that throbbed enough to try and make her head ache. Mora sat up and grabbed the tankard on the table by the bed, having a long drink of the cider left for her. She then reached up and felt around her head before finding a bump on the back. Try as hard as she could, she could not think of where she might have gotten it.

Gybbon opened his eyes and watched as Mora rubbed the spot on her head that had hit the floor. He had begun to wake up when she had started moving around, a little afraid she would panic when she found him there. Mora had either figured out why he was there or she was still groggy.

"Morning," he said, and looked at Freya. "Ye were supposed to wake me when the sun rose."

Mora laughed and watched as her cat patted him on the face. "The sun has just risen and ye should be glad I was slow this morning or ye might be the one needing a wound tended."

"Ye were shivering from the cold, although it was warm enough in here."

"I could remember that much. My mither got the chills bad once and my da climbed into the bed with her, then had me and Andrew crawl in as well.

However," she said sternly and looked at him, "we kept all our clothes on."

"I believe I mentioned once that I dinnae wear them when climbing into a proper bed."

She just harrumphed in a soft way, then rubbed her head again. "Why does my head hurt?"

"It didnae like the floor it met with." When she looked at him in confusion, he just smiled.

"I fell?"

"Like a stone. Ye were right outside the door to the hall and headed to the stairs when ye went down. Ye had the fever again. Annys thinks it was simply because ye did too much too soon, had too much weighing on your mind and heart." He reached around her, grabbed the tankard, and used the last of the cider to rinse away the taste of the night from his mouth.

"I didnae ride a horse and that was all Jolene said I couldnae do."

"Aye, I ken it, but Annys thinks ye have had far too much to deal with for a while now and that may have made the cart ride enough to make ye sick again. Your wound is just fine—before ye ask. Your head didnae split open or the like, so that will stop being painful soon."

"Well, I guess that was lucky as that floor is hard."

"Ye could put a cold cloth on the spot. I dinnae ken why, but it can help." He reached out to find the spot giving her trouble. "'Tis a sizeable knot ye have there."

She sighed as he wrapped his arm around her and pulled her close. When she did not immediately protest, he kissed her. This was how a man should wake up in the morning, he thought, as he deepened the kiss and she responded, wrapping her arms around his neck.

He moved his kisses to her throat and she murmured with an enjoyment that tempted him to kiss her again. He stroked her back as he gently brought her even closer. Gybbon heartily wished there were not so many bedcovers between them.

Mora knew she should pull away and put a stop to this, but she held him tighter and returned his kiss. She also knew she should put an end to the way he was stroking her anywhere he could reach. It was not until she felt the heat of his hand move over her breast that alarm crept into the pleasure he was stirring.

Gybbon silently cursed as he felt her body stiffen, but he stole one last caress before he pulled back. She was a lady and an innocent. Greedy though he was feeling, he knew he had to move slowly.

"Weel, that was a fine good morning," he drawled, then winked at her. "But ye better turn away because I am about to get out from under these cursed covers. Unless ye have a wish to bask in my beauty."

Mora rolled her eyes and turned around, ignoring the part of her that urged her to look. If nothing else, that could make him think she was ready for something she knew she should not indulge in. From what little she had glimpsed when lifting the covers a bit to peek at him, he was a very nicely put together man.

"Does Andrew ken I fell down and got the fever again?"

"Aye, I am afraid so. He is with the other boys though and kenned I was going to watch ye during the night."

"He slept with some of the boys?"

"Aye. They put him with Benet and Joan's lads."

"How lovely. He rarely gets to be with boys near his age."

"Nay only near his age but ones who have shared some of the troubles he is having now." He grabbed her gently by the arm and tugged her over to him, then gave her a quick hard kiss on the mouth. "Do ye want a maid sent?"

"Nay, I could too easily get spoiled."

"Then I shall see ye in the hall." He walked to the door.

"Do ye think it was the bath that brought the fever on?" she asked as she watched him reach for the handle of the door.

"Nay, I doubt that. For all we ken, it could have aided in it leaving ye so quickly. Nay, I think Annys is right. Ye have just carried too much all on your own for far too long."

Mora thought on that as she rose to get dressed, moving slowly until she felt certain she was steady on her feet. Her mind was inclined to drift to the sweetness of his kisses, the way they made her feel, but she forced it to stay on the matter of what had caused her to swoon like some weak maid. She would think about Gybbon, his kisses and caresses, later. And those feelings much later than that, she decided. It would be important to know if she would refuse or accept them, but there was time for all that later.

He was right; she had been carrying a lot of weight for a long time now and had had little time to deal with all of it. There was her grief over her parents, her added grief over the likely fate of her brothers, and being the head of a household, a household her thieving cousins thought should be theirs. There had been no time to sort out any of these concerns, and it had been exhausting her. It was a shock to realize her own cousins were willing to kill off her entire family, people who had always been kind to him and his family, just to take back what their grandfather had willingly and legally given to his youngest son.

Somehow, she had to get their father, her uncle, to heed her. She had not seen the man for a fortnight or more, but perhaps he had improved to where he could, and would listen to her. Jolene was certain the mon was being poisoned. Mora could not bring herself to disbelieve that, but did wonder if Robert's brothers knew of it.

If not, then she needed to try and do something to save them, especially Murdoch. She knew he had no knowledge of his brother's crimes. She could still see that look of horror on his face when Robert had openly admitted to killing and stealing from her parents. She was not as certain about Lachlan and Duncan and their part in all of it.

She finally yanked off her night shift and began to get dressed. A quick look at her wound was enough to tell her she had done it no harm when she had fallen. It was ugly but not infected at all. Mora took a moment to dig out the cream Jolene had packed for her and rubbed it on her wound.

Mora was going to have to ask Jolene how she made it. It soothed the itch of healing that still bothered her occasionally, and she was certain it was easing the scarring such a wound could leave her with. There had been no poisoning in the wound, either. This was a salve she definitely wanted to be able to make and always have at hand.

Leaving the bedchamber, she headed down the stairs, going carefully and keeping a firm grip on the rail at the side. She could hear that the morning meal was being put out and almost laughed when her stomach rumbled softly. It was all so wonderfully normal and she hungered for normal. Normal and calm. She gave a start when a hand gently grasped her by the arm.

"Sorry," said Annys. "I had thought ye kenned I was following ye."

"I thought ye were already down there. I could hear that the food was being served."

"I had to go change my gown. Bit of an accident in the kitchens." Annys looked at her. "So ye are feeling better?"

"Aye. Much. E'en put Jolene's cream on my wound myself and decided I need to learn how to make some. It is marvelous."

"It is, and I keep meaning to do the same, but she keeps giving me some so I forget. Sigimor's people are doing better?"

"Aye. He just felt the need to get Jolene and his son away from there."

"If I had suffered what he went through when he was a young mon, I would have done the same. But what about his twin girls?"

"At one of their kinsmen's with about seven nurse-maids to, as was said, keep them out of trouble." She grinned when Annys laughed heartily. "They cannae be that bad, can they?"

"Aye, they can, but they are adorable. I have only met with them once and they were younger, but e'en then I could see it. They are definitely Sigimor's girls."

"I seem to have met with so many people since Gybbon came into my life."

"And there are more to come if ye stay in it. Many more. And they are already planning on whom to get in touch with to try and find out what happened to your brothers."

"It would be wondrous if they could and e'en more so if they were found alive."

Annys patted her arm. "Keep that hope."

Niall Ogilvy groaned and rubbed his backside when his brother David had them stop for a brief meal. "Why are we rushing there?" he asked.

"Because something is wrong. Verra wrong. I ken it and need to ken what it is."

"If 'tis trouble we are galloping toward mayhap we should have brought some of the other men."

"I ken where they are. Made certain of it before we left them. Have their promise to come and help if help is needed."

Niall stopped the pacing he had begun to limber up his legs and sat down to look at David. "Ye are truly worried."

"Someone tried to kill us, Niall. We cannae forget that. I dinnae e'en need to look at the scar I have to keep it in mind. Except for the French we were fighting, there was no one o'er there who kenned us weel enough to want us dead. And did it ne'er trouble ye that we got no news from home? That our parents or sister ne'er once sent us word to ask about us or tell us about them? They can all write."

"Aye"—he shrugged—"but I just assumed it was because we were nay easy to find and we were far from home."

"I did, too, until I spoke to the men awaiting a hanging for their trying to murder us. They were hired by Scots just before they boarded the boat to go to France. They gave a description of the one who did the talking and it sounded verra much like our dear cousin Robert."

"Jesu," Niall whispered. "Why? We ne'er did anything to him."

"Nay, but I do ken that he has always resented the fact that Grandfather gave our father that house and several acres of land. It took a bite out of what he saw as his."

"It wasnae his; it was the old laird's and then became his father's."

"And will soon be his. Rabbit is near done. We eat, then continue."

"Mora might need us?"

"Aye. Her and wee Andrew." David could see that Niall was puzzled and asked, "Why would our cousin hire men to kill us? Why nay just wait and see if fighting in France will end us?"

"Because he is getting rid of heirs to that bit of land until it has to be drawn back into the big lot his father holds?" Niall asked the question in a quiet, nervous voice.

"Aye. It is all that makes any sense."

"I pray ye are wrong."

"Nay harder than I do, but just the thought has me anxious to get back home. I need to see if I am wrong or right. Until I can see what awaits, I cannae rest. The question of why did he try to have us killed preys on me."

"Then we willnae rest. Much. We will go get your answers."

Chapter Thirteen

Mora blushed faintly as Gybbon hooked her arm through his and led her out into the garden. It was dark but there were a few torches lit to give light to the area, and the moon shone bright. She suspected everyone who had seen them leave the hall knew why he was taking her for a walk in the gardens when one could barely see what grew there, and that did embarrass her a bit.

They had been at Glenfuerach for a week and she loved the keep. It was well run and sturdy, with a guard obviously trained to watch and battle any trouble that came along. Annys was already a friend and Andrew was happy to be with other boys in a place behind big, thick walls.

"Triona, Brett's wife, has done a lot of work here," Gybbon said, sounding quite proud of his brother's wife as he looked around. "She and Annys worked hard, although Annys was cautious because she carried her child. It was an overgrown, snarled mess. They even put in the herb garden. Then Triona returned to her home and Brett."

"Why did they have to do so much work?"

"'Twas left alone for too long. The new laird cared naught about gardens. He did like to hunt down the meat for the table but cared nothing about all the rest ye need for a fine meal. 'Twas much the same with the whole keep. It all needed work. The laird here wanted Triona's keep. He probably planned on living there and just allowing this one to rot and expanding his land holdings."

"Annys told me some of the tale." She shook her head. "I just find it difficult to understand. Aye, your brother and Annys have cleaned things, but the mon had a fine, sturdy keep and land. Why try so hard to grab even more? Why nay just make this one finer?"

"Annys's lands were far more fertile and she had excellent grazing lands, so her husband's cousin came after them. He thought to make his hold on the place more firm by wedding her, but that failed so he just tried to take them. He had the backing of his family, too, for they had always resented her late husband being given the lands. She has a lot of skilled people on her lands and their market day produced a nice profit. He wanted that, too. He even put all her fighting men in prison to rot. So, after the battle and after Harcourt got himself named laird of this place with Brett's blessings.

"With Triona, it was her neighbor Sir John, with his family's quiet backing at the start, as they all disliked the fact that their ancestor lost the lands and they had ended up in the possession of her late husband, Boyd. They felt it should be theirs. Brett had kenned her years before but came the moment she wrote him of trouble. There was e'en a battle o'er it all, but then that ended when her husband's elder brother, Nigel, appeared from the dead and joined in. It appears France is a good place to try and rid oneself of unwanted relatives as Adam had paid someone to put Nigel in a prison to rot. So Brett weds her and is suddenly Laird of Banuilt, the keep John held. Annys and her son came here to be with Harcourt."

"Ye didnae lie when ye said your kin had experience with greedy relations trying to enrich themselves. Seeing this, all I can think of is that Robert seeks to steal a pittance. It seems that the surest way to trouble for a woman is to be in possession of some lands."

He laughed and led her to a bench set between two trees with gently arching branches. Gybbon sat and tugged her down beside him. He put his arm around her shoulders and pulled her up close to his side. It pleased him when she snuggled closer and rested her head against his chest.

He kissed her temple. "Ye are safe here. Andrew is safe here as weel."

"Just being behind such thick, high walls has done a lot to ease the fear riding me so hard."

Nodding, Gybbon listened to the sounds of the keep, the slow softening of the usual noise as the light faded. Harcourt had gained himself a good solid place here with people who were more than happy to call him their laird and bow to Annys as their lady. He also now had a well-trained fighting force.

As he slowly rubbed his cheek against Mora's hair, he began to ponder about what he needed to do to have a place to live, some work to do, and get some coin. He had gathered a hefty purse during his travels, but more would help. Gybbon realized such thoughts told him he was done wandering around the land fighting other people's battles. If he had to fight again it should be to protect something he owned.

Mora looked up at Gybbon and frowned. He had a look that told her he was meandering through a lot of thoughts and memories. She was not sure she wanted to know what they were but felt compelled to ask.

"Gybbon, where have ye gone?" she asked softly, and reached up to stroke his cheek.

Mora's gentle question and touch yanked him out of his rambling thoughts. "Just thinking over the last year or two and all the places I have been."

"Ye were doing a lot of wandering around? Selling your sword?" she asked warily, afraid that might be an insulting question.

"At times. But I often would wonder if I was really fighting for the right side, and that troubled me. Mostly I would ride to a kinsmon when he needed aid and lend a hand. Sold Jester's services as stud to a few people."

"They liked his coloring, didnae they?"

"Aye, that was mostly what they hoped to get, but he is also a good, strong stallion who can run fast, and any mon with men to seat cannae resist that either." He nodded and said, "I ken everywhere he might end up having left a wee Jester."

"Then ye had best hope he cannae pass on his temperament."

Gybbon laughed. "True. Although tossing the wrong person out of the saddle is nay always such a bad thing."

He picked her up, ignoring her gasp of shock, and set her on his lap, facing him, her legs settled just where he had wanted them to, on either side of his legs. He looked at her blushing face and then kissed her frowning mouth, feeling it soften beneath his lips.

"This is verra, weel, indecent, isnae it?" She looked around the garden but could not see anyone.

"There is no one here, Mora. No one to see your wee bird legs."

"Oh! I dinnae have bird legs." She smacked him on the arm knowing he did not even feel it.

Laughing, Gybbon pulled her closer and began to kiss her neck. This was why he was suddenly thinking of all he needed to do so that he could settle in one place. If anyone would have suggested such a thing would happen to him and because of a slender woman who carried a cat around, he would have laughed heartily.

It was true that his family lines were rife with what many would call strange marriages, ones where the husband and wife were friends, partners, and lovers. Even stranger to many was the fact that most Murray men considered a vow taken was a vow held, so there were no tidy rows of houses holding discarded mistresses. He blamed his parents and, to be precise, all of the elder Murrays.

Mora was startled when Gybbon set her on his lap. The way he had settled her there made her all too aware of the fact that he wanted her. When she had turned fourteen she had been vigorously pursued by the miller's son despite her higher station in life. Her mother had taken her aside to give her a talk about men and women. Privacy was a rare luxury few could afford, so Mora had not been completely ignorant about the fact that something went on between men and women, but her mother had very carefully told her precisely what happened. It had nearly been enough to make her want to look closer when she saw some couple wrestling up against a wall, but she had resisted the temptation, sensing it might taint something in her.

She knew what Gybbon had her straddling, why he was gently moving against her. What troubled her was that she liked it. She wanted to move against him as well, his kisses and the stroking of his hands clouding her mind and making her body ache. Mora knew she should put a stop to this and was thinking on a way to do that when he ended the kiss he had been giving her, leaned back, and took several deep breaths, then letting them out slowly.

"We are in the gardens," he muttered, surprised at how firmly he had to remind himself of that fact.

"I ken it," she said, resting her head against his chest as she tried to banish the feelings that were making her body tremble.

Gybbon gently stroked her face and tucked the few stray locks of her hair that had come loose from her braid behind her ears. "Time to go inside."

She let him set her down and then stand up. He took her by the hand and began to lead her back to the doors they had slipped out through. Mora wondered if anyone would still be in the kitchens.

They slipped in with only one lone kitchen maid noticing them and then went up the stairs. By the time they reached the top of the stairs, Gybbon had his arm around her waist. They had reached her door when he suddenly pulled her into his arms and kissed her.

Mora let herself sink into the kiss and enjoyed the heat it stirred within her. She knew what he wanted and she was uneasy. A large part of her wanted it, too, but she was neither a widow nor a tavern maid and she knew she should not. There had been no words of love or even need. No promises she could cling to for a future.

Then she thought of all that had happened. What good were promises to her when she had a man determined to kill her? She was filled with a grief and anger that had little place to go and his kisses eased all that, gave her a moment to forget them. He was evidently a man who liked to wander and she was one who ached to settle. So what harm was there in allowing herself to just forget all of it in his arms?

He looked at her and she was certain there was a question in his eyes. A strong reckless and rebellious part of her rose up to answer that question and she opened her door. His eyes widened when she tugged him into her room. Delighted by his surprise, she curled her arms around his neck and kissed him with all the fierce desire she had fought to keep under control.

As he held the kiss, Gybbon unlaced her dress. He did not know what had possessed her to become so bold, but he was not about to argue with her. He had not been looking forward to a long night twisted up with unrelieved desire. If she had doubts after, he would do his best to ease them.

He stripped her of her clothing piece by piece, kissing her between each removal. When he dropped the last piece of her clothing to the floor, he picked her up in his arms, flipped back the covers on the bed, and set her down. He kept a close eye on her, watching for any sign that she might be changing her mind, as he hurriedly shed his own clothing. He had to smile at the way she had cocked her leg to hide the red curls at the juncture of her thighs and crossed her arms over her breasts. Gybbon would have liked to stand there and openly look at her, but he did not wish to make her nervous.

Once he had stripped off his own clothing, he got on the bed with her. He tugged up the covers and then pulled her into his arms. For a moment, he feared the trembling he felt in her was due to fear. Then she wriggled closer to him and he knew it was a need that might well be as strong as his. Her eyes, however, were wide with unease and he gently kissed the corner of each one.

"Any time ye wish me to cease, just say so," he told her softly, all the while praying she would not say the words, and he began to slide his hands over all that soft, pale skin he had hungered for.

Mora tried to relax as he kissed her ears, her neck, her shoulders. His hands, a little roughened from sword use, kept stroking her. When he cupped her breast in one hand, she shivered, and then his lips were there. She gave a soft cry as he sucked and licked at her nipple. When he moved to the other breast to do the same, she felt the grip of nerves and fear leave her, but a strange ache took its place. She stroked his back and held him close and he continued to feast.

So intent was she about how he felt beneath her hands, how his skin felt as it lightly rubbed against her, she lay there and just savored it all. Even the brush of his hair on her skin was a caress. It all put her into a daze of pleasure. Then he slid his hand over her belly and between her legs. She tensed, unaware of what was going on now. He whispered to her even though she only heard the whisper of words, not what he said, and then kissed her as his fingers continued to taunt and stroke her. That ache that had puzzled her grew stronger with each teasing stroke. She held him tighter, wanting something but not sure what that something was.

"Gybbon," she said on a sigh.

"Aye, loving, I ken it." He settled himself between her legs. "I am sorry, love, but it is going to hurt some."

She was just thinking how unfair that was when the pain struck. As quickly as it came it was gone, save for a slight sting, and all she felt was an unusual fullness. He lifted her legs and silently prompted her to put them around his hips. Mora hugged him tightly with arms and legs, then he began to thrust inside her. Gybbon watched her for a while, but she finally had to just close her eyes and feel.

Soon Gybbon felt her body rise to meet his every thrust. He gave himself over to the pleasure of it, trying very hard to make sure she felt some pleasure as well. As he bent his head to her breasts and sucked, he knew he was reaching the end and he really wanted her to be there with him. Then her heels dug into his back and he knew. He was right there with her when she arched and made a strange little sound that was half moan, half cry. He thrust into her a few more times and felt her body clench around him as he spilled himself inside her. Once done, he tried to get out of her quickly and managed in time to collapse beside her instead of on top of her.

"Aye," Mora said suddenly, after several moments of lying with him while they both gasped to catch their breath, "it wouldnae have been a good idea to do that in the garden."

Gybbon looked at her, saw the faint smile on her face, and rolling over to hug her, started laughing. "Nay, it wouldnae have been," was all he managed to gasp out before laughing some more.

A few moments passed and he realized she had gone to sleep. He glanced around and found Freya curled up at the end of the bed, staring at him. When he felt the heat of a blush on his cheeks, he cursed. He got up to dampen a cloth, cleaned himself, then rinsed it and went to clean off Mora, ignoring her blushes when she woke enough to realize what he was doing. Freya watched him the whole way. He did not like what she eyed with interest and covered himself with his hand as he went back to bed.

"'Tis but a cursed cat," he grumbled as he curled himself around Mora, her back hard up against his front.

He then closed his eyes. His body was hinting at interest in going another round, but he ignored it. She had been a virgin, and the door had required a good battering to open, so he expected there would be some tenderness in the morning. Despite his wants and needs, he was determined to be a gentleman.

As he forced his body to relax, he thought on what needed to be done about Robert. Instinct told him Robert was not a man one could reason with, could probably not even be tortured into seeing reason. He was going to have to kill the fool but, unless he got the old laird to see it as a needed justice, that could cause a lot of trouble for his family, Sigimor's as well. This area was an odd cluster of clan holdings, and what affected one could all too easily affect another.

All he could do was hope someone else would do it. The man had to have a lot of enemies.

Robert could be dealt with, Gybbon decided, determined to push the problem aside for now. No matter how the problem was settled, there would be trouble. He was feeling too satisfied and content to worry about that now.

The sun was breaking over the horizon when Gybbon woke and he slipped out of bed. He gathered up his clothes and stepped behind the privacy screen, to relieve himself, wash up, and then dress. When done he walked out and moved over to the bed.

He was just contemplating kissing Mora awake when he heard the door open. His brother Harcourt stood there with a half smile on his face and crooked his finger in a gesture to tell him to come along. Gybbon sighed and went.

"Are ye sure that was wise?" Harcourt asked as they started down the stairs.

"Did someone ask ye that?"

"Nay." Harcourt laughed, but it was not a happy sound. "Sometimes I wish they had, but then I realize if they had, and I had listened, there would be no Benet."

"Aye, and ye cannae want that. Weel, it probably wasnae wise, but I find I simply dinnae care." He frowned. "Unless she frets o'er it."

"Weel, ye were sneaky enough last night that Annys was shocked to find ye were gone from your bedchamber. She woke me up to ask if ye had told me ye were leaving. So ye lost me a nice sleep and some morning time with Annys."

"Since I didnae get any morning time, I dinnae think I can work up any sorrow for ye."

"All that roaming ye have done has made your heart cold, brother." He grinned when Gybbon laughed. "Are ye done with it?"

"I am thinking I might be. Will have to see how matters go."

"Ah, so she has ye thinking of staying in one place."

Gybbon shook his head. "I just started thinking on it and have made no decision. Just wondered while doing it, if she was why I suddenly started thinking on it. One usually needs a reason to stop and settle in one spot. But then I would have that silly cat."

"Roban is up with Annys, so we dinnae have to worry about Freya."

Gybbon looked down to see the cat strutting along with them. "I didnae e'en see her get out."

"She slipped out the moment I opened the door. She has seen Roban but then ran up the stairs and disappeared. I just dinnae want her getting hurt by the bigger cat."

"Oh, nay. Mora adores the fool cat."

"The moment a woman or a child names an animal, it becomes important and sometimes a great pet."

"Like Roberta, who is not for the pot."

"Exactly, although the stupid beast is near full grown now." He walked into the hall and hailed Nicolas, who moved to the head table to sit next to Harcourt while Gybbon sat on his other side.

"The offer to be my second still stands."

"As does Nicolas," said Gybbon.

"Then ye can be my third."

"I dinnae think ye can have a third."

"I can have anything I want; I am a laird." Harcourt grinned at them, and both Nicolas and Gybbon laughed.

"That ye certainly are. And how often do ye tell your wife?"

"All the time, and she listens raptly."

"Then does as she pleases."

"Aye." He laughed along with the other men, then grew serious. "Then what about the bit of land I talked on?" Harcourt said abruptly, as he heaped some porridge into his bowl.

"That I might consider, but nay now. I did earn a nice purse of money, but it will take time to collect it all, as I left it at various kinsmen's to keep it safe from thieves."

"Ye could have some of what is between us and the border."

"Nay. I would choose a patch between ye and Nigel. I dinnae want, nor can afford to build a big keep, Harcourt. A nice fortified house would be it and better it be placed between two weel-fortified keeps. Gives me two places to choose between if I have to get to safety."

Nicolas nodded. "Aye, good plan."

Harcourt lightly smacked Nicolas on the back of his head. "A keep would be better."

"I would be ready for my grave before I got the coin to build one of those," Gybbon said.

Sighing heavily, Harcourt nodded. "True. Might be better to just make sure the manor is as strong as it can be."

"That can be done. Time to think on it, anyway. Now, I need to keep my mind on how to end this threat from Robert Ogilvy."

"I am nay sure ye can," said Nicolas. "The mon has already killed a number of people, is trying to kill his own father, to get what he wants. Any mon who is willing to do such things is nay going to end his campaign because it does nay make sense or has grown too hard. If he was, he would have stepped back when he realized Sigimor was involved in protecting the lady and that boy. Any sane mon would."

Gybbon laughed. "True enough."

For a while, they discussed several ideas concerning what could be done about Robert. Tiring of that, they went out to indulge in some sword practice. It was between him and Nicolas because Harcourt had to sit down due to his healing foot. His men watched and occasionally took a turn. Gybbon realized how much he had missed such comradery while roaming the country. It was just another reason to stop roving, he decided.

By the time it ended, Gybbon was weary and needed a wash but had to admit it had been a good way to pass the time. He went to his bedchamber and washed up, then went to Mora's bedchamber. All he found was a maid who directed him down to the lady's sitting room. Annys had seen Jolene's and had decided she needed one. He could see the reason behind such a thing as he suspected it was a nice place to go when men started their boasting or talk of old battles.

He stepped inside and saw Mora immediately. She looked healthy again and was deep into a discussion over the making of a shirt. As quietly as he could he walked over and sat in the chair facing the two women on the settle.

"Are ye done clashing swords together?" asked Annys.

"Aye and nay. Harcourt didnae try to join in. He sat

down and delighted us all with his opinions on our skills." Gybbon smiled when Annys laughed.

"I am sure ye enjoyed that."

"And he is arguing about me setting up some place to live near here. This time I at least came to the decision that, if I did, it would be a manor house, well fortified, set between here and Nigel."

"There is a lovely spot there, almost right at the halfway mark."

"I ken it. Have often studied it." He grinned at Annys and she smiled back at him. "But there is nay a hurry to do it. And," he added as he looked at Mora, "there is a certain problem that needs to be ended."

"'Tis my trouble. Ye must nay hold back any plans ye had for it. Besides he is three days away so how much trouble can he be?" Mora asked.

"A lot. He is but a day's ride from here."

"He is? But it took us nearly three days to reach here."

"Ah, weel, we came a circuitous route and were in a cart. We also wanted to go carefully, slowly, because of ye and the boy, and needed to keep a close watch for Robert and his men."

"Oh. I hadnae realized he was so close to us here."

Mora began to think of how she could get to her uncle if it was only that far away. She was not sure how much it would take to get to Robert's father, but it could at least be considered. Then she could get in and speak with her uncle. He had always been a reasonable, friendly, and understanding man. Mora did not think that had all changed. She felt certain she could get him to believe her if she could just talk to him.

Annys got up to leave, breaking into her thoughts.

Mora watched as the woman gracefully walked away, stepped out the door, and was grabbed by her hobbling husband. She then listened to the woman scolding Harcourt on walking and carrying something on his broken foot.

"I hope he isnae injuring it," Mora murmured.

"Nay, he wouldnae do that," Gybbon said. "He believes in what she says when it comes to healing. And, she is light so I doubt carrying her off somewhere is going to damage him, but he will put her down quickly if he feels it is doing damage. And what are ye doing?"

"Fixing a few of Andrew's shirts. He can be verra hard on clothes."

"Aye, my mither used to complain about that with all of us. Freya went up to the bedchamber and Mary told me she let her in. She didnae wish to go out and watch us practice. So, are ye feeling better?"

"Oh, aye. I am nay certain why I got feverish again, but it has passed."

"Just as long as ye dinnae do too much."

"Aye," she replied, and pushed aside the thought of going to face her uncle.

She began to pack up what she had brought into the room and soon had Gybbon escorting her back to her bedchamber. Mora did not know if she was to offer an invitation or leave it until he made some move to join her. Then Andrew skipped up and took her by the hand, ending all debate. Despite his presence, however, she leaned forward and intended to kiss Gybbon on the cheek. Gybbon turned enough to make her kiss land on his mouth, and Andrew made a noise of childish disgust.

Grinning, Gybbon said, "I will see ye later."

Mora walked off to see where Andrew was sleeping and wondered if she was right in thinking he was saying he would be back in her bed. She would readily accept him, too, for she was determined to enjoy that as much as she could before she attempted to go and speak with her uncle.

Chapter Fourteen

David frowned up at the sky as he and Niall rode into the small village. They had only been gone two, almost three years, but there were visible changes in the village. Riding along easily in the open air was a pleasure, especially after the many times he and Niall had had to hide after fleeing the place where they had been held prisoner. The vast, starlit sky was now just black, the soft light shed by the moon vanquished. He could feel the touch of a damp coolness in the air.

"'Tis going to rain soon," he muttered to Niall, who rode at his side.

"Aye. We have been wet before. Filthy too," Niall said, scowling down at his travel-worn clothing.

"True enough, but I would prefer to avoid being so again. We will go to the inn."

"We could go to Aunt Maggie's."

Glancing at the row of the old laird's leman cottages with the one burned out shell in its midst, David felt his heart clench with a sorrow he had no answer for, although he had cared for Aunt Maggie. "Nay, we cannae."

Niall looked where David did and cursed with a

fluency in three languages that David had to admire. "Sad to say, cottages burn all the time," Niall said with a slight lilt at the end, which made it less of a statement and more of a question he wanted an answer to.

"Aye, they do," said David, "but I have a verra bad feeling about this time and this cottage."

"Ye have had a bad feeling since we left France."

"I have and it hasnae faded, just grown stronger with each mile we have drawn closer to our home." David turned toward the stables next to the inn. "Mayhap we can get some news while we are at the inn."

"Nay sure I want to hear any," muttered Niall as he reined in next to his brother and let David chat with the lad who would put the horses up in the stable.

Just as they stepped inside the inn the sky opened and let go of the rain the clouds had been holding. David hastily shut the doors. He got a room for them both to share and ordered their meals. The innkeeper would have been someone he could ask, but he was so gregarious and talkative, David decided not to chance it. He then chose a table near to the windows and Niall sat on the small bench across the heavy wooden table from him.

"Now what has ye frowning?" asked Niall as he nodded his thanks for the tankards of cider a girl brought them. "I have learned to worry when ye frown like that."

"'Tis just that I thought I would be happy and eager to get home, yet I am not. I keep waiting for the feeling but it just doesnae come."

"It has been two cursed years. Near three."

"True. Yet, some touch of those feelings should be there when we are so verra close to home."

"Mayhap it was seeing Aunt Maggie's house burnt

down and nay kenning why or e'en if she got to safety."
Niall smiled widely at the plate brimming with meat
and a few vegetables set in front of him by a shy serving maid. "Some food will help."

"I dinnae think so, but my belly is telling me to cease
fretting and eat." He grinned when Niall laughed.

For a while Niall and David quietly enjoyed their
meal. David kept looking out the window and he was
not sure why. He watched one of the maids hurry by
with full tankards, caught Niall doing the same, and
they shared a grin. A moment later he was staring
out the window again and suddenly he knew why.
Four men rode up and dismounted. They stood by
while one argued with the stable lad. The torches
lighting the front of the inn gave off enough light to
show him the man's face, and David cursed.

"Grab your food and cider," he told Niall as he
collected his own. "We will finish this in our room."

Niall picked up his plate and drink, then frowned
at David. "Why?"

"The Ogilvy brothers have just arrived."

Niall cursed and gently grabbed the arm of the
busy serving maid as she started past them. He asked
if there was another way to get to their room and, after
she refilled their tankards, she quickly led them to the
back stairs the servants often used. Once David and
Niall were in their room, they locked the door and
settled at the small table there to finish their meal.

"Are ye certain it was them?" Niall asked as he finished his meal and sat back to sip at his cider.

"Oh, aye. It was them." David carefully stacked their
plates, then sat back to savor his own tankard of cider.
"Robert was arguing with the stable lad. The other
three just stood there watching him and getting wet."

"Do ye think they are all in it together?"

"If they are, the other three are in it due to fear of Robert. They have always feared that fool."

"Aye, that is true. Yet, to follow him when he is trying to kill off his own blood kin is rather odd."

"We dinnae ken how or for how long he has kept his boot on their necks. I do ken that the laird made certain young Murdoch was guarded weel until he learned how to fight with some skill. Also recall often thinking that the three, Duncan, Lachlan, and even Murdoch, should just get together and beat the meanness out of him."

"How did ye learn that about Murdoch?"

"Heard Maman and Da talking about it once. Something happened that made putting a guard on the boy a necessity. Da said he was of the opinion one should be put on Robert." He grinned when Niall laughed, but his expression grew worried. "We should have gone home."

"Aye, but now we need to ken what happened to Aunt Maggie and why her house was burned."

"We will despite how strongly my innards tell me I dinnae want to ken."

"We could just ask one of the people here."

"And I would if Robert and his brothers were nay here."

"Ah, weel, best we get some sleep as I feel we will have a lot to do come the morning."

David stood up and went to the door to set the plates and tankards outside. To his delight one of the serving maids was there collecting other things set outside the doors, and he requested the full breakfast for two in the morning plus a small jug of cider for the night.

She returned with an admirable speed, so he gave her a coin in thanks, and he set the jug and small tankards on the table. Her prompt cheerfulness was quickly explained when she made it clear she thought they were Camerons. David did not correct her because he did not want their real names mentioned where Robert might overhear.

Locking the door securely, he stripped off his clothes, washed up with the water and cloth left out for guests, and then went to the bed. He kicked at Niall, who was taking up more than his share of the bed, and then settled down. It was going to be a long night, he decided. He had too many questions and no answers. David knew they would prey on his mind for most of the night. It was time for them to find out the fate of Aunt Maggie and then get home.

Mora was just climbing into bed when Gybbon slipped into her room. She just smiled and he began to strip out of his clothing. Although she knew it was bold, she could not stop watching as he undressed. He truly was a fine-looking man. Lean yet well-muscled and all of it covered in smooth, slightly swarthy skin with only a few scars.

When he was naked, and she was trying very hard not to stare at his groin, he reached out and yanked off her shift. Mora squeaked and slid down beneath the covers. Her sudden attack of shyness faded when he grabbed hold of her and held her close.

Leaning into him, she decided she really liked the two of them sharing a bed. He was warm and the sound of his breathing or his heart beating was comforting.

She knew what they did was wrong, but she simply could not find the heart to care.

Gybbon doubted she had any idea of how badly he wanted her. He was very pleased that she had not backed away after their last time together, but welcomed him into her arms again. As he smoothed his hands over her slight yet temptingly curvy shape, he kissed her and kept kissing her until she got that faintly dazed look in her eyes that he liked.

Nudging her onto her back, he began to kiss her breasts. Plump and soft, they filled his palms, her nipples growing hard and inviting quickly. He took one into his mouth, teasing it with his tongue and sucking on it. Mora made a noise and arched into him. He kept at her until she began to writhe beneath him, then began to kiss his way down to her stomach.

Mora threaded her fingers in his hair and tried not to pull on it. She pushed away a touch of fear of how much of her he was seeing and concentrated only on how he made her feel. Then he kissed the inside of her thigh and she shuddered. The feel of his hair brushing against her groin was similar to a light caress and she closed her eyes, promising herself that she would not consider what he was doing or seeing but just enjoy what he was making her feel, how his kisses made her blood run hot, and how his touch made her breathing grow shaky. Then he kissed the red curls between her thighs and her body jerked in shock, but before she could react and push him away, he tightened his hold on her thighs slightly and began to torment her with his tongue.

When he kissed her there as if he was kissing her mouth, she felt her body begin to tremble faintly. Mora remembered that from the last time he had bedded her. She knew she was nearing the edge of that fall that had left her panting and weak. She called his name and realized she was whispering, but the way he began to kiss his way back up her body told her he had heard her.

Finally, he pressed his forehead to hers and eased himself inside her. "Pain?" he asked.

"Nay. None."

"Ye have no soreness?"

"Nay. None," she said, and reached down to clasp him by the buttocks and push him toward her.

He chuckled and began to move. Mora wrapped her arms and legs around him and held on tight. Gybbon kissed her even as he began to move harder and faster. Mora decided she loved the feel of him moving inside her, even loved the feel of holding him as they were both naked. It was odd for she was actually very modest, had always been so. Then that feeling that she suspected she could come to want all the time started to sweep over her and she tightened her hold even more, rising to meet him, and he thrust hard a few times until she cried out.

She closed her eyes and enjoyed the strange rush of feeling in her thighs and the release of the tense ache low in her belly. Her grip on him eased as it all slowly slid away leaving her warm and content. Releasing him when he slipped away, she then tensed as he returned to wash her off. Placing her hands over her face, she attempted to just ignore that very practical act after such pleasure.

Gybbon got into bed and pulled her into his arms. "Dinnae fret so, sweetling. 'Tis better to do that than to just lie about in the mess."

"One shouldnae have to consider mess after such a thing."

"Few things in life dinnae have some mess," he said, and nuzzled the side of her neck. "One of those hard facts of life. We are a messy lot, we people."

"Sad. I dinnae understand any of this anyway, so I shall take your word for it."

"Thank ye."

She patted his chest. "Ye are welcome." She smiled when he laughed, then blushed because she suddenly had a question she was not sure she should ask. "Is what ye did, weel, normal?" She ignored his choked laughter.

"Aye. Why?"

She shrugged and began to lightly stroke his belly. "I was just curious. I also wondered if it is done to men."

His entire body tensed. "Aye, in a way. Some men with a wife back home try to claim it is nay being unfaithful to have a woman do that instead of making love to them."

"I doubt the wife thinks so. I saw an army once and I saw the wagons following it. The hard women always follow the army. My mother used to cluck and condemn them, nay because of what they did to make a living but because they did it with husbands. I did wonder at the time if my da was one of the husbands she thought of, but I didnae ask."

"Probably a good idea."

"Aye. I dinnae think I really wanted to ken anyway. Then Da would have just been a mon instead of Da, if that makes any sense."

"It does. Suddenly he has all the faults of any mon, is nay better than the cooper down the road."

Mora nodded as she gently caressed him down his chest and over his taut belly, inching ever closer to his groin. Then taking a deep breath, she slipped down that little bit more and lightly grasped him in her hand. He jerked but did not pull away.

As she thought of doing what he had done, he kissed her and Mora knew she could do it. She might not do it well, but she could try. The moment his kiss ended she began to kiss her way down his body. She could feel him tensing beneath her and prayed it was not because she was doing something wrong. When she reached her goal she ran her tongue over him and he groaned. Taking that as approval, she continued, even slipping her hand between his legs to caress that other part of him. As curious as she was interested in giving him pleasure.

When she kissed the top he caught her head in his hands and suddenly he was in her mouth. Her shock came and went quickly and she began to imitate his movements in her body. Then she gasped when he grabbed her foot and swung her around so that he could torment her again. When that feeling began to sweep over her again, she gasped, and then he tossed her to her back, plunging into her with no hesitation. Mora sat, then took his hint when he grabbed her by the hips and began to move her. She rode him and was soon rising to those strange heights all over again.

Gybbon held her still on him as he felt her release seize her and let his own loose. She slumped into his arms when she was done and he worked up enough strength to pat her on the back. When she slid off he kept his arm around her.

It was several moments before Mora found the

strength and breath to speak. "I think we should only do that on special occasions," she said, and could hear the lingering breathlessness in her voice.

"Good idea," he answered, and was not surprised at the hint of hoarseness in his voice because he knew he had held back a lot of shouts. "My Saint's Day, your Saint's Day, Andrew's Saint's Day . . ." He paused. "Michaelmas, Twelfth Night, New Year's Day, New Year's Eve . . ." He felt her start to laugh and grinned. "Lammas, All Saint's Day . . ."

"Hush," she choked out. "I think some of those might require a hefty penance if we celebrated them that way."

"I will pay it."

She snuggled up to his side and wondered if he would be there in the morning. "Hush. I am tired now."

"Oh, I see. Ye have had your use of me and now ye mean to just rest."

"Aye." She patted his chest. "I believe ye have had your use of me as weel, so ye probably need rest, too," she said as she closed her eyes.

He looked down at her and grinned. She had fallen asleep already. It was pleasant to think he had worn her out with pleasure, he decided, and closed his eyes. He would just have a short rest, he thought, then get dressed and go to his own room.

The light of the sun shone right into his eyes and Gybbon woke with a groan. He had forgotten to close the curtains. Suddenly realizing he was still in bed with Mora, he groaned again. It was nice to wake up with her, but it was not a particularly smart idea. While he suspected a lot of people had undoubtedly guessed he had taken her as his lover, he did not think she would be comfortable with them seeing the proof of it.

As quietly as he could, he washed and dressed, then crept out of the room. It did not surprise him to find Harcourt waiting for him in the hall. His brother looked amused, not angry, so he relaxed. He knew he could relax more if he did not have the suspicion that Harcourt knew something he did not.

"Ye are up early," he said, as they started to make their way down to the hall.

"Young ones. They have no understanding of the joys of lying about in bed with one's wife," Harcourt bemoaned.

"And by the time they reach your age, ye will probably be too old and bent to have that enjoyment anyway."

"Nay, I intend to remain strong and virile right up to the last day."

Gybbon laughed. If anyone could, it would be Harcourt. He would do it just out of stubbornness. "So, what is to be done today?"

"I thought we might go have a look at that bit of land ye said ye would want if ye came to live here."

With the thrill of the pleasure he had enjoyed last night still humming in his veins, Gybbon did not shy away from any talk of settling in one place as he might have done a week ago. "Sounds like a good idea."

Mora was surprised when she woke up to a bedchamber filled with sunlight. She could not see any sign of Gybbon; she looked over the side of the bed and saw his clothes were gone. No surprise, she thought, as it was late in the morning. Mary must have stopped in, as well, for her clothes were tidily laid out over the back of a chair.

Slipping out of bed, Mora ran to the chair and pulled on her shift. It felt odd to wake up without him, which she found strange. She had only been in bed with him twice. Perhaps that was what lovers did, she thought, then blushed when Mary peeked in and immediately hurried over to help her dress and do her hair.

As she worked with Mary, Mora tried to recall all her mother had told her about the matter of men and women. Rona had spoken of honor but only briefly. Her mother had spoken more about feelings, about love, and how it was wrong to waste such a gift on a man with no honor. At the time she had wondered if her mother had suffered at the hands of such a man. She knew Gybbon was not unworthy even though she had no idea if he cared for her in any way.

She shook away such thoughts. It was too much thinking. She would make herself dizzy. She and Gybbon were lovers and that alone made her happy. Mora promised herself she would not ruin the good of that by thinking it to death or worrying needlessly about something she could not change.

Settled in her mind for the moment, she thanked Mary for her help and headed down to the hall. She realized that she was very hungry. When she walked into the hall and saw little Freya next to Gybbon helping herself to bits of meat, she smiled. Things were fine right now and she would not disturb the harmony with deep or dark thoughts. There was enough in her life to make her sad, so for now she would hold tight to what made her happy.

* * *

"Are they gone?" asked Niall as he pulled on his boots.

"Aye, just riding off now," said David as he watched Robert lead the others away. "If I judge it correct they are riding back to the Ogilvy keep. Surprised they are up and about so early."

"So, we will be able to go and see what may have happened to Aunt Maggie."

"Aye, after we eat," David said when there was a rap at their door.

The maid brought in full plates of food, and both brothers made quick work of it. After clearing his plate, David sat back in his chair and sipped at his ale. He finally felt some pleasure at being back in Scotland, but it was dimmed with the news he believed they would soon be given.

When the meal was done and cleared away and the maid given a coin, he went down and took care of their bill. Niall joined him just as he gave the call for their horses to be brought round. When they went outside, David looked down the road and sighed.

"Dinnae need to ride there," David said, and caught up his mount's reins.

"Nay, and it might be good to walk a bit after such a large meal."

"It cannae hurt."

He walked toward the burnt hulk that was all that was left of Aunt Maggie's home. David could think of no one who would want to hurt the woman. If it was Robert there was a reason he had gone hunting for Aunt Maggie and all David could think of was that young Andrew or Mora had been here with her.

For a while they stood in front of her house and just stared. Neither of them felt inclined to go poking around in the charred mess left behind. He heard a door open and glanced around until he spotted Morag Sinclair on her step, wearing only her night shift and a large shawl, gaping at them. Just as he was about to greet her and apologize for waking her so early, she ran up to him and hugged him, then hugged Niall.

"Take your horses round the back and I will let ye in that way. There is a lot I have to tell ye. But get out of sight. The sheriff occasionally takes a verra early morning walk to make himself look as if he is doing important business."

When they were seated and she had served them some cool cider, Morag began to tell them everything that she knew as gently as possible. She comforted them when she gave them the hard news about their parents, promising to show them the graves as soon as it was safe again.

"Go see Laird Sigimor. He will lay it all out better than I can. He and that Murray lad were dealing with getting Mora and Andrew someplace safe. If naught else, he will ken where they are."

They went to their horses and started toward Sigimor's keep, but a mile or two down the road, David stopped. He looked and saw Niall right beside him, his head down. "I am sad that my bad feelings proved all too true."

"Nay sadder than I am. We shouldnae have left. If we had been here . . ."

"We would have been the first ones killed. We could fight, so it would have made us the first target. What we can do," he said, and his voice hardened, "is kill Robert. Mayhap his brothers."

"Why only mayhap?"

"I am nay sure, but something tells me they have been dragged into this mess, and while they dinnae dare stop him, they have nay helped him."

"Then they shouldnae die. But Robert . . ."

"Robert is dead, and the harder we make that death for him, the better. Now we go speak to Sigimor and find out what has happened to Mora and Andrew."

"And see if we can find out who the devil this Murray lad taking care of Mora is."

David grunted in the affirmative.

Chapter Fifteen

Mora had watched carefully as the men had ridden off. They had all been going to see Nigel at Glencullaich. They thought they would be gone for two to three days. Once she had heard that, she had stopped listening closely. All she could think of was that she could slip away to talk to her uncle. If she was very lucky she would be back before they would, with all her troubles solved. Her hope was not high for that, but she had to try.

As she made her way back to her bedchamber, she wondered if she was being too reckless. She had waited one day to make certain they had gotten there so she would not meet them on the road, and to think of what she needed for such a journey. She had only been recovered from her last fever for a week and Gybbon had made it clear he thought she needed longer. She also knew he would insist she not go or only go with a troop of men at her side.

Slipping into her bedchamber, she fought a strong sense of guilt as she collected up what she thought she would need and put the items in a small sack before grabbing her cloak. She stopped by the bed to stroke her cat. It would be the first time she had ever left her pet alone since she had held that soaking wet, too small kitten down by the burn, but she knew she was leaving her with good people and Andrew would love her.

"I cannae take ye with me this time, Freya. If Robert sees ye, he will kill ye."

Even though she told herself she was being silly, tears stung her eyes, so she dashed quickly to the door and hastily shut it behind her. She heard a soft, scratchy yowl and saw a little gray paw sticking out under the door. Resisting the strong urge to take her pet with her, Mora turned and hurried down the stairs.

Getting to the stable proved to be easy. She walked there with no more interest from others than an occasional greeting. There was only one man inside the stable and he hurried to saddle the mare she had been practicing her riding on before she even asked him to. She patted the horse, hooked her sack onto the saddle, and then mounted.

"Ye sure ye are ready to be riding all by yourself?" the man asked.

"Aye." She frowned. "Nay. I dinnae ken. I have to try at some time though, dinnae I?"

"Aye, ye do. Good luck, lass. Where is your wee cat?"

"I thought I would leave her in my room until I am certain I can ride around by myself."

"She isnae going to like that."

Mora laughed, but it was not really funny. No, Freya was not going to like it at all. All Mora could do was get as far away as possible before her cat made enough fuss to rouse everyone, who would then wonder where she was. If she got out of this alive it was going to be a long time before Freya forgave her, she thought as she rode out through the gates.

As she rode along, she took out the scrap of paper she had written all the directions she had gotten. It had been a long, slow process to gather the information she needed, and the need to be secretive had worn on her. The slow process of getting a little piece of information from each one she had a talk with had also been irritating, but she had finally gotten enough.

Mora wondered why the men had not heartily complained or even mutinied when they had been made to take such a long, winding route home while toting her, Andrew, and a cat in a cart pulled by sturdy ponies. If they had gone the straight route they could have done it in a day, as Geordie had said. She had not realized her family had lived so near to so many clans.

In the hope of remaining unseen, she kept off to the side of the path, using the trees and shadows to hide her. She could only pray no one from Glencullaich or Dubheidland was out for a ride. As she passed by a lot of open land on the other side of the small, rutted road, she wondered if that was the land Harcourt and Gybbon had discussed. It was beautiful and a nice manor would look equally as beautiful set in there. If she got back to Glenfeurach she would have to tell Gybbon.

Nibbling on a cake, she decided riding slowly along was enjoyable. Avoiding a cairn that she suspected was a boundary marker, she noted that she was coming to a building site. Not seeing anything to indicate any of the workers were around, she trotted by. What little was there suggested someone was having a small church built. She grinned; putting one of them between two large keeps and a short ride to two others told her someone hoped to tempt some of the guard to attend services. It was the only explanation for why it was not being built in the village, the more usual choice for a church.

It was growing late, the light failing by the time she reached the trail she needed to follow. She was not surprised Geordie had known exactly how to reach the Ogilvy keep as the men had done a lot of complaining about the habit of theft the clan had suddenly developed. It appeared Robert was already taking control, and Mora worried about how ill her uncle had grown. She wondered if she should go back home, then gritted her teeth and turned down the trail by the cairn and the crooked rowan tree.

For just a moment, she wished her brothers were with her. She could almost see the three of them riding up to the keep, perhaps with a small force of Murrays and Camerons behind them. It was a splendid thought, but she shook it away. She fixed her eyes on the large stone keep in the distance and rode determinedly toward it, knowing that her only shield was that she was a woman and the laird's niece.

When she reached the keep the gates were wide open, which struck her as odd for they should be shutting them at this late time of the day. As she rode through them, a man ran up to take her reins, then held out his hand to assist her in dismounting. She was glad of the aid when she was finally standing on the ground for it took a moment for her legs to cooperate. Looking at the man, she suddenly recognized him and smiled.

"Greetings, Manus," she said, wondering at his dark frown and noticing how he kept casting worried looks at the other men. "Something wrong? Is the laird worse?"

"Nay, lass. He isnae hale but he is awake and can move about with aid. Laird Cameron's English wife came to tend him and he has improved every day since then." He handed her horse over to a stable boy.

"Oh, good. I have come to speak to him."

He sighed. "This isnae a safe place for ye now, lass. Half the fools here believe ye killed Old William and have been poisoning the laird. About all they dinnae believe is that ye stole Robert's sword. Fool still has it."

"Do ye believe it?"

Manus leaned closer. "Nary a word but things are wrong here, lass. 'Tis a bad time for ye to come for a visit."

"I have to. I have to make Uncle listen to me. Andrew and I are all that is left."

"All? Ye had twa other brothers."

"They went to France to fight for coin." She ignored Manus's swearing. "We havenae had a word of their fate in about three years. Robert strongly implied he kenned they would ne'er be coming home."

"Ye talked to Robert and still live?"

"Weel, I ran and got Andrew away. We are now with the Murrays. Laird Cameron helped us, too." Mora was not sure why that news was making him more nervous. "I have to talk to the laird. Nay, to my uncle. I have to get him to see what is happening."

"I will let ye talk to him. Just hope I can get ye out safely," he muttered.

She had to move fast to keep up with his long strides. He marched to the keep all the while keeping his men back with a fierce look or a flick of his hand. Mora did not understand why all the men glared at her. How could they believe Robert? How could they believe she had done the things Robert tried to blame on her?

They went into the hall and she saw her uncle. He sat at the head of the table and looked old and haggard. The poison had drained him of vigor. She prayed it had not also drained him of sense.

"What is she doing here?" her uncle bellowed, then fell into a fit of coughing. "Lock her up," he demanded when he stopped.

Manus released her but stayed close when she moved to hurry to her uncle. When the man looked at her, she hastily stepped back. There was such fury and hatred in his eyes she felt stung by it. This was definitely not going to go as she had hoped, and suddenly she wished with all her heart that she was back at Gormfeurach with Gybbon.

"I have come to plead my innocence of all the sins your son tries to blame me for. To tell ye the truth of what has been happening."

"Have ye—or have ye come to make sure there is enough left to finish me with your foul poison?"

"How would I have gotten in to do that? To do anything to poison you? Have your men seen me about the place? Have the women or lassies in the kitchens e'er seen me in there? Have ye e'en asked? How did I do it?"

"Old William kenned it, which is why ye killed him."

"With Robert's sword. Aye, he told me at the same time he told me he had the blood of my parents on his hands."

"David and Rona are dead?"

"Aye, Robert killed them as they came home from market. No one told ye?"

"Robert probably felt I was too weak for such sad news."

Mora doubted that. If Robert had thought it would take his father off sooner than the poison he would have told him immediately. The man did look sad though, so she held her tongue.

"And then ye came and killed William with Robert's sword. Did ye think he had done it?"

"Nay, not him but Robert. And why does he still have the sword if I stole it?"

"Ye dropped it as ye ran."

"Ran from where?"

"From the ledger room where ye killed Old William!"

"The room just down the hall? And I ran down this hall yet no one saw me? None heard me drop the sword on the stone? Ye truly think"—she held up her arm—"that this wee bird arm could pick up a mon's sword and use it with enough strength and skill to kill Old William?" She saw a glimpse of sadness and confusion on his face, but then his expression quickly returned to one of anger.

"Manus, why havenae ye put this lass in the dungeon?"

"Uncle! Listen to me. Think on what I say!" She felt Manus grasp her arm and her heart sank.

"Nay! Ye will just lie. Like your mother! I told David nay to wed her but he wouldnae listen to me. Married the ruined wench and turned his back on me. Fool. Now he is dead, too. Get her out of here, Manus. Get her out."

"Come along, lass." Manus tugged her out of the hall, but she noticed the men in the hall would not look at her. She decided they were beginning to see the truth, see at least some of the game Robert was playing. There was also something about her mother and father's past that was causing her further trouble, because it still gnawed at the sick laird.

A plump woman ran up to walk on her other side as Manus led Mora down to the dungeon. She wondered what Hilda, Manus's wife, wanted, and then the woman said, "Manus, ye cannae do this."

"I have to do it and I am going to. And ye are going to see that she has everything she needs." Manus looked at Mora. "I am sorry, lass, but I am nay going to die for ye and that is just what I will do if I dinnae lock ye up."

"'Tis all right, Manus. I would ne'er ask it of ye. He is mad, isnae he?"

"A wee bit, I am thinking. Gets lost in bad memories, too. He willnae face the truth about Robert. Ne'er has."

"Ye think he already kens the truth?"

"Oh, aye," said Hilda, "but what mon wishes to face the fact that his firstborn son is naught but a killer and a brute or is the verra one trying to kill him? I worry for the other lads now that their da is sunk in his own misery."

"Do ye think Robert would kill them? What would it gain him?"

"Nary a thing, but I wouldnae be surprised if he plans to kill young Murdoch. Soon after his da goes, too, so he can toss them into the same hole. He was always jealous of the boy because his da kept him close. Mon still had all his wits about him and kenned Robert would harm the child."

"Hilda!" snapped Manus. "Dinnae forget he will be your laird!"

"Nay mine," Hilda muttered as she watched Manus put Mora in a cell and slowly lock the door.

"Are your new friends coming for ye, lass?" Manus asked.

"Nay, but I wouldnae tell ye if they were just so ye could prepare all the men to kill them."

"Ye would let our men die?"

She looked around the cell she was in, then said, "Aye, but I will say this, my friends would try to talk to someone, try to sort it all out and keep blood from being spilt. From what I just saw of my uncle, he will-nae care. And, if ye two are right, and he clings to all the lies his son has told just to save face and some long-held false hopes he wants fulfilled, he is near as mad as his foul son." Out of the corner of her eye she saw Hilda nod.

Manus marched off shaking his head, but Hilda looked at her. "Who are your friends, lass?"

"The Murrays on either side of ye and the Camerons."

"Oh, my. A handsome lot of friends ye have found. My spit boy is the nephew of the laird's cook," said Hilda.

"Oh, that's nice." Mora wondered what that had to do with anything.

"It could be, lass, it could be a verra nice thing indeed. I will be down in a few moments with a meal for ye."

Mora sat on the narrow, hard bed and sighed. It had seemed like a good idea. Come and talk to her uncle, a man she could recall as being nice, funny at times, and welcoming. She suspected it was that memory that had pushed her to come as her uncle was no longer any of those things. She did not think it was all caused by the illness, either. Her uncle had had things go very wrong in his life and had been abed long enough to brood on them.

Why would he think her mother was a liar? Her mother never lied. And what did he mean by calling her mother a ruined woman? Mora clenched her fists and fought the urge to get up and stomp out her fury. He seemed to think matters had been ruined between him and his brother yet, if that was so, why did her mother take all of them to visit him?

She ran her hand over the stone wall behind her, discovered it was surprisingly dry, and leaned back against it. It was not an easy thing to do since it had been an ugly confrontation, but she carefully thought over what her uncle had said. The third time she did so, she abruptly sat up, seeing what was firmly stuck in his memory and tormenting him. It was not that her mother had been ruined but that his brother had married her anyway. It all had little to do with her mother. It had to do with his father, with the brothers' bond breaking until they were little more than coldly polite strangers.

Her uncle had been the man who had ruined her mother. David was the one who had married her, giving her back the honor his own brother had stolen from her. Mora suspected it had been a rape, harsh and ugly. There was the unworthy man her mother had referred to when she had given Mora the talk about women and men. Mora had to wonder how hard it must have been for her mother to see Tomas, even if the visits had been rare. Then she had an alarming thought. Had her mother been left with child? Was one of her brothers actually her cousin?

"Idiot," she muttered, and shook her head, trying to push away such thoughts. One thing she was sure of concerning her mother and father was that they had loved each other, had loved all their children. It might have been started by something ugly, but it had become beautiful and stayed that way until the day Robert had killed them.

Her poor father, she thought, and closed her eyes to push back the tears. How had such a sweet, gentle man come from such a family? A man who could carve such beauty into a piece of wood most would have just used for kindling should have had a better lot. She thought of him showing a fascinated Andrew about carving and then smiled. His second family had given him a better life.

Robert had stolen it, ended it before its time. For that alone Robert had to pay. Even if she could not escape the trap she had walked into, she would do her best to make sure Robert paid dearly for the innocent blood on his hands.

"Here ye go, lass," said Hilda, holding a large tray while her husband unlocked the door. "A nice full meal and dinnae try to say ye are nay hungry. Nay matter

what is happening one should always remember it
could change."

"Things could get better?" asked Mora in a dis-
believing tone as she looked over what was on the tray
Hilda set down on the bed beside her.

"Ye can ne'er ken and ye willnae want to be swoon-
ing with hunger just when ye should run."

"Och, nay, that would be bad."

"Hilda, what are ye babbling about?" asked Manus.

"Nary a thing, love. Someone will be by in a while
to take away the empty tray."

Puzzled by the woman, Mora shrugged as the door
was locked again and the couple walked away. She
tasted the chicken and found it very palatable. Then
the sound of a disturbance echoed down the stairs.

She watched as Hilda came running down the
stairs, then thrust her hand through the bars. Mora
frowned at what the woman was holding out to her.
What game was the woman playing?

"Take it," hissed Hilda, and Mora took what revealed itself to be a piece of parchment, a pen, and a
tiny bottle of ink. "Write out what has happened to ye
and hide it in the napkin. Ye have about an hour at
best before some lad is sent to collect the tray." Hilda
then dashed back off up the stairs.

Mora set it aside, tucking it just under the very thin
blanket on the bed, and ate her meal as she thought
on what to write. When she finished the afters of
stewed apples, she turned her full attention to writing
a letter. She had no idea what Hilda planned to do
with it, but the woman was acting very secretive, so she
would just do as she was told and see what happened.

Carefully folding the letter into the napkin, she prayed it would not smudge badly.

A young boy, perhaps just entering his teens, came to take the tray. She wondered if she should feel insulted that they believed she was not worth a bigger, well-armed guard. It would not be too hard for her to trick or overpower the thin lad but she did not. It would humiliate him and she could not do that. She simply hoped she would not deeply regret that restraint later.

Lying down and wishing she was bold enough and felt safe enough to strip for bed, she stared up at the ceiling, studying the shadows cast by the torches. She was not sure what her uncle had planned for her but suspected it would not be good. The anger and mean spirit in the man appeared to have been strengthened or freed by the poisoning. Yawning, she closed her eyes and forced herself to stop thinking so hard. What was happening made no sense, so she needed to cease trying to sort it out or understand it.

Instead, she thought of Gybbon. He was going to be so angry about this. And, if her uncle and cousin physically harmed her, she could be certain they would pay very dearly. Slowly, feeling oddly reassured by that, she fell asleep.

A loud clattering startled Mora awake. She sat up and stared at the bars. A sneering Robert stood there with a stick, running it along the bars. Behind him stood his three brothers. He obviously kept them on a very tight tether, she thought. None of them looked happy. She did not think she had ever seen such a sullen, miserable lot.

"Ah, Cousin, weel met. Ye decided it was time for ye to torment the prisoner?"

"I thought we could have a wee talk before ye are hanged."

"I cannae think of anything ye could discuss that I would be interested in. But, hanged? Ye dinnae believe I will win at the trial?"

"Trial? What trial? Why should time and effort be wasted on such a trial?"

"The law?"

"Did ye forget? My father is the law here. He was declared so years ago. He is also the laird and rules this land."

She studied him for a moment. "'Tis a shame that I willnae be around on that day when he discovers all your lies. Just how many people do ye consider an obstacle or an enemy and have ye managed to get the mon to kill them all for you?" There was a flash of shock on all three of his brothers' faces, and she felt sad, for it was confirmation that he had done just that.

"What does that matter? And, the mon is dying."

"He didnae look like it when I saw him and he spouted all your lies at me." Robert looked so proud of that she was tempted to spit on him.

"Enough talk."

"Oh, dear, and it was all so riveting," she murmured, and while his brothers quickly grinned, Robert glared at her.

"I will be standing right up in the front of the crowd when ye hang."

She watched as he strode away. His brothers looked

at her before following him, and the sadness in their eyes told her she would get no help there. Murdoch looked close to tears. And she prayed he had the wit to hide that quickly.

Mora laid back down and sighed. There was nothing she could do. Her uncle was not interested in hearing the truth about his heir, so he listened to only lies. She had been a fool to think she could cut through that kind of blindness just because she was armed with the truth.

She should just go back to sleep, she thought, but that seemed a waste of what little time she had left. All she could do was keep stating the truth and pray there was at least one person at Wasterburn who would be bold and step up to at least cause the laird to wait until he made absolutely certain that she was guilty of what she had been accused of. Mora knew it was foolish to rest any hope on that. Her mother had often complained that her brother by law too often thought he was a king and not just a laird.

Closing her eyes, she thought on Gybbon. She really wanted to go back to him but feared she never would. Nor would she see Andrew or Freya ever again. It seemed odd to her that when she faced the end of her short life, all she could think of was the people she would miss.

Or never know, a soft voice whispered in her mind. That made her eyes burn with tears, but she refused to let them fall. She would never know her child, never be blessed with one. The fact that the child who came to mind was a lovely boy sired by Gybbon made her even sadder. That would never happen. She would never even learn if he cared for her as more than a bed warmer.

Mora decided she would pray for whatever scheme Hilda was so happy about to actually work. The woman appeared to think she could do something that would help, but Mora did not know her well enough to judge if that confidence was warranted. Hilda could be one of those people who always thought they had a good plan only to watch it fail and then they would come up with another one. Whatever the woman thought she could do, Mora feared there would not be enough time to do it, but she had some time to pray that the kitchen maid had really come up with an idea that would work. She would add the hope that her uncle could be deterred long enough to make that happen.

Chapter Sixteen

Gybbon looked around the keep and wondered why people were keeping their eyes down and others appeared to be looking for something. He followed Harcourt to the door and a frantic Annys met them in the hall. Then he heard a strange scratchy yowl and frowned.

"What is that noise?"

"It is Freya. She is shut in Mora's bedchamber and is nay happy about it."

"Where is Mora?"

"I dinnae ken. Harry in the stables said he saddled that mare for her yesterday as she said she was going to practice her riding and she ne'er came back. We sent men out to look but there was nary a sign of her. We were just about to begin the search again when ye returned. I shouldnae have let her go. She has trained, but she wasnae trained enough if there was trouble."

"She wanted to go. I doubt ye could have stopped her. She just would have found another way."

"That cat has been in a frenzy since she left."

"That why it sounds so scratchy?"

"Nay. She didnae make many sounds as a cat does,

but she has been doing that constantly since Mora rode off. Without her."

Gybbon ran up to Mora's bedchamber and cautiously opened the door. He barely managed to dart inside before the cat was there. He looked all around and the sight of her bag made him frown, for some of her things were missing, yet she had to have carried them in something else. He had never seen her without that bag. The more he thought on her disappearance, the more he felt sure he knew what she had done. He went to the door and sighed when Freya leapt onto his shoulder and wrapped her tail around his neck.

"Dinnae get comfortable because ye are nay coming with me," he said, and hurried back down to the others. "I ken where she went."

"To talk to our uncle," said a small voice from behind him, and he looked at Andrew.

"Did she tell ye that?" Gybbon asked as the boy reached up and took Freya in his arms.

"Nay, but she felt she should do it, so I figured that was where she slipped off to. Mentioned it a few times and one of the boys we played ball with yesterday is kin to one of the Ogilvy guards. He told me he saw my sister ride into the keep just before the gates were shut for the night, so I kenned I had guessed right. She wants to tell Uncle the truth."

"That is what I fear she has done, too," Gybbon said.

"Oh, nay. That old mon willnae listen to anything she says, especially if it is a criticism of his eldest son. She will ne'er convince him that Robert lies or killed her parents and tries to kill her and Andrew," Annys said, and shook her head. "If she had just mentioned what she planned, I could have told her, given her good solid reasons for why I think it, too. She has put herself in danger with no chance of success."

"I have to go after her. If the mon still has the sense to give orders, she has walked into a trap. Robert will make sure she cannae leave and will allow his da to kill her for him."

"I will come with ye and we can stop at the manor and pull in Sigimor," Harcourt said.

"Why do we need Sigimor?"

"Aside from the fact that I promised I would tell him if something new happened about all this mess, he is keen on getting the old mon to finally see what his son is. His clan has lost some animals to the mon and so have others. All our allies. The laird just willnae listen to the truth—that 'tis the son's doing. There are also Camerons at the keep, as men-at-arms, and some in the village. And at the manor are some guards we may be able to make use of. Robert willnae be able to get many of his men to face off against Sigimor's. Plus, he probably has a few MacFingals with him."

"Then I will get Freya and let us ride to get Sigimor."

"Why get the cat?"

"She will want to see it when she is freed and I think all that scratchy yowling might be bothering Annys."

"Ye get the cat then and I will get Andrew so she can have both when we get her free."

"Aiden! What are ye doing here, laddie?" asked Annie, Dubheidland's cook, as she hastily dried her hands so she could hug the boy.

"She brought me." He pointed toward the woman standing behind him.

"Hilda? Why have ye come here so early? Ye ken I love to see the lad, but today isnae a good day. I am just finishing the meal to break the night's fast, then I must pack up things as we will return to Dubheidland today."

"I need to speak with the laird."

"Weel, I fear ye may have to stand in a line and wait as we already have visitors and more stepped in just as ye did. Ian popped in to tell me."

"If the visitors are who I think they might be, then I may speak with them, too?" She reached out and ruffled Aiden's bone-straight black hair, which too often fell into his eyes. "Are ye ready, lad?"

The boy held on to a piece of paper and nodded, then looked at his aunt. "Is the laird in the hall, Aunt Annie?"

"Aye, but ye cannae go there. He has men with him and they are doing whate'er it is men born higher than we are do when they get together."

"I have to. I have an important letter for him." He walked out of the kitchen and Hilda smiled at Annie.

"Hilda, he shouldnae be interrupting the laird!"

"Dinnae fret. The laird willnae care after he reads the letter."

"What is in it?"

"Wheesht, how would I ken that? I cannae read. Now, what can I help ye with?"

Niall frowned at the manor as he and David were about to ride past it. "That doesnae look empty anymore. I wonder whom Sigimor allowed to live there."

"Himself," David replied, and turned his mount toward the large stone house when a tall, red-haired man stepped out. "Those guards must have told him about us riding by. Hope nothing happened to Dubheidland," he said as he reined in before Sigimor.

"Nay, save for the fact that all my people fell ill with something, so I brought my wife and bairn here. I am looking and I am sure I ken who ye are, but no name is coming to mind. Havenae broken my fast yet. Ye arenae kin, are ye?"

David dismounted as he laughed. "Only verra distantly. David Ogilvy." He held out his hand to shake Sigimor's as Niall dismounted and came to stand beside him.

Shaking Niall's hand, Sigimor then turned and opened the door. "Guards didnae recognize ye, either, so I will take some comfort in that. Come in. Food will soon be served. I fear I have some verra bad news for ye."

As they followed him in, David said, "We have heard it. We talked to Morag Sinclair. She told us but she also had some good news. Aunt Maggie made it to her sister's. She had some burns though, so will be staying there for a while."

"For the best. Things are nay right here as yet. Now what?" he grumbled as a boy walked into the hall and headed straight for Sigimor. "Who are ye, lad?"

"I am Aiden, the cook's nephew. I have a letter for ye." He thrust it toward Sigimor.

"What does it say?"

"I dinnae ken. Cannae read, can I. Ye can. Ye are a laird."

"Who sent it?"

"A lady. Our laird has put her in the dungeons."

Sigimor just grunted as he watched Jolene hesitate briefly in the doorway before she walked toward him.

"A lady in the dungeon? Hurry and read it, Sigimor."
She smiled when the boy bowed to her, then she sat
down next to Sigimor and whispered to him, "Why is
there a scullion boy in here?"

"Brought the letter," he whispered back, and kissed
her ear. "After I present ye to these two fools so they
can sit down again. Jolene, meet Niall and David
Ogilvy, Mora's brothers who couldnae seem to find
their way out of France."

"Oh! Mora will be so delighted!"

She pretended not to notice the little boy had slid
onto the bench next to her and was filling his plate
with food but handed him the right utensil as he studied all that was standing around the plate. Jolene
knew she should be outraged and order him to leave,
but he looked like he could use a good meal, so she
said nothing, just made certain her skirts were well
away from his clothing.

Then she studied Mora's brothers. Both were tall,
lean, and handsome enough to draw many ladies to
their side. The one called Niall had brown hair, but it
was liberally sprinkled with red and some gold. David
had dark red hair. She could actually see a small
similarity to Mora in them, especially in the blue of
their eyes.

"Uh, Sigimor, she is English," said Niall as he sat
down, and earned a slap on the back of his head from
David.

"I ken it but I decided I would forgive that flaw," he
said, and leaned out of reach when Jolene tried to hit
him. "Let me read this letter, woman!"

David watched as Sigimor read the letter and his
expression grew darker and darker. He suddenly understood why the man's name could be enough to

unsettle people. That was the face of a man who would ride into a gathering of the enemy and cut them to pieces, then go home, wash the blood off, and bed his wife with no lingering remorse about what he had done.

"Sigimor, what is wrong?" Jolene asked, and lightly rubbed his arm.

"I believe ye will see your sister soon," said Sigimor, and handed David the letter before turning to his wife. "We will need to ride within the hour."

Jolene nodded slowly, realizing he meant they might have to fight. She was about to ask some important questions, such as who, why, and where, when there was a sound in the hallway that drew her attention. Several men walked in and she wondered why so many people were coming to see Sigimor so early in the morning. It could not be good.

Her eyes widened as Gybbon, Harcourt, a young boy, and a few MacFingals walked into the room. The MacFingals were the ones who seemed to have made Sigimor's home theirs, yet they stood with the two Murray men looking as deadly stern as the Murrays did. She did wonder who the young boy was until he squealed and raced toward the two Ogilvy brothers. The Murrays also looked as if they had ridden hard to get to Sigimor. Jolene was getting a very bad feeling about all of this.

"Sorry to disturb ye so early," said Gybbon.

"Ye didnae rouse us out of bed, so no bother," said Sigimor. "Lost your lass, have ye?"

"How did ye ken that?"

"She wrote to me. Though it isnae addressed to me, so she may have just been writing to anyone who would be taken the letter. Seems her uncle didnae feel inclined to hear bad things said about his wee boy. He ne'er has listened to any bad said about that son. Sit. Have some food. We will leave, as I have said, within the hour."

Gybbon sat, setting Mora's bag down next to him and opening it so Freya could slip out. "Are ye sure we should wait?"

"Aye. Old men do nothing fast. Mon probably hasnae e'en got out of bed. Robert willnae do anything because he obviously would prefer his father to take any blame that might come. Aye, we have time to finish breaking our fast." He glanced at the MacFingals, who were already devouring full plates of food. "And ye need to let those lads eat or they might be too weak and frail from hunger to fight. And mayhap the boy should go to bed, aye?"

"Can I take the cat?" he asked when Jolene walked over to him.

"Of course ye can. I will see to a box for the animal," Jolene said as she led the boy away.

When the MacFingals merely looked up from their food and smiled, Gybbon felt a smile tugging at his lips as well. Sigimor did have a skill of making one feel less frantic. He noticed a dark, furious look on the face of one of the young men who had been there when they arrived. Curious as to who they were, although Andrew's reaction made him strongly suspect they were the long-lost brothers, he looked at Sigimor.

"Ah, forgot to introduce ye. Lads," Sigimor said to the two young men, "meet Harcourt Murray, Laird of Gormfeurach, and his brother, Gybbon. Harcourt, Gybbon, these two fellows Andrew latched onto are Mora's long-lost brothers."

"Why did they ne'er hear from ye?" asked Gybbon,

as Jolene returned, having left Andrew in the capable hands of her maids.

"Because someone tried to kill us, almost from the moment we got there. Nearly succeeded once with me. And we wrote. The letters were clearly caught and tossed away before they reached my parents. We ne'er got word from them."

"Ye didnae question that?"

"Oh, aye, we did. Constantly, but we couldnae find any way they were doing it. When I healed from the third . . ."

"Fourth," muttered Niall.

". . . attempt to kill me," continued David, "we decided to start to make our way home. The attempts to end us continued and I pray it cost Robert a lot of his money. We did get a few men hanged for what they did, but it didnae stop the attempts."

"Even tried once to get us locked up and hanged," said Niall. "Fortunately, David was charming the daughter of the mon who would have come after us and she gave us enough warning to get away. Along with some weeping and wailing." He flinched when David elbowed him in the side.

"Robert has been a verra busy boy," muttered Sigimor. "Mon is more clever than I thought."

"And now," David said in a hard voice, "he plays much the same game with our sister."

"Which would leave Andrew with no one," said Niall.

"And there he finally makes his mistake," said Harcourt.

"What do ye mean?" asked David.

"The lad is nay alone. He has the Murrays."

"And the Camerons," said Sigimor. "Nay, the boy

willnae be alone. He will also have his sister back soon."
Sigimor looked at the MacFingals, who made a noise
that indicated insult over not being included. "And I
guess he has these fools, too. Sweet Mary help him."

"An impressive guard for a small lad," murmured
Niall, obviously moved by the show of support. Then
he grinned and looked at the MacFingals. "I think he
would really like the MacFingals."

"Not if he has a horse he favors," drawled Harcourt.

Ned tossed a piece of bread at him, but he caught
it. Then Jolene started to lecture them on table matters. Gybbon watched Mora's two brothers calm and
held his hand out to them.

"May I see the letter?"

"Why?" asked David even as he held it out.

"To see what trouble she has gotten into, her view
of it all."

"How can that help?"

"She is inside. We are not. She has spoken to the
old mon. We have not."

When David frowned and nodded, Gybbon took
the letter and looked at it. She had a very neat hand,
he thought as he began to read:

*Greetings! I am in the dungeon in my uncle's keep.
The bed is hard and the blanket is thin. Uncle is
better in body, but I worry about his mind. He is
very angry and he refuses to believe any wrong about
Robert. I pointed out that several questions should be
asked, that the answers would prove Robert was
lying, even asked them myself, and answered them,
questions that show Robert's tale is nonsense, but he
bellowed at me that I lied just as my mother had.
That made me angry, but I could see then that he*

*will just not listen. And so, I am locked up and
Manus has the keys. Robert came by to gloat and
sneer and tell me I am to be hanged and said that he
will be in the fore of the crowd watching it. Hilda
believes this letter will help, but I cannot see how.
Who can she give it to? I hope Freya did not cause
Annys too much trouble and that someone can take
care of her. Tell Gybbon I am sorry I did not heed him
about this. Please watch over Andrew. Ink is done.
Mora*

Gybbon shook his head. "She babbles. How can
one babble in a letter?"

Niall laughed. "Never had a letter from her, have
ye. She writes down whatever goes through her mind.
We actually missed getting one while in France."

Jolene took the letter and read it, smiling most of
the time, but then she sighed and looked at the men.
"She is also scared."

"How can ye see that? I suspect she is scared, but I
didnae see that in the letter." Gybbon took it back
from Jolene and glanced over it. "She does speak of
Robert gloating over her hanging, but I cannae really
see fear. She sees that they mean for her to die, which
is why she asks someone to care for that foolish cat
and for Andrew."

"I cannae tell ye why I see that she is scared here,
I just do."

"One of those things women claim they ken e'en
when they have no proof," Sigimor said, and softly
grunted when Jolene hit him in the arm.

"What cat? And who is Freya?" asked Niall.

"Freya is her cat. The one Andrew was stroking?"

"That was the wee runt that someone tried to drown?" David asked, and Gybbon nodded. "It survived?"

"Aye, and dinnae ask me any more about it as I cannae explain that animal except to say it is badly spoiled and doesnae seem to realize it is a cat. Ye will just have to see for yourselves."

"Then mayhap ye can explain how ye met our sister?"

"She tried to steal my horse." Gybbon just smiled at the brothers' shocked faces and helped himself to some bread.

"How long did she stay on him?" asked Harcourt, smiling faintly.

"She didnae e'en get the chance to pick up the reins. He didnae toss her hard though, but she was wounded at the time and that made it a bit worse."

"Your horse tosses people off?" David asked in surprise.

"Unless ye are properly introduced and approved, if ye get in the saddle, he will toss ye to the ground."

"What wound did she have?"

"When she first ran from Robert he tried to stick a knife in her. Jolene said it looked like he was trying to gut her. 'Tis closed now and healed. Jolene"—he raised his tankard of cider to the woman in a silent toast—"is a skilled healer." He could see the fury on the brothers' faces and nodded in approval.

"I think we had best get over to Wasterburn. We dinnae ken when the laird will rise and make his decision."

"He doesnae get up until after the noon meal is served," said Aiden, then blushed deeply when all the adults looked at him. "They say 'tis because he was so sick," he added, looking at Jolene. "He got better after ye saw him and gave him that potion. Colin still moans about being stuck in the room while it did its work." He grinned and Jolene laughed.

"Aiden!" called Hilda from the door. "Ye shouldnae be sitting there."

"Oh, 'tis fine. Are you the woman who got the letter from Mora?" asked Jolene.

"Aye. I thought it might help the lass."

"Come here then." Jolene indicated the seat next to the little bench she and Aiden shared, then looked at Sigimor. "This woman has seen Mora." She then nodded toward Niall and David. "The young men across from us are her brothers. And, you are Hilda?"

"Aye, m'lady."

Jolene poured the woman a tankard of cider. "Sigimor, this woman can probably tell you a lot of useful things about what is happening, who is trouble, and maybe e'en the best way to get Mora out."

Sigimor frowned at her. "Jo, ye are the wife. I am the one who goes about all matters of battle. I am the one who makes the plans."

"Of course, love. I understand," she murmured, and was not surprised when he stole the sweet cake she had just put on her plate.

Gybbon hid his grin by sipping his cider, then listened as Sigimor gently questioned the woman. She was nervous at first and hesitant to answer until he assured her he had no plans to wantonly slaughter the garrison since some of them were related to him. Gybbon was a little amazed at the questions Sigimor asked, revealing that the man well understood the ways of battle. He glanced at Harcourt, who was watching and listening carefully to the exchange. When he was done, Sigimor dismissed the woman, who was going to take the boy with her, and Jolene made certain they both had a small sweet cake before they left.

"Sometimes I forget how clever and sneaky ye can be," said Harcourt.

"Then 'tis a good thing we are allies."

Then Sigimor laid out his plan and Gybbon felt the hint of hope. Glancing at Mora's brothers, he could see they did as well. It was indeed good that they had such a man as an ally, he thought. Sigimor planned for everything, every step that needed to be taken, and even for what might go wrong. He planned in a way to bring back as many of his own people as possible, all while destroying the enemy. It was easy to see why Sigimor still lived, despite his tendency to make people angry, and all his siblings were still hale.

"So, when do we ride out again?"

"Soon, Gybbon. Verra soon. I want us all in place when the judgment is given. Then we can make our judgment and bring the lass back."

Chapter Seventeen

Mora woke to Manus opening the cell door, a wide awake and somewhat flushed Hilda standing behind him with a tray. "Is it morning already?" Mora asked as she sat up and rubbed her eyes.

"This is when the laird says all working in the keep must eat. Prisoners too," Manus answered in a voice sharp with annoyance. "I think he hopes it will keep us out of his way once he hobbles down to break his fast."

She widened her eyes a little. That was the angriest Manus had ever sounded when talking about the laird. It was almost a complaint about the man, and the man had always been careful never to say anything bad about his laird. As Hilda set down her tray, Mora could see the laughter in the woman's eyes.

"I will tell ye this much, lass," said Manus as Hilda walked out of the cell and he began to lock the door, "rest and think because naught will happen until midday or later. Laird doesnae do any business till then."

"Ah, weel, he is still fighting to get his strength back after the poisoning."

Manus nodded and shuddered a little. "Aye, but he began improving after Lady Cameron made him, er, gave him a potion so he would, weel, throw it off."

"Expel it. She said expel." Hilda crossed her arms over her chest and shook her head. "He expelled all over the place. Didnae ken a body could hold that much. Colin looked as if he would join him and Matron didnae look much better e'en though she has taken care of the ill many times. It was truly a horrible time."

"Cameron's English lady called it cleansing." Manus shrugged and sighed. "Messy, foul business. I was surprised it didnae finish the mon off."

"It worked. That is what one must keep in mind, that it worked."

"True, but I dinnae think he came back right."

"Nay." Mora sighed. "I am nay sure he did, either, but I am nay sure that is from the illness. How he is behaving could be the anger I saw in him, a fierce anger, and I think he cannae, or willnae, expel that. It taints all he does and thinks."

"Ye think he does ken what Robert is and has done, dinnae ye?" said Hilda.

"Aye, I do. There is a big part of him that has already accepted that Robert is wrong. He recognized that enough, at some point, to do what he could to keep Murdoch safe. I would wager he kenned why he was ill, as weel. The mon is nay weak-minded. It has just proven too much. He doesnae want to see it, doesnae want to hear about it, doesnae want to admit it."

"Weel, the old fool will have to soon or he will be condemning all of Wasterburn because we will have

to live under Robert's rule." Hilda shrugged her
shoulders and rubbed at her arms as if she had suddenly been buffeted by a chill wind.

"Robert! Stop! Stop now!" cried Murdoch as he
rushed across his brother's bedchamber and pulled
him away from the girl he had been beating. "She is
little more than a child." He avoided looking at the
naked girl when she crouched down and tried to
cover herself.

Robert swung toward Murdoch, a knife in his hand.
Murdoch tensed for the pain of it piercing his flesh.
To his surprise, Robert stopped, the knife point em-
bedding into his shirt and tickling his flesh, but he did
not push it in. He just stared at it with a blank look on
his face that chilled him, and Murdoch signaled to the
girl to run. A quick glance showed her picking up her
clothes, then running to the door.

"Why hesitate now, brother?" he asked as he tried
to think of a way to disarm Robert without being
killed.

"'Tis nay time," Robert said, a distant look in his
eyes. "Need to keep the order straight and there are
still two left." He sheathed his knife and gave Murdoch a sharp slap on the cheek. "Your time will come.
Shame ye sent away the lass. Now I shall have to find
another one."

Murdoch watched Robert leave, then ran to the pot
in the corner and emptied his belly. He finally had to
accept that his eldest brother was mad. It had long appeared to be simply a deep meanness and an easily
stirred anger, but the last year it had settled in hard

and his thoughts and actions had become less precise or clever.

Staggering to his feet, Murdoch washed his face, cleaned his teeth, and rinsed out his mouth, continuing to think on how all the signs had been there years ago. Robert had always been arrogant, always insisted things go his way, and had been vicious if they had not. Too often that viciousness had been aimed at Murdoch. He still carried some of the scars and might well have died if not for Lachlan and Duncan.

He had been very young when he had realized that Robert was more than just a mean, angry brother; he was someone to be very careful around, even to avoid as much as possible. Being just a boy, Murdoch had become attached to an animal, and of all things to care for, he had gone and loved a rabbit, one of the ones the cook raised so they had meat handy. Cook had not minded and had even helped him learn how to tend to its care. He had even named it Bruce after their great king his father had told him so many stories about.

Then it had gone missing. After searching everywhere, he had gone to the kitchens to get something to eat before searching some more and there had sat Robert, grinning and eating what Murdoch had known was his rabbit. Just in case he had proven to be too stupid to know it, Robert chuckled and loudly demanded the weeping kitchen maid cut him some more of Bruce.

Murdoch had just stared at him until Robert had offered him some. That was when he had vomited all over the table and on Robert. He had then run as fast as he could to his father's side. The man had asked no questions but kept him close to protect him, and had done so until last year when he had considered Murdoch old enough and big enough to adequately defend himself.

His father had begun to change shortly after that day. The pleasant, even funny man he had known had faded away into an angry man. Then Murdoch's mother had drowned and the only witness had been Robert. Everyone had been puzzled because his mother had been terrified of water and never went near the burn. His father must have seen something, or Robert had said something, but Murdoch was certain that was when the laird had realized that his heir was mad and would always have to be watched closely. His father had done nothing then either, except to grow even angrier. Murdoch had always wondered if the anger was because his son was wrong or because he had to keep hiding crimes to protect him. Murdoch also had to wonder how many of the dead at Wasterburn in the last ten years had actually been caused by Robert.

Walking outside to find Lachlan and Duncan, he kept an eye on how the other men acted around Robert. There were no cheerful greetings when the man walked up, most of the men keeping their eyes downcast. Any woman near him slipped away as fast as she could without actually running. Then Murdoch saw the gallows Robert was carefully inspecting, despite the fact that it had stood in the bailey for years, and his heart sank. He could not let this happen.

When Jonathan, the man who had taken Old William's place, called them inside for the judgment, Murdoch hurried to follow Lachlan and Duncan and prayed he could find the backbone to speak up in Mora's defense. He glanced at Robert, who had chosen a seat in the front, and his heart sank. The man was smirking, and Murdoch knew he would do all he could to make the judgment move quickly and give him what he wanted.

Mora wished there was a window in the cell she could look out, but then realized there never would be such a thing. It could allow a prisoner a way to escape. There were certainly many men taller and much stronger than she was who would make their way out of the window.

She had managed to sleep for a while after breaking her fast, but nothing could help her sleep now. Although she did not have the sun to look out at, she was certain the time for the laird to make his judgment was swiftly approaching. The hope she had held, that someone would put a stop to this, was long dead. No one knew she was innocent of what she had been blamed for.

The one she had a difficult time understanding was her uncle. While it was true that he was still sickly, even fragile, after the poisoning, his unrelenting belief in his son was absurd. There was just so much evidence against Robert. How could the laird ignore it? Lachlan, Murdoch, and Duncan may not have accused Robert of anything immediately provable, but they had certainly tried many ways to fight his father's blind belief in his heir.

"I am sorry, Maman," she whispered. "I did try to give Andrew a good life, but I havenae had him long. Still, I believe he will have protection. Gybbon Murray kens the danger Andrew is in and he has a lot of allies. Good, strong allies like Laird Cameron."

"Who are ye talking to, lass?"

Mora was startled and held a hand over her rapidly pounding heart as she looked at Hilda. "Oh, ye startled me. I was just talking to my mother."

Hilda's eyes widened and she looked around. "Ye can see her?"

"Och, nay! I just thought I would speak my thoughts to her aloud."

"Ah, hoping she will hear ye in heaven. That would be helpful. Manus will be here before long, once the laird's done eating and decides he needs to do some judging. Already made his sons come in and they are waiting. I remember your mither. Rona? Aye?"

"Aye, she came here a few times."

Hilda nodded. "She did, but I was speaking of when she was young. Sent here to learn how to run a keep and mayhap marry the heir. The old laird wanted a match."

"He wanted my mother to marry the laird? But she wed David."

Hilda leaned up against the bars and crossed her arms. "It was the plan, but she liked David. Any fool could see it, and the old laird was no fool. Our laird wanted her, too, because she was a bonnie lass, so the old laird told his eldest son to mark her as his, show her what she would be missing if she chose David. The old laird was a mon who felt women had but one purpose, to serve a mon however he felt she should. Taught his sons that, too. David didnae learn the lesson; he was a gentle soul. Our laird followed his da's teachings."

"So, the laird did as his da said and raped my mother." Mora felt like weeping for her mother.

"But then how did she wed David if the laird had claimed her?"

"Because David caught him. Sadly, after and nay before he did it, and nearly killed his own brother."

"My da did?"

"Difficult for me to believe, too, but aye, David beat him badly, then he took your mither away and wed her. His da decided David had finally shown that he was a mon and gifted him with the manor house and lands. I suspect he was going to do it anyway as he only had the two sons, weel, two sons by his lawful wife. Took your da nearly a year before he moved back and settled in the manor. He ne'er set foot in this place again, except for a time or two when your mither wanted him to, though I dinnae ken why she would want to."

"She felt it was important and I think she believed Da needed to try to mend the break between him and his brother. She gave that up though."

"Nay surprised. The laird is nay a forgiving mon or one who apologizes for doing wrong. David never much liked his brother, hated him after what he did. And the laird ne'er made any effort to change. I think she had a small hope that the laird would change and could prove to be some help to her lads. Ye still have no word on their fate?"

"Nay. Nothing." She smiled faintly at the worried Hilda.

"What are ye doing down here, Hilda?" demanded Manus as he hurried down the steps.

"Just keeping the lass company."

"Weel, they are waiting upstairs for her." He walked up to the cell and began to unlock the door.

"Sorry, lass," Hilda said as Mora stepped out. "I have

thought on little else save how to stop this and have nary one good idea. The one I did try hasnae brought any results, though I thought for certain it would. The old fool kens this is wrong, but he willnae allow that cursed son of his to take any blame. Ne'er has."

"Thank ye for trying, Hilda."

"Weel she can just stop trying," Manus snapped. "He is our laird, woman!"

"God help us," Hilda muttered, and she looked close to tears as Manus tied Mora's hands in front of her.

Manus sighed and nodded. "Ye dinnae have to come, Hilda."

"Oh, aye, I do, though the old fool might try to shoo me away."

Manus led her up the stairs, something Mora found it difficult to do with her hands tied. Hilda followed close behind. Mora knew without looking that the woman was there to catch her if she stumbled or even tried to hurl herself down the stairs. She doubted she would be fortunate to just break her neck if she tried it. These last few months she had found very little luck.

"Hold on, Manus," said Hilda as they began down the corridor that led to the great hall.

"What now, woman?"

"I need to fix her hair."

"What? Why now?"

"Because, ye old fool, they will cut it if it is hanging free like this, and she doesnae need that humiliation."

"Go on then, but be quick about it."

"Why would they cut off my hair?" Mora asked.

"Dinnae ken," mumbled Hilda as she began to twist

up and pin up Mora's hair. "Something to do with getting the noose on right," she mumbled.

The woman choked out the words so Mora asked no more questions. She stared at the doors at the far end of the hall. Lachlan, Duncan, and Murdoch walked in and went straight into the great hall. Murdoch cast an anguished look her way and she sighed. He could not stop this on his own and she knew it would trouble him for a long time.

It troubled her that the three brothers could not unite against the one making their lives a misery. She had given up trying to understand why her uncle was so determined to ignore the monster that was his son. He did not overtly dote over the young man yet did so much to cover over all the signs that the son was rotten to the core. How could he not see that he was condemning his other sons to misery, perhaps even death, by doing nothing about Robert? He was also condemning his own people. Instead of a fine, strong keep and a good laird as his legacy, the old laird could leave behind a place filled with misery, cruelty, and death.

"How can he nay see it?" she asked herself, and then realized she had spoken aloud.

"See what, lass?" asked Hilda.

"That what every mon hopes to leave behind is something good, something that will be remembered. What he has fought so hard to hide still lives in Robert and it will taint everything the Ogilvys have built here."

"Aye," said Manus. "'Tis why I have been looking for a place Hilda and I can go to."

Hilda stared at her husband in shock. "Ye have?

Why? Ye are the one who always reminds me he is our laird!"

"If he dies he willnae be anymore, will he? Robert will," he said, and lowered his voice, glancing around nervously. "And I willnae serve him. Ye think he is bad now? He will turn monstrous cruel when his da is dead and no longer has to worry about what the mon might say and do. Nay, I dinnae plan for me and mine to be here for that. I want us out of his reach, especially our girls."

"Oh, Manus." Hilda hugged him and the man turned a brilliant red. "I was so afraid for our girls."

He awkwardly patted her on the back. "Did ye really think I would chance them ending up like poor Mary? Or alive but broken like so many of the lassies here? Nay, not our lassies. I didnae ken what to think so I thought, get out of here, Manus. So just calm your mind, loving."

"Thank ye, love. Thank ye."

"Who is poor Mary?" Mora asked, touched by the man's efforts to ease his wife's worry.

"Mary was a kitchen maid. Murdoch was a lad and he loved this rabbit and Robert made her prepare the lad's rabbit for the spit. Then Murdoch came in, obviously upset, and Robert gloated, told the girl to cut him more. He had beaten on her—the bruises showed for weeks—so she did, crying all the time. Poor little Murdoch emptied his belly all over the table and Robert. Mary was so upset, so bothered by what Robert had made her do, she went and told the laird. He actually did something about that and gave Robert a terrible thrashing. Then about a fortnight later, Mary disappeared. We found her down by the burn, beaten, raped, and then hanged from a tree. Oh, and her tongue cut out."

Mora shook her head. "How does a mon get so twisted about?"

"Born that way," said Manus. "Got it from his mama. The laird's first wife was mad or sick or something. She would rage at time over nothing worth such anger and other times would weep and wail as if she was watching her bairn die. There were times when she was fine though and could be the sweetest lass. That's when the laird fell in love with her and wed her. Then she had Robert. As a bairn, Robert was much like any other. The laird himself took over the bairn's care with the help of some of the women here because his wife tried to smother her child during one of her weepy spells. She killed herself a few weeks later. It wasnae until Robert got older that one began to notice that something was not quite right with the lad. Robert was mean, bone-deep mean.

"Laird married again and the lass was fine, except that she hadnae wanted to wed him. She had Duncan and Lachlan and she was good enough as a mother but 'twas certain she didnae want to be one to Robert. She died in a fall from her horse. It was whispered about that it happened as she had been riding back from her lover's arms.

"Then we had Murdoch's mither. Sweet, sweet girl, a lot younger than the laird, scared of everything, but tried hard to be a mother to the laird's boys. Then she had Murdoch. She adored that child, played with him all the time but ne'er ignored the other lads. Laird was real fond of her. Murdoch had his mother the longest, too, right up until he was walking and talking. Then the lass who wouldnae e'en stroll by the burn she was so afraid of the moving water, went to the burn and drowned. Robert was the only witness to it."

"What a sad life my uncle has had," murmured Mora. "So, Robert killed more than Murdoch's pet, didnae he? He killed the poor lad's mither."

"Aye, I think he did," said Hilda. "Near the end she was afraid of him and kept him away from Murdoch."

"I dinnae understand why the brothers dinnae unite against him."

"I have been here all my life, lass, and I have seen how Robert keeps them down," said Manus. "Ridding the keep of anyone or anything they love. Just as he did with Murdoch. Then he showed them how easily he can get to them when they are sleeping. He has ground Lachlan and Duncan beneath his boot since the day they were born. The only rebellion they have ever shown is how they try hard to defend Murdoch in some way. They are tugging on a wee scrap of bravery to do even that much."

"It is a horrifying tale," Mora whispered, then stiffened in shock when she saw who entered the keep next. "Gybbon," she whispered, and took a step toward him only to feel Manus's grip tighten on her arm.

Hilda turned, putting herself between Mora and the men at the door, probably to keep her from acting on seeing Gybbon, so Mora took a moment to collect herself. Just because Gybbon was here did not mean she would be freed. She caught the glimpse of a redhead over Hilda's shoulder and smiled a little. It was Sigimor and he was holding the doors to the hall open for someone to go through. He was at least on a standing with her uncle, so there might be a bit of hope.

"Weel, I didnae expect such a fine answer to your

letter, lass." Hilda turned and smiled at Mora. "It is hopeful, aye."

"Aye, but I am nay allowing it to be too hopeful. I think the disappointment would be more than I could bear and I am trying to look brave and calm."

"That is probably wise. But, ne'er underestimate the Laird of Dubheidland."

"Oh, I would ne'er be that foolish. I am verra sorry I have brought him this trouble, however."

"I doubt he is bothered. If he was, he would have just sent ye on your way. The mon doesnae bother with all that politeness some folk do."

Mora could not believe she could, but she laughed softly. "Ah, nay, he isnae. He has married a woman who kens how to deal with him verra weel indeed though."

Hilda nodded. "The English lady. She has spirit. It showed when he brought her here to look at the laird and she said he was being poisoned. No one argued and have done all she told them to. Laird's better, too."

"If ye are done gossiping, ladies," Manus said, "Jonathan is signaling us to go in."

Mora looked toward the doors to the hall. Jonathan stood there angrily signaling them to come along. She did not know what he had to be angry about. She was the one who faced hanging for lies told by Robert.

"Does he expect me to run over there just to hear the laird condemn me?" she muttered.

"Probably." Manus started walking and she hurried along with him. "Mon is so proud of his new station and fears any mistake will lose him the post."

Mora took a deep breath to steady herself as they walked through the doors.

* * *

Sigimor reined in when the Ogilvy keep came into view. Harcourt and Gybbon reined in on either side of him and Mora's brothers reined in beside Gybbon. "Sigimor, why are we just staring at the keep?"

"Weel, Gybbon, I think ye have kenned me long enough to ken I dinnae just storm a place. I have to think on it and plot the best approach."

"I would wager that hurts. Why make your head ache before a battle?" drawled Harcourt.

Harcourt let out a quickly muffled yelp as he suddenly went flying out of the saddle. Gybbon was impressed. He had not seen Sigimor move, yet the small grin on the man's face as he looked down at Harcourt was proof enough that he had done it. Mora's brothers chuckled, but softly. Sigimor's men laughed freely.

"Curse ye, Sigimor. I hate it when ye do that," muttered Harcourt.

"Then ye should ken when to keep your clever remarks to yourself."

"Ye must kick a lot of people out of the saddle," he murmured, "because ye do inspire the remarks."

"I did find that it had become a habit and I should be more careful when I suddenly saw my wife on the ground once and realized I had kicked her out of the saddle. She wasnae pleased with me. I even got down to help her up and she punched me in the face." He sounded outraged.

"How did she reach it?" Harcourt asked in a voice that told everyone he was fighting hard not to laugh.

"Slammed her tiny fist right into my eye as I was bending over to lift her up and saying . . ."

"'Stiffen your wee backbone and grit your tiny teeth,'" the MacFingals called out, then laughed.

Sigimor shook his head. "I often wonder why I have them around so much."

"They are your kin."

"I should look more carefully into that claim of relation," Sigimor muttered, then went back to staring at the keep.

Harcourt rode ahead of Sigimor, out of kicking reach, and said, "They may nay have the red hair, but the relationship is glaringly apparent."

Gybbon waited with a swiftly dwindling patience as Sigimor studied the place. He was amazed by how calmly Niall and David waited, sitting quietly on their horses as the time slipped by. He suspected they had a much deeper faith in Sigimor than he did.

The gates were wide open and he wondered about that. Only two men stood near them watching, and he was certain they could see Sigimor and his small army. He wondered if the men of Wasterburn no longer cared much for the place they protected. Glancing at Harcourt, he could see his brother staring at those open gates nearly as hard as Sigimor was.

Sigimor finally nodded a little, then looked at Harcourt. "Ye and I and Gybbon are going to ride right in. If we are questioned we will say we have heard of what has happened and have come to speak for the accused."

"And ye think they will just let us in?" asked Gybbon.

"Aye. We are two neighboring lairds and ye are the brother to one of us. Then there are her brothers, whom someone might recognize. I think those men willnae dare to stand firm before us and will let the laird deal with us."

"What do we do when we get in there?" asked Harcourt.

"Just what I said, and Nanty will slip in to speak to the ones in the bailey that are our kin or simply have no stomach for what is happening. Slowly the rest of the men will slip in, either because none of these fools are watching or because they just let them do so. The rest of the men will follow directions from Nanty."

"And when we are all within the bailey?" asked Ciaran MacFingal.

"I want that scaffold the old fool ne'er takes down surrounded. Put one of us behind each mon standing nearest to it. I want Camerons standing behind anyone who is our kin just in case a fight breaks out. I want someone up behind the men at the top so nary a one of them can act as they believe the laird wants before they can be stopped. I want as little blood spilled in this as possible."

"Why so careful?" asked Gybbon.

"I told ye we are very intertwined. That old fool is pushing his people into standing against friend and family just to protect a son who probably should have been strangled at birth. I want those people who are only doing as they swore to—protect their laird—nay harmed by this idiocy. In truth, I only want one in there to be killed. Robert. He is a poison to what had become a very quiet, peaceful area."

"If it works, it is a verra clever plan," said Harcourt, then grinned and shook his head when Sigimor just nodded. "I dinnae want to fight these people either. Alliances such as we have here mean more choices for all our people. A wider selection when a mon wants a bride and for when they need work they like."

"Aye. Customers for the goods one makes and the crops one grows. If we nurture this we may soon reach the time where we dinnae much need the rest of the world to survive verra nicely."

"Which would suit ye fine," said Gybbon. "Ye have ne'er had much use for the rest of the world."

Sigimor shrugged. "It hasnae done much for me and mine. Nanty?" The young man rode up to Sigimor and then the two had an intense but very quiet talk.

Gybbon watched Nanty ride to the gates and then dismount. It looked as if he was having a pleasant conversation with the two men there. Then they shook hands and Nanty slipped inside the gates. Gybbon knew that if he walked into the bailey right now he could search for a very long time and never see the man. It was the younger man's gift and Sigimor made good use of it.

Sigimor made good use of every connection he had, blood or marriage or even just friendship, because they had fought on the same side at one time. And that, he realized, was Sigimor's real strength. He never let the connection fade away, kept it strong and friendly. Gybbon was not even certain of how many connections or alliances the man could claim.

He was diverted from his meager attempt to try and figure out the many connections Sigimor had when he saw several of the men dismount and walk to the keep. "What has happened?"

"Naught. We just saw Nanty signal for the men to start going in. My cousins now watch the gates." Sigimor turned and ordered the two youngest to gather up and watch the horses.

"Are ye certain the others willnae notice them? Make some outcry?"

"Nay, but I do doubt it. Word has spread of a hanging and a lot of folk round here would walk to the keep just to watch. So, seeing a stranger willnae make them panic. They will be expecting some to come in. Ne'er have understood people thinking a hanging is something ye want to watch, but some do. If word got out that it could be a woman being hanged that would bring even more."

"Sick bastards," muttered Ciaran, and Gybbon wondered when the boy had ridden up close to him.

"Sad to say there are a lot of them in this world," Sigimor said, then watched as Ciaran dismounted, sheathed his sword at his back, and donned a long, flowing cloak. "Ye be careful in there. I dinnae want to have to explain why ye are bleeding to your parents."

"Aye, neither do I," Ciaran said, and ambled toward the gates.

"Who are his parents?" asked Gybbon.

"Ewan MacFingal and Fiona MacEnroy, who is also affectionately kenned as Fiona of the eleven knives. She is very good with knives."

"Ah, nay. It would be difficult to explain their son's wounding to them and still be breathing afterward."

"Aye, and ye probably wouldnae be able to find your horse to run away."

Gybbon laughed and returned to watching the men they had brought with them make their way into the keep. Finally, it was time for them to ride up. The others had gotten in so easily he was rather surprised when they were halted.

"I thought ye said they were your cousins," he muttered to Sigimor.

"They are, but I can see two of the brothers standing back by the door so they have to play the good guards now." He frowned down at his cousins. "Has it begun?"

"She is just being brought in for judgment, but everyone kens what it will be."

"All to protect a son who isnae worth the spit in my mouth."

"Aye, I fear so, though I ken ye have the final part of this nonsense covered."

"As weel as I can. Ah, the brothers have gone back in."

"Then go ahead. Just try to nay kill the old fool. We all have the feeling that once that boil named Robert is properly lanced the old mon will go back to what he was. If ye kill the old mon it will just be worse, nay better."

"Because Robert would be your laird then."

"Aye, and doesnae that just terrify the whole lot of us. Good luck!"

"Scares me," murmured Harcourt as they rode through the gates. "Be the end of our peaceful time."

"Doubt the last shovel of dirt will be put in the old mon's grave before Robert stirs up at least one of the clans round here. He has been trying for a while already by stealing things."

Two young men came to take their horses, and Sigimor, Mora's brothers, Gybbon, then Harcourt dismounted. Another man opened the doors for them and they walked in. Gybbon started to the door to the great hall. Then he glanced down the hall and stopped, Sigimor walking into the back of him.

"Mora?" He started to step forward, headed toward Mora, when Sigimor grabbed him by the arm and held him still.

There was a tall, stern man in the door to the great hall. He nodded at Sigimor and then looked at Gybbon and Harcourt. Gybbon thought he looked like a stiff-necked elder fellow but just smiled as Sigimor introduced him and Harcourt.

"The prisoner will be brought in in a moment if ye will come and take a seat." The man spoke very politely and waved them inside. "The boy said ye came to speak for the accused?"

"Aye," replied Sigimor. "Is there a special space for such ones to sit?"

"Nay, for none were expected. Simply find some place to sit. This shouldnae take much of your time." He walked toward the table at the far end of the hall and faced the door.

"Weel, that tells us the verdict is all planned nay matter what anyone says," said Sigimor, and he walked forward to an empty bench.

"Then how can they call this a judgment? They are not making one; they have one. She is being brought in just to hear their opinion."

"Aye, doesnae mean we cannae argue it."

"I am nay sure anything would help her."

"Nay, but that is why we are here, isnae it."

Gybbon sat down next to Harcourt, who was staring at Robert. He looked at the brothers and sighed. Robert looked smug and satisfied and the other three looked miserable, especially Murdoch. He glanced at

Mora's brothers and saw that their hands were clenched tight into fists, revealing they were not as calm as they wanted people to believe. He heard the doors to the great hall open and looked back.

Mora was brought in by a man and a woman. Her hair was piled up on her head and he wondered why someone had bothered with that. He felt a little sick when he thought of one reason it might have been forced into that style, and it had to do with the placement of the noose. The gown she wore was stained but clean. He saw no bruises or cuts. She did look tired and sad. She was marched down to stand in front of the table where the laird sat.

Chapter Eighteen

Mora looked to the table at the back of the hall. Her uncle looked much better than he had when she had last seen him, but he looked angry. That did not bode well for her.

Then she glanced toward her cousins. Robert was sneering in that way he seemed to favor, and the other three brothers looked miserable, especially Murdoch. Since her uncle was busy fumbling with a bunch of papers, she decided to have a look at the surprisingly large crowd that had come to see this.

She did not realize a hanging was such a crowd pleaser, she thought angrily. Then she tried to push the anger away, except it would not leave. This was so unfair and her uncle knew it.

Suddenly Robert tensed and looked behind them. It was enough to have his brothers looking, too, and there were almost smiles on their faces. Robert looked as if he wished he could take up his sword and go after whatever, or whomever, he saw.

Curious as to what they were all looking at, she looked over her shoulder. A faint smile curved her lips when she saw Gybbon, Sigimor, and Harcourt all sitting there with their arms crossed. The looks they were sending her uncle and his sons would certainly make her rethink whatever she was about to do. Unfortunately, all they could do was glare, as they would have been disarmed before entering the hall.

Then she noticed two men at Harcourt's side in the same pose. It took her a moment to recognize them as, in the nearly three years they had been gone, there had been changes. She took a step toward them and Manus again tightened his grip.

"My brothers," she whispered, and Hilda was suddenly at her side.

"Lass, ye have to face the laird."

Then her brothers looked at her and smiled. It was not a dream. Somehow her brothers had arrived home, safe, just when she needed them. The roaring in her ears grew loud and, with a soft sigh, she gave in to the blackness sweeping over her mind.

Gybbon and Mora's two brothers leapt to their feet, but they had to wrestle with a few of Ogilvy's guards to get out of their seats. Gybbon was surprised when every one of the brothers save Robert also stood up, but it was Murdoch who acted. He moved fast, sliding on his knees over the floor until he could catch Mora. Sigimor moved the guards blocking them out of the way simply by picking up one and tossing him into the others.

By the time they reached Mora's side, Murdoch had roused her and she stared wide-eyed at her brothers. "Ye have come home."

"Aye, Mora. Ye have gotten yourself in a tangle, havenae ye?" said Niall as he chaffed her hand between his.

"Oh, aye, I have indeed. But I did get some friends that may help," she said as he helped her sit up.

"We have met. Perhaps later we can have a chat about who that fellow Gybbon is." He nodded when she blushed.

Mora suddenly had to get away from Niall as she was in no state to be answering any questions about Gybbon. That was a conversation she needed to have with all her wits clear and working at their sharpest. Finally getting on her feet, she hugged David as best as she could with her wrists tied together.

"Has Andrew seen ye?" she asked David.

"Aye, Harcourt brought him to Sigimor's manor. We have been rather busy trying to get ye free of this trap. We ken he is protected and that is enough for now."

"Is your little family moment done now?" Robert drawled. "Can we get back to the judgment?"

Mora gripped Niall's arm when she felt his body tense and looked at Robert. "Aye. Let us get to this." She went back to standing in front of the table where the laird sat. "M'laird."

"Ye are here to answer for charges of murder and theft," he said.

"I see. And who brought such charges against me?"

"Robert Ogilvy."

"Of course, and ye believe him to be an honest source?"

He glared at her. "He is my son."

"Aye, and I am but your niece."

She just stood as he went through all the things Robert was trying to blame on her. Her brothers protested and several times Gybbon pointed out she could not have done that because she was with him or at Sigimor's, but it still left enough to hang her with. Mora felt her heart sink as her uncle declared her guilty and read her punishment out. Even when one knew they were innocent, she discovered it was hard to be charged, convicted, and even sentenced to hang.

As Jonathan and her uncle stepped out from behind the table and proceeded to walk her outside, Mora noticed that her brothers, Sigimor, Gybbon, and Harcourt were gone. That five such sizeable men had slipped out so silently surprised her. She hoped they were not planning something too dangerous to free her. She did not want to be the reason that the tight circle of alliances that made the area so peaceful had been destroyed.

Once outside, she blinked at the sunlight. She had not realized how she had missed it, but was annoyed that she had been in the dark long enough to react badly to its return. She looked at the scaffold and resisted the strong urge to fight the hold the two men had on her arms.

Then she noticed all the men circling the scaffold and wondered why they were two deep. She was no threat. One of the men standing behind a man leaned around the man and winked at her quickly before ducking back behind the man. The man he was behind was shaking in a way that told her he was badly smothering a laugh. Mora was sure that had been one of the MacFingals that hung around Sigimor. Looking around at each of the ones with a man behind them, she realized that a lot of them had red hair, and from what she saw, a lot of them were actually having a pleasant conversation with their guard.

Her uncle tugged her up the steps and Robert skipped by them, nearly nudging them off the steps.

Robert went and stood by the hangman, who looked extremely displeased with his presence. The moment she was placed by the noose, and the hangman began to slip it on, her uncle let her go and faced the crowd to repeat her sentence and what she was being punished for. While her uncle's back was turned, the men on the platform disappeared rather abruptly and were replaced with others. Even the hangman, she realized, when the strong smell of leeks had disappeared to be replaced by a scent she knew all too well.

Then her uncle turned to tell the hangman to do it, and she saw in his eyes such sorrow she actually felt bad for him. Glancing at Robert, she saw only glee, but right behind him stood Harcourt, sword in hand. She tensed, but instead of the noose being tightened it was taken off her neck and put around Robert's, who stood there openmouthed with shock but unable to move because he had a sword at his back.

"What is happening!" demanded her uncle.

"We are about to hang the guilty man," said Sigimor as he got up on the platform with the others. "Is that nay why we are here?"

"But, we had her . . ."

"Nay, ye didnae, and ye ken it. This lass has ne'er killed anyone and ne'er stolen a thing. So, what are ye doing here? Protecting Robert yet again? Do ye really believe he is worth an innocent lassie's life, the lives of your own brother and his wife, the life of your nephews for he tried to end them too and made certain their family could not get in touch with them? Or your own life? This lass didnae poison ye. She wasnae around here often enough to do so, and ye ken it weel."

Mora saw the tears fill her uncle's eyes and moved

to try and comfort him, but Gybbon tightened his hold on her, preventing her. "Uncle, I ne'er did these things."

"I ken it," he whispered in a broken voice, "but he is my son. *Was* my son. I am so sorry, lass."

Robert tried to scream that he was innocent, but Harcourt clapped his hand over his mouth. Then Duncan stepped forward to tell of the murder of Rona and David. A woman from the kitchens talked of how often Robert was in the kitchens while the laird was ill and always insisted upon seeing his meals. Sigimor told of the burning of Maggie's home while Andrew was there. Her brothers told of Robert's attempts to have them killed in France and his effort to make certain they could neither get nor send any news to their family. It was as if everyone had suddenly been freed of the bonds that had held them silent. Then Gybbon told the man to think of all the other things that had happened and revealed he had had a good talk with many of the people at Wasterburn.

By the time they were done, the bailey was silent except for her uncle's weeping. He mumbled something to Jonathan and then staggered back down the steps. Mora noticed it was Manus who moved to help the man continue on until he disappeared into the keep.

Gybbon pulled a badly trembling Mora away from the gibbet and untied her hands, handing the rope to Harcourt, who had Sigimor tie Robert's hands. When Harcourt removed his hand from Robert's mouth the man called out to his brothers, who, almost as one, turned their backs on him and walked away. Mora pressed her face into Gybbon's chest and refused to watch Robert die, despite how his wrongs had harmed her family, and the fact that he had tried to get her to suffer the same fate by taking the blame for all he had done.

After helping her down from the scaffold, Gybbon led her through the crowd in the bailey, keeping a firm arm around her trembling body, and out through the gates. "Ye are safe now, love."

"I ken it. I also ken it is silly to worry about my uncle, but I cannae seem to help it. This could break him. He was crying in front of all his clan, Gybbon, and he was always such a proud mon."

"He lost the right to be proud with his attempts to blame the innocent for what Robert had done and to ignore all the wrong that fool committed. There comes a time when ye just have to face the fact that your child is wrong and allow him to pay for what he has done."

She nodded. "I ken it. I truly do. May we go home now?"

"Aye. To Sigimor's for tonight and then we will decide what to do tomorrow."

As he got his horse and brought it to her, Mora took the opportunity to hug her brothers properly. She felt bad that she had gained so much from this tragedy while her uncle had lost so much. It was her hope that one day he would see that he had also gained. She really hoped he would find peace with what he had now that Robert was gone. Then, ignoring her brothers' attempts to get her to ride with one of them, she went and let Gybbon put her on Jester, then settle in behind her.

Chapter Nineteen

Gybbon rode up to Sigimor's manor and, after dismounting, helped Mora down. Her brothers were right there and then Andrew hurried out of the house and flung himself into David's arms while wrapping an arm around his sister's neck. After hugging the boy hard, David handed him over to Niall once Andrew released Mora. Mora started to edge closer to him only to have David intervene. Gybbon watched Sigimor head into the manor, the laird giving him the quick flash of a grin before ducking inside. Gybbon decided to follow him inside and, if Jolene was not there, punch him right in his irritating grin.

Once inside, Gybbon saw that Jolene appeared, so he had to satisfy his annoyance by just glaring at the man. That only widened Sigimor's grin. Gybbon watched as the brothers came in with Mora and Andrew. It was good to see the boy so happy, he thought. Glancing toward Mora, settled snugly between her two brothers, Gybbon sighed. He was the only one not completely pleased with the situation. He sat down next to Sigimor and helped himself to some food.

Mora was delighted to have her brothers home safe and alive, but she was getting the urge to bang their heads together. She had spent a lot of time in that cell recalling the private times she had shared with Gybbon, remembering how his touch had made her feel and hungering to feel that way again. Her brothers, however, made it clear with their actions that they were determined to protect her virtue from this big, bad man. She was tempted to tell them that what they so assiduously protected was gone days ago.

Suddenly she remembered that the bedchamber she had had was right next to Gybbon's. If he wished to come to her, she would fulfill what had been a sustaining dream during her time in that dungeon. She just hoped her brothers would not go so far as to guard her door. If they did, Mora thought she just might have to beat them with a stick.

"I think Freya has missed ye," said Andrew.

"Oh, I ken it." She looked at Harcourt. "I hope she has nay been bothering Annys too much."

"Nay anymore. Brought her here."

"Then, where is she?"

"Upstairs in your bedchamber. I had not meant to put her there, but I picked up the bag and she was in it. Held the door open and she would not come, just sat there next to that bag."

"Oh, dear." Mora watched David put some meat on her plate and wished it was Gybbon doing it. "She will be showing her displeasure with me."

Niall laughed. "Mora, it is just a cat."

"A cat that eats at the table when she feels inclined. Gets my wife to cut up some food for her." Sigimor frowned down at his full plate. "She doesnae cut up my meat."

"Of course not, you have hands," Jolene pointed out.

"Aye, clever things." He wiggled his fingers in her face, then slipped his hand under the table and Jolene squealed. She then blushed bright red and slapped him on the arm. "Rude, rude man!"

Ignoring her, Sigimor went back to eating and Mora shook her head. They were a wonderful couple but as mismatched as any could be. Jolene was a very proper lady and Sigimor was a rough, somewhat uncivilized man, but they suited. She realized she really wanted to meet the daughters they had made together.

"We will be leaving tomorrow if it doesnae rain," said Sigimor as he helped himself to more bread. "Need to get my lassies back from Ilsa before they drive her mad."

"She has been raising Odo, so I think she can manage our girls. And we sent her plenty of help."

"Aye, mayhap, but there is only one of Odo."

"Who is Odo? Her child?"

"Nay. He is hers now, but he was a foundling," replied Jolene.

Mora listened in fascination about Ilsa's husband, who had taken in bairns left at his gates, claiming them as his or accepting the blame the women claimed was his, and raising them. Her life suddenly seemed very boring, ordinary, despite the tragedy that had struck it. She had certainly not seen much of the world and could now see that she had not experienced a large part of what life offered. The truth had to be faced, she decided. She simply was not a person who sought out adventure. Mora loved the stories, however, and Jolene was in the mood to tell a lot.

When she finally made her way to her bedchamber,

Mora had had enough of men. Sigimor was taunting Gybbon in some strange, mostly silent way she did not understand, and her brothers had kept poking at Gybbon trying to discover what his interest in their sister might be. She thought it very arrogant of Niall and David to think that, after three years away, they could walk back in and control her life. She had never much liked their bonding together on such a matter before they had left to go trotting all over France.

She stepped into the room she had been given and saw her bag with an angry-looking Freya sitting next to it, her tail flicking wildly. Running over to the bed, she picked up her cat, ignoring the growls of displeasure, and stroked her. Silly as it was to get so attached to an animal, she had missed her cat while stuck in her uncle's cell. Just petting the cat calmed her.

"Now, Freya, calm down. I hadnae expected to be gone so long. Thought I could talk sense to my uncle, but I should have kenned better. He is a mon. Men dinnae heed what a woman says. If ye feel like scratching someone to show your displeasure just give me a moment to fetch Niall and David."

She got up and got ready for bed. Donning her night shift, she washed up, then cleaned her teeth. She took a moment to rub some of Jolene's cream on her scar and firmly reminded herself to get the instructions for making it before she left. Hurrying back to bed, she got beneath the covers, welcoming the warmth, and smiled when Freya curled up beside her.

Mora wished she was curling up with Gybbon. It was odd that she would pine for something she had only known twice. Yet, she did. She closed her eyes and reached out for sleep. Keeping her breathing deep and even, she soon felt the tug of sleep. Soon she would have to go home with her brothers and might never see Gybbon again. Mora fought to push that thought away for it interrupted her slide into sleep.

Gybbon was walking to his bedchamber wondering how he could get in to be with Mora when he was surprised to find Sigimor there waiting for him. "Why are ye lurking around my door? Shouldnae ye be with Jolene?"

"She will wait for me. Mora's brothers are watching ye verra closely."

"I ken it."

"So mayhap ye should make up your mind about what ye want to do with the lass." He held up his hand to stop Gybbon's reply. "Aside from that. They catch ye at that and ye will be beaten and toted to a priest. So be certain ye are ready to run that risk."

"Weel, nay sure what I want in the end, but I at least have some land to build a good, solid, fortified manor on. To be honest, I dinnae ken if I am looking to stay in one place, settle with one woman, maybe have a bairn or twa, or if 'tis just an urge to stop for a wee while. Yet I find myself nay concerned if those two lads drag me and Mora before a priest."

"At least ye have thought on it. Get in your room and, if ye are a daring fool, walk up to the hearth and push on the wall to the right of it. See ye in the morning. Oh, and lock the doors."

Gybbon shook his head and went into the room. He shut the door and stared at it for a moment, then took the key off the hook on the door frame and locked the door. He was surprised Sigimor had some of the more expensive types of locks on his inside doors, but the man did like some things that displayed

"I have money" to anyone who came round. Gybbon bet the man had the most elaborate and costly lock on his own bedchamber.

Next, he walked over to the hearth and stared at the wall but could see nothing. He pushed on the wall and it slowly opened. He grinned and stepped into Mora's bedchamber. Gybbon had the feeling that little door was from the time of Sigimor's father, and hoped the mon had not used it to be false to his wife.

He thought about that for a moment and doubted it. There was such a horde of Cameron brothers he did not think the man would have the time or the energy to bed any other woman. Then he recalled that there was a passage that led down to the dungeons in one of the bedrooms and he bet it was in Mora's room. The clever door in the wall had been a way to escape if needed. It could be even older than he thought it was, and he also decided he would have one in his manor when he had it built.

Gybbon noticed Mora had not banked the fire or even shut the heavy drapes over the window, so both firelight and moonlight gave him more than enough light to see by. Softly, he walked over to her bed and saw that she was sound asleep, her strange cat curled up in one arm and staring at him. He thought about just letting her sleep as she was most likely worn out from being imprisoned and facing a certain hanging for crimes she had not committed. It took but a moment for him to decide he simply was not that generous and walked over to her door to lock it, frowning when he found it was simply a latch and bolt, not as strong a lock as he had. Her brothers could easily break through.

After a moment of thinking what would happen if

they did, he found he did not care. Gybbon was not sure what he felt for Mora, but the thought of being pressed into a marriage with her did not make him shy away. In truth, he faced the possibility very calmly, his only worry being that he would prove a poor husband because the urge to wander might return and he would leave her alone too often.

At some point, and soon, he was going to have to think hard on what he felt for this woman. He started to walk back to the bed, shedding his clothes as he went. Finally, he stood right next to the bed, naked and frowning as his mind started puzzling over the problem now, not ready to wait.

He had known her for only a short while, but he had wanted her from the start, even though he had only seen her in the firelight. She was not a buxom woman but, for once, he did not care about that but still craved her. The passion he found in her arms was the fiercest and most satisfying he could recall enjoying. He found her company welcome even when there was no immediate need or opportunity for lovemaking. And, he realized with a curse, he thought of it as lovemaking, not rutting or sex.

Gybbon nearly groaned aloud as he lifted the covers and slid into bed beside her. It was clear that he had inherited what some males in his family called the Murray curse. They were also sure it had been passed down from the women in their family. When he tugged Mora into his arms and it felt as if his whole body sighed in pleasure, he doubted the "curse" was all the fault of the woman. Then he heard himself whisper an apology to her cat as it stalked away to a bed someone had left to the right of the fireplace for it, and he knew he was lost.

Mora woke up slowly as she became aware of the hard warmth she was pressed against, the sound of a heartbeat she already recognized thumping in her ears. She took a deep breath, savoring the scent of him, and realized she now truly felt as if she was safe and had come home. It was going to shatter her heart when he finally left her, but she pushed the thought aside. He was here now and she would not taint the moment with a sadness for what would come.

"Mmmmm, is that ye, William?" She felt his body jerk slightly as her words shocked him and could not stop herself; she began to giggle and felt a light but sharp slap on her backside.

"Wretched woman," he grumbled, but had to grin.

She opened her eyes to look at him and grinned. "Sorry, I could not resist. Ye shouldnae be here. My brothers might find ye."

"Only if they kick in Sigimor's fine door. Door is locked."

"I have a lock on the door?"

"Aye. So do I, but 'tis a better one than this."

"How did ye get here without my brothers seeing ye?"

"Seems there is a hidden door between the bedchambers. Right by the fireplace." He frowned when he watched her stare at the fireplace, then suddenly blush. "What has ye blushing like that?" He kissed her cheek. "Did ye just wonder if Sigimor's da had lovers? I did, and then apologized to the mon in my head."

"Nay, I didnae think that. I just thought that Jolene may have put us in here apurpose, and I found that a little embarrassing for it meant she already thought we were lovers and thinks we have been skipping back and forth all the while we have stayed here."

He chuckled. "The door there is to escape into here where I believe the opening to a passageway to the dungeons is. 'Tis an escape route. Although, she may have already thought us lovers, but she didnae tell me about the door."

"Ah. Weel, that is clever if the passageway is here." She tried to move, thinking about going to look for the door to that passageway.

"Nay, we can look later. I want to look at it anyway for I am thinking it would be a good thing to have in the manor house I mean to build."

"Ye have a house planned?"

"Aye, Harcourt is giving me some land and I plan to put one between his keep and Nigel MacQueen's. He gave me the choice of the land between him and the border or the other side. I chose the other side."

"That was verra kind of him."

"Aye, but 'tis also a custom amongst my clan. If ye end up with a lot of land ye mark off a place for a brother or cousin to make their place. It has worked verra weel for us. No one expects a lot of land and some pay some money toward it, which I intend to do, but it does mean ye have a strong ally right at hand and that is slowly making us a clan to reckon with."

"Aye, I can see that. Where e'er one settles ye actually end up with two."

He let go of her and tugged off her night shift, then pulled her back into his arms. "There. That is much better."

"Oh, weel, aye," she muttered when she relaxed against him.

He chuckled. She was still a bit shy when naked, but he suspected she always would be, at least when she was first disrobed. He smoothed his hands up and down her back and felt the tension of shyness leave her.

Gybbon kissed her, letting his hunger for her show in his kiss. She slid her arms around his neck and returned the kiss. He could almost taste her own hunger, which pleased him and quickly heightened his need for her. Kissing his way down to her breasts, he took the hard tip of one deep into his mouth. The soft noises of pleasure she made stoked the fire of his own passion.

Mora tensed a little when he began to kiss his way down her belly. She knew what he was planning to do as he nudged the covers aside as he went. Try as she might, she could not completely hide the tensions of embarrassment. It drove her wild but she just felt it was too much, too deeply personal. Then his mouth was almost there.

"'Tis nay a Saint's Day," she murmured, and felt the light touch of his breath as he laughed.

"It must be someone's," he said, and licked her.

Mora lost all ability to speak and threaded her hands through his hair. It allowed her to tug on him, trying to bring him back into her arms as she felt that strange but fierce feeling building, which she knew would soon sweep over her. She wanted him inside her when it did.

Instead he turned onto his back and pulled her down his body. "Ride me, love."

She did not have time to ask what he meant before he had settled her on top of him, and slid into her. He grasped her by the hips and moved her and she finally understood what she had to do. Although she was not sure she was doing it with any skill, she rode him and felt that urge to shatter grow with every stroke. When it came she had to bite her lip to keep from yelling out, then slumped down onto him as she rode that wave of weakening delight. Her eyes widened when she heard herself tell him she loved him.

It was too soon, she thought, panicked by what she had said and only partly comforted by how his hold on her tightened. There were no immediate words of assurance or of a return of that feeling, and his tighter hold could be born of panic as easily as it could be a sign of acceptance. Mora feared she may have just completely ruined what she had with him. She felt how he had hardened against her and she decided to take that as something aside from rejection of her feelings.

"Ah, lass, are ye sure it isnae because we just shared a delight?"

"Nay, it isnae. I suspect I could get that from most men."

"Only if ye want them killed," he suddenly said in a very hard voice, and she risked looking at him.

Gybbon looked into her eyes, which were wide with uncertainty, pulling her back into his arms and close to him. Jealousy, he thought. He had felt pure, white-hot jealousy when she had said she could get it from another man. He was caught, he thought, and almost smiled. Caught tight and hard.

"Dinnae look so afraid, love. I have also been puzzling over the question of do I or dinnae I."

Resting her head on his chest, she asked softly, "Ye havenae decided yet?"

"I havenae kenned what I want since the day ye

tried to steal my horse," he grumbled as he rubbed her back. "When ye said it, my heart grabbed the words greedily."

"Oh, all right then."

"That is enough?"

She smiled at the slight note of hope in his voice. "Nay, but I am willing to wait for ye to be certain." *But, nay for long,* she added silently.

"That is verra kind of ye."

And now he was teasing her, she thought, and slapped his chest. She had just convinced herself she could wait for him to return her love but she was not happy about that. Just felt it was best that he knew his own heart and was sure before he said the words. Teasing her about it was not acceptable.

She wondered how he could not know. It seemed to her to be something one should recognize as soon as it struck. Her love was a part of her; she knew it was there every time she looked at him. Even his scent was enough to stir it in her heart.

Gybbon watched her face and could tell she was thinking hard, fretting over it. He suspected every female in his family would happily thump him into the ground right now. The moment he had heard her say she loved him, he had known he loved her, too. He was still trying to calm his heart down.

They had not known each other long and he had thought such a thing as love took a while to settle in. To a Murray it was usually so life changing he had believed it was one of those things that required time to grow and get hold of you. He went through a list of the whys in his head and sighed. Now he was just being mean, he decided. Every time he tried to think of what he would do in the future, she was there at his side.

"Lass, dinnae fret so." He ran his fingers through her hair. "I ken what I feel weel enough, but I am one who feels the need to think hard before I commit myself to e'en the smallest thing. And this is nay a small thing."

"Nay, it isnae."

"But, I need to cease puzzling o'er something that is clear for most everyone to see. Yet, suddenly, I am thinking of building a strong manor house, even of putting in escape routes and setting it right between two strong keeps one should be able to run to if there is trouble. And do ye ken who I always see at my side?" She looked up at him and he smiled. "Ye. Ye are in every vision of what is to come for me. I just chose nay to look at that too closely."

"And ye just did? Look at it closely?"

"Aye. Takes a mon a while, I suspect."

"Takes ye even longer," she mumbled, and was not surprised when he laughed.

"Aye, it appears so." He put his hand under her chin and tipped up her face so he could give her a kiss on the forehead and then on the mouth. "Aye, lass, I love ye." He saw the glint of tears in her eyes and sighed. "'Tis nay something to weep about. If anyone should be weeping, 'tis I, for I will be giving up the roving life and I rather enjoyed it." He grunted when she lightly punched him in the side. "And already ye begin to abuse me." He held her tight when she laughed.

"I would ne'er stop ye from doing a wee bit of roving."

"That is what I kenned but the urge is gone. Willnae

swear it will stay gone, but for now, aye, no itch to ride off."

She snuggled up close to him. "Good."

"Will have to let my family ken what is happening. That may take a wee bit of time and I cannae promise we willnae suddenly have more of them about than one would wish for."

"Is your family that large?"

"Aye, because it tends to include all of them, nay just mither and fither and siblings but cousins and aunties and uncles and whome'er they wed and what children they have. Weel, it is a lot, aye."

"That's lovely."

He looked to where the cat was and found it sitting up and staring at him. "I suppose I must take the cat in, too."

"Without a doubt."

"Fair enough. Ye will have to claim Jester as one of your stable."

"She likes Jester."

He laughed and pressed her head against his shoulder. "Sleep, lass. I ken ye need it and 'tis too soon for me to celebrate this moment." He caught her puzzled look. "Men need a bit of a rest between bouts."

Mora felt herself blush and just nodded. "I didnae ken that."

"And glad I am to hear that," said a deep voice.

Mora squealed and ducked under the covers. Gybbon sighed and turned to look at Niall and David. He had not even heard them come in. They looked angry, yet he did not have the feeling they were prepared to beat him close to death. He hoped his judgment was right on that.

Chapter Twenty

Mora stayed hidden under the covers even though she knew it was cowardly of her. If nothing else, she was leaving poor Gybbon to face her brothers alone. Realizing she could not leap out while naked to defend him if her brothers decided to beat him, she wriggled over to the edge of the bed to grab her night shift from the floor where Gybbon had dropped it. She wriggled around as she tugged it on.

"What the devil is she doing under there?" asked David.

Lifting the covers a little to peek, Gybbon grinned. "Trying to put her night shift back on."

"I didnae think I wanted to be naked if I had to leap up to defend ye," she snapped as she slipped her arm into the sleeve.

"Ye were going to try and defend me? That is sweet, but I dinnae think ye will need to bother."

She was about to call him arrogant when he was suddenly yanked out of the bed. Even as she pulled on the other sleeve, she popped out from beneath the covers. Her brothers stood by the bed, David with a good hard grip on Gybbon's arm as Niall started to toss his clothes at him.

"What are ye doing here?" she demanded.

"Good question, love. Better one, just how did ye get in here?" asked Gybbon.

"We ken about Sigimor's escape passage and came up that way after we found the doors locked."

Gybbon looked around as he tried to put his clothes on while still being held firm by David and found a door partly open near the hearth. "Sigimor isnae keeping that secret verra weel."

"We are his kin so he told my mither about it. Ye will wed my sister."

"He doesnae have to," Mora snapped, then wondered why she said that when she wanted nothing more than that.

"Oh, aye, he does," said Niall.

"That is a verra interesting place," said a young voice, and Andrew stepped out of the door to the passageway.

Mora groaned and covered her face. "Did ye nay see that he followed ye?" she asked her brothers.

Niall and David shook their heads. "He must have seen us leave our bedchamber," said Niall.

"Why are ye holding Gybbon?" Andrew asked as he paused to pat the cat, then started walking over to them.

"Because I am thinking of beating on him," said David.

"I would rather ye didnae," said Sigimor as he walked in behind Andrew. "I have no wish to have the far too numerous Murrays descend upon me."

"Oh, sweet Mary," muttered Mora, and buried her

head in the pillow. "Is the whole cursed house going to wander in?"

"Nay, lass," Sigimor said, and patted her on the head. "I just got curious about who was wandering through my walls." He looked at Gybbon. "Guess locking the doors wasnae enough."

"Nay. Nice locks ye have, though."

"Thank ye. Started putting them on certain doors once I could afford them as I was weary of my whole family walking into my room whene'er they pleased."

"Oh, I can understand that."

"Now, everyone out." He looked at Gybbon. "And that includes ye."

"But . . ." Gybbon began.

"Nay, we will go down to the hall and have some ale to calm tempers and discuss what happens next, then back to our own beds till morning. Mora, I warn ye, ye will have Jolene in here first thing in the morning."

"Why?"

"To plan your wedding," Sigimor said, and her brothers nodded, and then he went and shut the door to the passageway and locked it.

"But . . ."

"Sleep weel, Mora," said Sigimor as he ushered everyone out the door only to poke his head back in a moment later. "Lock the door."

She sighed when he left but got up and locked the door. She did not know why that was necessary as it appeared there were all sorts of places in this room for someone to sneak up on them. And how would Jolene get in if she locked the door?

"Not my problem," she said as she climbed back into bed.

She lay on her back, scratched her cat's ears when

it jumped up to curl at her side. It appeared she would soon be married. Gybbon had not looked overly distressed by that, but she was annoyed. She had always hated it when she was ordered to do something. She just prayed Gybbon did not have any resentment over being dragged before an altar.

They had deprived her of the chance to have Gybbon ask her to be his wife and any of the loving that might have come after that. It should have been a lovely, romantic moment and they had stolen that away. Mora decided she would find a way to make her interfering brothers pay for that.

Gybbon sipped his ale and tried to ignore the way Niall and David were glaring at him. He did not like the fact that he was being pushed to the altar but knew he would have been going there soon anyway. Then again, he had only just begun to think of how to ask Mora to marry him and had a small sense of relief that he did not have to come up with something a woman would think was suitable. He had not been gifted with the skill at romantic talk such as some of his relatives were.

"I want Harcourt there," he abruptly said as the brothers and Sigimor talked about the wedding they were busy planning for him.

"Already sent him word. The priest, too, and just received the reply from him." Sigimor scowled. "Didnae need the sermonizing he put in, just an aye or a nay. He will be here in time to wed the sinners." He grinned at Gybbon. "So be sure to look appropriately shamed."

"I will do my best."

"Ye should look shamed," said David. "Mora is a proper lady."

"Who tried to steal a horse," Gybbon murmured, took another sip of ale and winked at a grinning Sigimor.

"That was under extreme circumstances."

"Doesnae matter, David," said Sigimor. "Now, I am eager to go back to my bed. Ye do not beat on him. I want him to look as handsome as possible when he stands afore the priest." He got up and walked out.

Gybbon decided he would also go back to bed and make himself resist the urge to go through that clever door. He stood up and so did her brothers. Gybbon could see how badly they wanted to hit him and he did understand that urge. He had enough sisters and female cousins who had lain with the man they married before the vows were said to understand how it made a man feel.

"Nay, sorry ye cannae, but Sigimor wants my face pretty for the wedding."

"Ye willnae be getting wed naked so we just need to avoid your face."

"True, Niall, but I think your sister would notice those bruises later." That remark made David take a swing at him, but Niall stopped it and Gybbon walked away.

Gybbon went up to his room and stripped off his clothes. He forced himself not to look at the door that would take him to Mora's side. It would be folly to give in to that temptation. He would have her as his, without question, after tomorrow, so he could just control himself for one night.

* * *

Mora woke to Jolene and Mary and another maid, their arms full of clothes and flowers. She was tugged out of bed as some servants came in and filled a bath. Jolene poured some pleasantly scented lotion into the water, then urged Mora to shed her night shift and get in. Unused to undressing before other people, even though these were other women, Mora tossed off her night shift and hopped right into the water, sinking down until she was somewhat shielded.

She scrubbed herself as Mary washed her hair. Then she was dragged out, dried off, and had cream rubbed into her until she thought she would swoon from the embarrassment. At last she was dressed again in a gown Jolene was lending her, but she had no time to admire it. She was sat down in a chair and her hair dried, then Mary set a wreath of flowers on her hair. The other maid, Anne, handed her a small bouquet.

"Now ye can look," said Jolene, and tugged Mora to her feet, then turned her so she faced a large looking glass.

Mora looked and lightly smoothed her hand down the fine gown Jolene had dressed her in. "It is beautiful."

"Are ye happy?" Jolene asked.

"Happy to be made so pretty?"

"Happy to be a bride."

"Aye and nay. Last night I thought on how I wished he could have had the time to ask me so I could always be certain this is what he wanted."

"Oh, he wants it, Mora, or he would have fought. This way he gets to wed the woman he wants and your brothers can feel like they have done what is right by you. 'Tis all manly nonsense though. I just wanted to be certain it was what you wanted."

"Aye, 'tis. I just bemoan nay hearing what he would have said."

"I ne'er heard a grand proposal from Sigimor, ye ken. He decided it was the best way to keep me safe and we got wed."

"Oh. I hadnae realized that. 'Tis a silly thing to fret over."

"Not really, but there is no purpose in it and no gain, so why do so?"

"True. The priest is waiting downstairs. I have met him and he is a stuffy, very pious fellow, so I would like to get down there before Sigimor says something that will get us both excommunicated."

Mora laughed and left the room with Jolene, but the woman made her stay at the top of the stairs until Mary signaled her to come down.

The priest was an older man and so pious and self-righteous it set Gybbon on edge. He was pleased to see that the man irritated Sigimor as well, only Jolene's hand on his arm keeping him even slightly polite. Jolene had arrived downstairs after helping Mora prepare just in time. Gybbon hoped Mora was not having second thoughts though, as he glanced at the door only to catch Mary waving someone in.

Mora stepped in just before he looked away and he had to admit, Jolene had done a wonderful job. Mora's hair was long and flowing, revealing what was almost stripes of red in her pale hair, and the blue gown that must have been Jolene's brought out the color of her eyes. She had a wreath of flowers in her hair and held a small bouquet in her hands as she walked toward him.

"They didnae hurt ye, did they?" she asked softly as she stepped up beside him and frowned at her brothers, before waving at Harcourt and Annys.

"Nay, Sigimor told them he wanted to see me as handsome as possible today." He grinned when she laughed softly.

The priest cleared his throat, drawing their attention, and out of the corner of his eye he saw Andrew scurry closer, holding two wedding bands on a small pillow. Gybbon wondered whose he was being given. When Mora's eyes widened and the hint of tears gleamed in them, he knew. They had been given her parents' rings.

"She always said they should go to the first one wed," said David.

"Oh, thank ye for bringing them," Mora whispered as she lightly touched them, and Gybbon nodded his thanks to the man.

He was surprised that she had not packed them in her bag, but then his attention was pulled back to the priest. The man droned on and on and suddenly Mora was nudging him to speak and he dutifully said aye. He listened as Mora repeated her vows and felt an odd swelling in his chest. This obviously meant more to him that he had anticipated. Soon enough it was over and he kissed the bride, doing his best to keep it a respectable kiss just to seal the vows.

Harcourt came over and clapped him on the back as Mora's brothers engulfed her with hugs and kisses on the cheek. "Feeling trapped?" he asked softly.

"Nay. Just annoyed that I wasnae the one to do the asking," Gybbon replied.

"Ah, good. Ye had planned on doing this anyway."

"Aye. Had just decided on it when those two rude fellows walked in."

"Hope ye were decent."

"Nay. Although Mora got that way by putting her night shift on under the covers." He smiled faintly when Harcourt laughed.

"Love to watch when they do that. I dinnae ken how they can see."

"Must be a woman thing."

"Aye." He looked at Sigimor and asked, "So now we can eat?" He then muttered a soft cry of pain and, seeing Annys right behind him, Gybbon decided he had just been pinched or hit for such rudeness.

Sigimor just grinned. "Aye. Now food." He mumbled a thanks to the priest, then walked over to the table, scowling a little when the priest followed and took a seat.

Gybbon smothered a laugh when he realized Sigimor had not intended to have a priest at his table, and he led Mora to a seat and then sat beside her. He nearly laughed at the priest's face when Freya jumped on the seat beside her. He did not think the priest would linger after the meal.

"Oh, dear, the priest is upset by the cat at the table," Mora whispered.

"Aye, so he will leave soon," Gybbon said quietly, and she smiled.

It was late in the afternoon before Gybbon got a chance to take Mora upstairs. Just at the bottom of the stairs, Harcourt stopped them and kissed Mora on the cheek and Annys did the same. Gybbon was pleased by this sign of welcome and shook his brother's hand.

"Starting on the manor house soon?" Harcourt asked.

"Aye, intend to draw out what I would like and then talk to some of the craftsmen in town tomorrow."

"Good. Just let me ken what ye plan as I have some craftsmen at the keep who wouldnae say nay to some extra work."

As soon as they left, Gybbon hurried Mora up the stairs so fast she was laughing by the time they went into his bedchamber. Their clothes quickly hit the floor although he noticed she was very careful about laying the blue gown over a chair. He then tumbled her into bed after locking the door.

"Locking that didnae help last night," she said as she curled her arms around his neck.

"Better lock, and no entrance to the escape tunnel in here."

"Oh. Good. I have no wish to see my brothers tonight." She smiled when he laughed. "I think they are no longer so angry."

"Nay, I married ye without complaint or force. I think they would still like to punch me in the face though."

"I dinnae understand that, as they are my brothers, nay my father."

He shrugged. "Ye have no father, so they have stepped in as your guardians."

"Weel, I am sorry they forced ye before a priest."

"I told ye. There was nary a complaint and it wasnae force. Aye, I kenned it was the only choice if I didnae wish to get in a long fight with your kinsmen, but no one forced me before the priest. In truth," he admitted reluctantly, "I was pleased I didnae have to think of a proper way to ask ye."

"What is so hard about asking a lass to marry ye?"

"I dinnae ken. Simple words, aye, but a difficult thing for men to do especially if they ken they have no skill with pretty flatteries and love words."

"I dinnae require any."

"Good, although I imagine I may come up with some now and then." He kissed her and held her close, loving the feel of her smooth skin against his.

Mora gave herself over to his slow lovemaking. He murmured things to her as he kissed and caressed her, and she decided he did not realize he had skill enough at pretty words when needed. Obviously, he needed some inspiration, she thought as she returned his caresses.

Wondering if it was because she was now legally married to the man, Mora felt daring and was soon kissing her way down his taut stomach. She made love to him with her mouth, savoring every groan of pleasure that escaped him. Then he turned her around so that he could do the same with her. As she felt her insides tauten and sensed what he had called her release rushing up on her, she pulled away and settled herself over him. He entered her a little roughly and she was proud that she had driven him to such desperation. This time she needed no direction and rode him until they both cried out softly from the strength and joy of their mutual release. She slumped down on top of him and felt him soften within her.

"Not a Saint's day," she said, not surprised by the breathless tone of her voice and smiling when he laughed.

"Nay, but we will add this day to the list."

"Aye. Probably the only respectable day." She pulled free and flopped down beside him.

For a while they lay quietly side by side, their breathing growing slower. He then turned on his side and began lazily stroking her. Mora liked it but was not sure she was ready to do anything all over again as she realized she was tired after a broken night's sleep and a long day.

"So, ye plan to get started on your grand manor house?"

"Aye. I think I will etch out what I have in mind on the morrow."

"So where do we stay while we wait?"

"Harcourt said we can stay with him and Annys, and Sigimor has offered us this place to stay in. I told him it could be a few years before what I want is built, and he just shrugged."

"That is kind of him."

"It is, aye, but ne'er forget what I told ye. Sigimor collects allies and favors. He especially likes it when they are close at hand. I build the manor house and he has an easy reach to two allies near at hand and all my family. But, 'tis a good offer and I told Harcourt I might take it. He agreed it was what he would choose if only to be alone with his wife."

"Oh. Aye, it wouldnae be so private at Harcourt's keep."

"Nay, not at all. So tomorrow we can plot out our manor house. I will even let ye decide on a few things," he said, and kissed her cheek.

"So verra kind of ye. Ye said it has some land?" She felt him nod as he kissed her shoulder. "So one might have a kitchen garden?"

"Oh, aye. It has a few acres just as your parents' had."

"That is verra generous of your brother." She frowned as she suddenly thought of something she had not considered before. "Did he think I trapped ye? That ye were forced into this?"

"Nay, not at all. Ye dinnae have to fret on that. Now, 'tis our wedding night."

"Aye, I believe I was there at the wedding."

"I ken ye are probably a bit tired, but I mean to celebrate properly."

"Oh, dear."

He just laughed and proceeded to celebrate three more times with an appropriate respite between each one. On the last round, he slumped at her side and was soon sound asleep. Mora grinned even as she felt her eyes closing. She had worn the man out. Something to be proud of, she decided, as she curled up next to him and went to sleep.

Epilogue

Four years later

Mora climbed down from the cart and Gybbon handed her their daughter, Caitlin. After only a few steps, the child demanded to be let down. Holding Caitlin's small hand, Mora made her slow way to the two stones that marked her parents' graves. She was just kneeling down before them when Gybbon came up with the boys, Logan and Reid.

Morag and Maggie had paid for the headstones and refused any attempt to pay them back. Tears stung Mora's eyes as she traced her parents' names etched neatly into the stone. It was something she did every time. She had brought her children here, quietly introducing them, as soon as it was safe to bring them outside. It hurt her heart to know her parents would never know their grandchildren.

The flowers on her mother's grave told her that her brothers had been there, and she carefully set hers between their bouquets. It was comforting to know she was not alone in stopping by on her mother's birthday. She said a little prayer, then accepted Gybbon's hand to help her stand up.

"The town picked a lovely spot to have consecrated ground," she said as she looked around, noting with approval the trees left to shade the graves.

Gybbon took her hand and walked her back to the cart. "Your brothers stopped by, aye?"

"Aye. They seem to do weel in raising Andrew. I was a wee bit concerned at first," she confessed, and was not surprised when he laughed.

"Och, aye. Just a wee bit. If ye hadnae been carrying the laddies, ye would have been o'er at the manor every single day."

She did not even attempt to argue with that statement but set Caitlin up on the cart seat, constantly telling the child to sit down as Gybbon lifted her up and sat her on the seat. As he climbed up, she turned to give the wrestling boys what Gybbon fondly called The Look, and they immediately sat down. She tugged Caitlin back down so the child again sat on the seat.

"And now we go to see what will soon be our home," said Gybbon, as he set the cart in motion.

"It has taken longer than ye thought it would, hasnae it?"

"Aye, but these things rarely go as planned. Too many things can go wrong, from the weather to supplies nay coming in when they were supposed to, and on and on."

"And we seem to have discovered every single thing that could go wrong."

"That we did, but I also had some things I wanted that caused a wee problem or twa. Still, 'tis nearly done and it will be perfect." Gybbon reached over his daughter to pat Mora on the shoulder.

"It certainly looked to be fine the last time I saw it, before the roof was to go on." She sighed. "I suspect Sigimor will be pleased to have his manor house back."

"He will, but he hasnae complained. Said ours is going much more smoothly than his did and he only wants his for one of his brothers. The mon is about to be wed, so that nudge could grow stronger, but he would ne'er suggest we leave just for that. He is too happy about having so many Murrays close to hand, plus thrilled that their arrival rid him of a few trouble-makers he figured he would soon have to confront."

She nodded and studied the land they were travel-ing through. It was going to take most of the day to get to the place where their manor was being built. Mora had assumed they would stay at Harcourt's keep, but she wished Gybbon would have let her pack what was needed. Glancing in the back, she frowned at the two chests and several bags he had put in the cart and could not help but wonder what was in them. Deciding not to worry about it, she went back to watch-ing the countryside and judged it as a pleasant place to live. Yawning, she tried to think of everything she wanted to do in her new home when it was finished, hoping it would be enough to keep her awake.

Something landed on her lap and Mora started in surprise. She stared down at Freya for a few moments before she realized she had fallen asleep. Frantically, she looked around for Caitlin and found her child in the back of the cart sleeping in a pile with her brothers. When she attempted to lean over and pick the child up, she realized she was tied to the seat. Mora glared at Gybbon.

"Ye tied me up again!"

"Aye, I did. Ye fell asleep. Again. Cannae have ye tumbling out of the cart."

"Untie me."

"Ye can untie yourself this time."

Muttering to herself, she found the knot and untied it. When she unwound it she found that it crossed over her chest and that the ropes were secured to the back of the seat. A closer study found cloth ties set up in the middle of the seat. The man had made harnesses for both her and Caitlin. It annoyed her that she found that touching and frowned at him.

"Ye have made harnesses for both me and Caitlin," she said, pleased by the hint of anger she had kept in her voice.

"I have. The two of ye keep falling asleep and 'tis a long way to the ground. Happens every time ye are in the cart. It gets rolling along and first one, then the other of ye go out like snuffed candles that snore."

"I dinnae snore."

"Weel, nay, not truly. 'Tis more like ye breathe loudly because your head is tipped back. Caitlin snores."

Mora leaned over the back of the seat and studied her little girl. Her wild mass of blond curls covered her face as she sprawled between her brothers, her legs and arms flung out over them. Then she heard it. She supposed that strange whistling sound could be called a snore, especially since she made the sound as she breathed in and made a louder similar one as she breathed out.

Sighing, Mora turned around and idly smoothed down her skirts. "She will outgrow that." She ignored his soft laughter. "She is going to be a fine lady one day."

"Och, aye, as soon as she grows out of snoring, playing in the mud until she fair drips with it, bellowing out commands like some war lord, and trying to pummel Reid." He laughed harder when she swatted him.

She looked around and realized they were now on the road that would go by their new house. "We are almost there."

"Aye. Ye had a nice nap."

She was going to have to figure out some way to stay awake, she decided. It would serve him right if she just kept talking for the whole ride. As they turned down a very rough trail toward the manor, she stared. It looked like there were a lot of people at the manor house, which, she noticed with pleasure, now had a fine slate roof on it.

Gybbon brought the cart to a halt, got down, then walked around to lift her out. A quick look into the back told Mora all the children were still sleeping, so she turned her attention to the people gathered. She gasped with delight when she saw all three of her brothers and ran over to hug Andrew.

"See, Mora? He is still alive," said David, and laughed when she stuck her tongue out at him.

After greeting Harcourt and Brett, Gybbon walked over to greet his brothers-in-law. They had been a great help to him in finishing the manor this last year. He now had to hope Mora appreciated all their efforts.

"We brought the cart of things we promised," said Niall.

"What things?" asked Mora as she glanced toward the cart to be sure the children still slept.

"Some things we thought ye would like from the

house. Passed ye on the road, but Gybbon was busy tying ye into place when ye fell asleep." He glanced over at the cart. "And I will go rescue my niece before she starts bellowing."

Mora looked at the cart and sighed as she saw Caitlin hanging on to the cart seat with her little legs kicking. Niall grabbed her and then the two boys popped up, rubbing their eyes. She took a deep breath and let it out slowly as she promised herself she would not worry about any of them right now.

"Thank ye," she said to David, and he gave her a quick kiss on the cheek, but not quick enough, because when he straightened up it was to find a grinning Niall standing in front of him with Caitlin in his arms and leaning toward him, pointing to her cheek.

"Seeing as your brithers have an eye on the bairns, let me show ye the inside," said Gybbon as both brothers muttered mild complaints.

Mora let him lead her away. She went through the thick oaken doors and gazed at the wide hallway. The dining hall was nice and large, and she had to suppress a sigh of pleasure when he led her into the kitchen. There would be few complaints from whomever they got in to work in such a space. As he led her from room to room she got a little uneasy. It was very luxurious. Then he took her to the master bedroom, which was obviously his pride and joy if she judged the expression on his face right.

He showed her the small bedchamber next to it, which had a door to theirs, and was intended for the youngest, and then the ledger room on the other side. But she could almost feel his excitement as he led her into that through a nearly hidden door by the hearth. Then he practically ran across the room to show her the other hidden door by that hearth.

"It leads down into the cellars," he said. "And they have already begun the tunnel that will lead to the other side of the wall that is being built."

She tried not to but she had to laugh. "So ye got your escape route."

"I did. And kenning our children, it can be locked way up at the top of the door."

"Oh, good." She did not mention her belief that they would somehow figure out how to undo it. "Sigimor has appreciated the one ye put on his door."

"Cannae have the little devils racing around inside the walls like rats."

"Nay, that would ne'er do. So, when do we move in?"

"Today."

"What? But, there are things we need to get," she stuttered. "Beds and chests, and something for the floors."

"And we will get them, but it appears we already have a lot. Given freely by all the others. Oh, aye, there are other things, but they can be gotten as ye decide what ye want or need. But, right now, we have more than enough to settle in."

"Mora!" called Annys from the door. "They are bringing in some beds. Ye might want to tell them where to put them."

Mora hurried off with Annys and fell into many hours of telling people where she wanted something put. Then she was caught up in the feast prepared and brought in. She was stunned when her uncle and his sons arrived bringing a few things, as well.

To her astonishment, the old man looked as hale as

he had in the earlier days, before Robert had gotten so bad. It pleased her even more when he told her that Murdoch would be the laird when he was gone, and it was obvious Lachlan and Duncan approved. Sigimor, Harcourt, and Brett all took the young man aside and she resisted the urge to go closer and eavesdrop.

Then Jolene walked up to her and gave her a hug. "Ye will make it all yours soon."

"I ken it. And, I have a gift for ye."

"Really? Why?"

"Because it seemed that ye really wanted one," said Mora as she hurried over to a chair in the corner of the hall and grabbed her bag. "Do ye recall I told ye that Freya would ne'er have kittens?" she asked as she returned to Jolene's side.

"Aye, because she didnae go outside so she would-nae be caught." Jolene's eyes widened. "She got caught?"

"She did, and by a male who didnae look much bigger than she was. I tried to catch him when it was over, but he was smart, because he ran from an extremely angry Freya as fast as he could." Grinning when Jolene laughed and smiled up at Sigimor, Mora reached into the bag and dragged out a very small black and white kitten. "I think I have a real runt cat for your wife. He is five months old and should be a lot bigger than this. I could wait a little longer to be certain if ye wish."

Jolene took it and held it, the kitten rubbing her face against Jolene's. "Nay. Oh, he is so cute."

Sigimor took it and checked between its legs before

handing it back to his wife. "He is so cute. Useless, but cute."

"I cannae promise it will be a runt," said Mora. "They can fool ye and suddenly grow big, but the chances are, this one will be small like my Freya."

"Just so long as it doesn't become another George."

"George was a fine cat," said Sigimor.

Mora left them to argue about how fine George the rat killer had been and went to find Gybbon.

It was very late before there was only her family left in the manor. She tucked the children into their beds and then went to the master bedroom and flopped down onto the bed. Gybbon came in and flopped down beside her. Mora smiled when he tugged her into his arms.

"Pleased?"

"Verra much so, but are ye sure we can afford this?"

"Aye. I made a fair amount of coin when I was wandering all over the country. A lot of the things, like the furniture and even some of the windows, were gifts or extra things someone had on hand. We only had to mend a few things. My family was always set on that. Ne'er threw anything away if it was still good or could be mended, and if something they had made wasnae exactly right, they would pay for the materials used and keep it anyway, then get what they really wanted. That is why some of the windows may strike ye as a bit odd when ye finally get a chance to have a good look. We made them to fit what we were given."

"Everyone was verra generous."

"Aye, and grateful. This land was an empty hole, nothing here. Now there is and there will soon be men to work and guard. All the keeps near us are allies and they are having trouble placing their men as the children grow. Now there is one more choice for them. And some of their lassies, too. This land will either be grazed or planted so more food is available. We serve a good purpose, lass, and they welcome it. And Jolene even brought a nice bed for Freya," he said, and pointed to the blanket-lined basket near the hearth where her cat was curled up.

Mora looked at her cat, then looked at her husband. "And ye have no urge to go awandering?"

"Why would I go anywhere? Everything I want is right here."

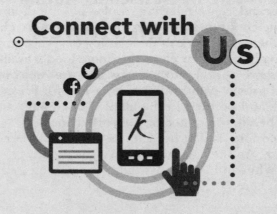